KEEPSAKE
SELF
STORAGE

T0161935

MARIANNE BANKS

Bella
BOOKS

2014

Bella Books, Inc.
P.O. Box 10543
Tallahassee, FL 32302

First Bella Books Edition 2014

Editor: Katherine V. Forrest
Cover Designer: Sandy Knowles

ISBN: 978-1-59493-395-0

Other Bella Books by Marianne Banks

Growing Up Delicious

Dedication

To Patricia. You are The One.

Acknowledgment

Many thanks for the weekly magic created by the Great Darkness Writing Group: Jeanne Borfitz, Jennifer Jacobson, Celia Jeffries, Lisa Drnec Kerr, Patricia Lee Lewis, Alan Lipp, Edie Lipp, Patricia Riggs, Jacqueline Sheehan, Morgan Sheehan-Bubla and Marion VanArsdell. Continued gratitude for the efforts of the good women of the Tuesday Night Manuscript Group: Jacqueline Sheehan, Ellen Meeropol, Celia Jeffries, Lydia Kann, Kris Holloway, Patricia Riggs and Kari Ridge. A huge thank you to Bella Books, Katherine V. Forrest and Karin Kallmaker.

I will be forever grateful for the good fortune that brought me to Dr. Michael Sisti, neurosurgeon, and Columbia Presbyterian Hospital and for the blessing of my wonderful family and many friends who made recovery possible and worthwhile.

CHAPTER ONE

May Hammond stood on the dike overlooking the Connecticut River and wondered what was floating in the water. It was caught in a tree beached on the shore a few months back during a particularly violent thunderstorm. It couldn't be a body could it? Too bad she hadn't brought her binoculars. She wondered if she could make it down there. The grade was kind of steep. Maybe she should call the police but she didn't want to be accused of being a hysterical old lady thinking she'd seen a body when it might turn out to be nothing more than a trash bag full of clothes.

Darn it all but she just didn't trust herself anymore. On her last birthday she'd turned eighty-three and generally felt fine. Her eyes were as blue as they'd ever been but now seemed to require glasses for everything, not just reading. Thankfully her hair was still thick though as white as dandelion fuzz. It was her knees that caused the greatest trouble, they just weren't what they used to be. The last thing she needed was to fall in the river. She had plans later with Avola and she had a few things to do around the house before that. In her younger days she wouldn't have hesitated. Things were different at this stage. She'd just go home and call the authorities, have breakfast, and let them handle it.

* * *

May could see from the dishes in the sink that her son, Earl, had had cereal for breakfast, Raisin Bran from the look of the crumbs on the counter. She popped a sugary raisin in her mouth. Would it ever be possible to get him to put his breakfast things in the dishwasher?

Just as she put the kettle on to boil she noticed the flash of a car pulling into the driveway. Gosh darn it. Now who could be here? She squinted through the crack in the kitchen curtains. It looked like Vera Henderson. What the gracious would bring Vera by on a Friday morning? Vera always cleaned her house on Fridays, no matter what. That kind of cleanliness tired May out. Not that she didn't appreciate a well-kept home but Vera took it a step, well a lot of steps, too far. Any woman who stripped and waxed her kitchen floor every week didn't have imagination for the more enjoyable aspects of life.

"What brings you out so early?" May asked, opening her kitchen door just as Vera raised her hand to knock.

Vera burst into tears.

After finding the Kleenex and helping Vera out of her overcoat, which was too warm for the weather, and getting her aspirin and pouring them both a cup of tea and then remembering Vera needed cream and sugar, after all that Vera said, "My Hoover gave up the ghost."

Vera's Hoover was a relic from the 1950s when Vera was raising her eight children. Vera's husband, Chester, was a devout Catholic who believed in habitual fornication without benefit of prophylactics.

"Do you think it can be fixed?" May asked, thinking it unlikely, as there weren't repairmen around anymore, let alone someone old enough to have ever seen a Hoover Canister with a roar like a cornered bear.

"Oh, May, I don't know. I plugged it in like usual and turned it on and it was working as good as ever. All of a sudden I smelled something burning. You know that electrical smell? I figured I vacuumed up some panty hose or something when the wall outlet exploded." Vera took a shuddering breath. "Next thing I knew, my drapes had caught fire. I ran to the phone and dialed 911 but you know that old rotary phone I have? It's been acting funny lately and it cut out on me after the 91. I had to dial three times before I could get the 911 out."

May realized she should have made a pot of tea. Usually one cup was enough but she had a feeling that wasn't going to be the case today.

"By the time I made the lady on the phone understand my draperies were gone and the fire was working on that rag rug I made out of Chester's old tweed suits, she told me to get out of the house. I just had time to grab my coat, purse and bag of crocheting."

So much for keeping a clean house, May thought. "How extensive is the damage?"

"Lots of smoke and water damage but the firemen were able to keep it all from going up in flames. I'll call my insurance company after nine o'clock; I don't imagine they're open before then."

"This is terrible news. Would you like some cinnamon toast, Vera? You need fortification."

"Thank you, May. But, what I really need is a place to stay. Could I use your guest room?"

* * *

Auction day at Keepsake Self Storage always brought out the weirdos. Fortunately Earl Hammond didn't mind weirdos. Good thing too because there was a bunch of them milling around the auctioneer, Bill Owens, like chickens pecking for grubs.

"Pursuant to Massachusetts General Law, Chapter 105A, Section 3…"

Earl slurped his coffee and listened to the auctioneer drone on. Bill was a stickler for doing things by the book. Even if everybody there had been to an auction before.

"…Unit number three-thirteen…"

Earl stepped forward and used his master key. He opened the door and stepped back so the prospective buyers could see what was visible. It was against the law to open any boxes or containers but nothing prevented them from shining high-powered flashlights over the contents.

"I see an air-conditioner and some pretty nice cedar boards. A ten-speed bike and a pair of hip boots," Bill intoned, craning his neck. Before Bill became an auctioneer he had been a regular, bidding at auctions when a unit's contents looked promising. He'd told Earl that he made more than a little bit of money selling the crap he picked up at auctions all around western Massachusetts, to say nothing of the money to be made in scrap metal. Earl wasn't sure he believed him. If there was so much money in buying delinquent units why did he become an auctioneer. Earl suspected Bill was one of those big talkers. The type who always got the best deal, ate the biggest steak, screwed the most gorgeous woman.

"Bidding to start at fifty dollars…"

Earl's mind drifted. As manager of the Keepsake he'd been to many of these. There was an auction every three or four months. Sometimes it was the only way to get people to pay. He felt sorry for some folks and tried to keep them off the list but his boss was a real bitch. Underneath her nice little old lady exterior was an A-Number-One Capitalist. Her favorite saying was, "I pay my bills and they can damn well pay theirs." Then she'd drive away in her old Caddie, country-western music blaring out of her CD player and cigarette smoke billowing behind her.

So, Earl did as he was told because he didn't want to lose his job. It wasn't that he liked the job so much but he didn't hate it either. Besides, everybody knew looking for a job was a real headache. It's not like there was a perfect job anywhere on the planet.

Earl had to admit he was a bit bored. There was only one interesting thing about his life and it wasn't his job and it wasn't his home. Sometimes that one thing wasn't enough to keep him interested and he found himself adrift from one end of the day to the other. He wondered how this had happened. It seemed like, last he remembered he was eighteen and ready for adventure and the next thing he knew he'd woken up this morning in a bed with sheets that needed changing and he was forty-seven. What happened to all that time in-between? Where had he been while it was passing?

Whew, the dairy farm up the road was really stinking this morning. They must be cleaning the barn or spreading manure. Some days cow shit was all you could smell though this odor seemed to have a little extra rank in it, kind of like when you got a whiff of road kill as you drove by.

"Sold to Mr. Walker for two hundred and fifteen dollars." Bill flipped to the next page on his clipboard. "Let's proceed to unit two-ten."

Earl led the way, squinting into the morning sun. He'd better adjust the timer for the security lights since it was only a couple weeks or so until the clocks turned back to Standard Time.

Time was another thing. It always bit you in the ass. Even if it was on your side for a while, it wouldn't stay that way forever. Like when he was in high school. He'd had no trouble staying in shape. He could eat whatever he'd wanted and his Levis always fit right. Now? Shit. Now, he had to take Lipitor for his high cholesterol and stay away from cheeseburgers and fries.

In a way, his father was lucky he died so young. Before some doctor told him to give up this and give up that. Pop just went out and got hit by a Hampshire County Transit bus one Wednesday morning after his standard breakfast from Harold's Diner. Earl thought of Pop's Breakfast as The Heart Attack Special. Three pieces of bacon, three sausages, three eggs fried hard because that was how he had liked them, white toast burned black and a quart of coffee with cream. Pop thought oatmeal was for sissies. What would his father think of Earl's Breakfast Special, Raisin

Bran? On Sundays, his one day off, he allowed himself a trip to Harold's and had Pop's breakfast and read the Sunday *Republican* except Harold fried his eggs over easy.

Sometimes he felt hopeless and he didn't like admitting that especially because you never knew if You-Know-Who was around. Whether she was around or not she always seemed to know what he was thinking. She'd say something like hopelessness wasn't a worthwhile emotion for human beings. Not very comforting. Next time they got together he would try to explain that he was having difficulty realizing that he was going to die, if not from a stroke or heart attack then surely from this dissatisfaction rumbling around inside him. He'd made a vow to have a heart-to-heart chat with You-Know-Who next time he saw her and see if she could offer any words of wisdom. He knew she had the power.

"Ahem?" Bill cleared his throat. Earl realized he had completely zoned out and he and everybody else were standing in front of unit two-ten. Whew. Something smelled to high heaven, definitely different than Mr. O'Brien's dairy. Jesus, it was enough to gag a maggot.

He unlocked and pulled up the door. The stench washed out of the unit like a tsunami. Earl fought the impulse to gag.

"What's that stink?" Bill asked no one in particular as he shined his high-powered flashlight over the contents of the storage unit. Nobody offered a guess though everybody did step back three paces.

That's when Earl noticed the shoes: cordovan wingtips, sole side out, toes pointing up with two legs coming out of them and disappearing under a twin mattress that had a bookcase and a box of Encyclopedia Britannicas leaning against it. The hairs on the back of Earl's neck stood up. He'd had a feeling when he got up that today was going to suck. No shampoo, his two percent curdled over his Raisin Bran and Dunkin' Donuts was out of cinnamon rolls, his special treat on auction days. And now this. Suspicious feet.

"Uh, Bill. Let's skip this one." Earl lowered the door.

"What do you mean skip it? Look at that nice Naugahyde recliner," some asshole with a goatee said.

"Yeah. I don't think you can stop one of these once they get started," another asshole said, waving the stem of his pipe at Earl.

"Bill?" Earl locked the door. "We'll do this one next time around, huh?"

Earl and Bill exchanged a look.

"Certainly. By all means. Well, that was our final unit. Anyone who has purchased the contents of a unit must remand payment to me in cash and clear out said unit by the close of business today…"

Earl walked back toward the office. If he remembered correctly, unit two-ten was owned by a Vietnam War vet who got behind on his payments during a hospitalization at the VA in Leeds. Earl had let him ride for months figuring the guy deserved a break. But, his boss had found out and pitched a hissy fit. Now, what was two-ten's name? Bob? No. Brad. That was it. Brad Nelson.

* * *

"Al-lo?" Avola had set down her hammer and upholstery tacks and answered the phone on the third ring.

"Hi, honey, it's me." May's voice crackled through the phone line.

"Oh, what a pleasant surprise. I thought you might be Mr. Alberti calling to see if his ugly recliner is ready. What explains a man's fascination with plaid?"

"I wonder if they like the dependability of a geometric design…" May's voice trailed off.

"It is hard to ascertain and though I was married to Louie Mr. Big-Boy-Liquors LeFebre more years than I care to admit I still do not understand men. He, too, was very fond of the plaid sport shirt so perhaps you speak the truth," Avola said.

"Frank was, too. Listen, honey, the reason I'm calling is to tell you that I have an unexpected houseguest."

"Yes? Who?"

"You remember my friend, Vera…we've known each other since school."

"Yes, I remember."

"Well, her house…she started a fire with her Hoover…"

"The vacuum?"

"Yes and what with the smoke and water damage she can't stay there until the contractor gets things fixed up," May said.

"So, she is staying with you, eh?" Avola thought Vera was a ditzy woman, reminding her very much of her sister Mary Christina, a woman who cared for appearances more than substance. They had never gotten along even as children. Avola's marriage to and then divorce from Mr. Big-Boy hadn't improved their relationship. Mary Christina was a nun and disapproved of divorce.

"Does she not have half a dozen children?" Avola turned on the coffeemaker she kept in the corner of her workshop.

"Yes, but only two of them live locally and she's fighting with those. What could I say? No to a woman who's lost the use of her home and her Hoover in the same morning?"

"My dear May, you could not say no to Attila the Hun if he asked you for help." Avola wasn't sure why she was being so uncharitable toward the unfortunate Vera. Perhaps it was nothing more than feeling ornery because she couldn't get the box pleat on Mr. Alberti's chair to hang correctly.

"I don't know why you're upset, Avi…I—"

"Upset! I am not—"

"Well, you sure sound upset. I don't know why I even called to tell you…"

"If you do not wish to speak to me then I will go back to this plaid monstrosity."

"It's not that I don't—"

Avola hung up. Not nice but she was afraid of what she might say. It was easier to apologize for hanging up than to say the wrong thing and have the words take on form and mass and become something no one could forget. Avola knew it was unreasonable to be jealous of Vera but jealousy did not seem ruled by the intellect. It grew like a dandelion, anywhere it could get a foothold. She knew she should call May back and she would, later, after she remedied Mr. Alberti's box pleat.

CHAPTER TWO

When he noticed a cruiser out in the parking lot, Earl opened the security gate. They must be here about unit two-ten. He ambled out to meet the cop, who rolled down his window but made no attempt to get himself out of the cruiser.

"Are you the individual who called about a unit having a peculiar smell?" The cop looked like he was about fourteen, though everybody looked fourteen to Earl since his forty-seventh birthday. The poor guy also had a wicked rash on the underside of his chin.

"Yes. I'm Earl Hammond."

"I'm Officer Deats. What's the trouble?"

"We had an auction this morning and when we unlocked unit two-ten there was a horrible smell and a pair of wingtips that seemed to be facing the wrong way. It looked to me like someone is dead in there."

Officer Deats unfolded himself from the cruiser.

"You related to a May Hammond over on East Street?"

Earl wondered what that had to do anything.

"Yes. She's my mother. Why? Is something wrong?"

"She called in a report of something floating in the river this morning. She wondered if it was a body or something." Officer Deats chuckled. "Turned out to be nothing more than a scarecrow got loose from somebody's garden."

Jesus, what were the chances. Some days it was hell living in a small town.

"My mother takes a walk almost every morning down by the river. But this isn't any scarecrow. Let me show you. It's kind of hard to explain."

Their feet crunched in unison on the gravel driveway. Earl unlocked two-ten and rolled open the door. The smell was more cloying than before.

"Hmmm. Whew, I see what you mean about the odor. Those must be the wingtips." Officer Deats removed his mirrored sunglasses.

"Yup."

"Wait here. I'm going to move these things out of the way."

Earl watched as Officer Deats pushed aside the box of encyclopedias and moved the bookcase. At that point the mattress slid down the wall revealing Brad Nelson, or what was left of him, reclining on an unrolled sleeping bag. His head rested on a sack of potting soil and he wore a T-shirt with a faded The Few, The Proud, The Marines across the chest. A pair of plaid shorts and the wingtips completed his outfit. There was an empty Jack Daniels bottle leaning against Brad's deflated thigh. The smell amplified. Earl wondered if he was going to puke.

He had never seen a dead body before. Well, take that back. He'd been to wakes and funerals and done the obligatory look-see into an open casket. All the deceased had been tidied up. Even Pop looked neat though a bit swollen. But Brad Nelson, the poor bastard, hadn't been tidied up. This was one of those things that a person could go their whole life without seeing and not be the worse for it. Well, at least he'd have something to report at dinner tonight when Mother asked him how his day went. Usually he had nothing to say. His mother had more going on than he did.

"You have an idea who this is, Mr. Hammond?"

"I think it's Brad Nelson, though it's hard to say with his face like that. He's the guy who rented the unit."

"I'm going to call this in." Officer Deats slid his shades back in place.

"I'll be in the office, if you don't mind, looking up his paperwork," Earl said to the twin reflections of himself in Officer Deats's sunglasses. He lowered the door and slid the lock into place giving the key to the officer.

Earl glanced at the security monitor and watched Officer Deats block off the access road around unit two-ten with yellow crime scene tape. He wondered if Officer Deats thought the death was foul play and that he'd done it. Thanks to the *Law & Order* reruns on cable, he knew the person who finds the body is the person the cops always suspect first. Thankfully he had no motive. He didn't really know Brad except to harass him on the phone whenever Brad got behind with his payments or say hello to him when he came by to access his unit and sometimes stopped in the office to pass the time of day. Sure, they got high a couple times behind the 700 building. But that was on a Saturday after closing time. And as for means, well, that would be the Jack Daniels, wouldn't it? Earl didn't drink Jack Daniels. Not since high school when he and his friend Jerry stole a quart from the package store and drank it one Sunday afternoon at Jerry's place when his folks were out of town. Nothing like puking your guts up to cure the whiskey habit.

The problem was pretty obvious even if you'd never seen an episode of *Law & Order*. It had to be murder. If that poor bastard Brad got so drunk he passed out, then who could have closed the door and locked it? The units weren't airtight. Brad couldn't have suffocated. So why didn't he come to and start yelling? Nope, it seemed pretty obvious that Brad was probably already dead when whoever it was closed the door and locked the padlock.

Who'd want to kill Brad Nelson?

* * *

Vera Henderson was dismayed at the condition of May's guest room. There were dead flies on the windowsills. How would she ever be able to close her eyes, much less sleep, in a room with dead flies on the windowsills? She hung her overcoat in the closet, which was empty except for a few boxes of Christmas decorations and some wire hangers.

Thank goodness she'd had the presence of mind to take her coat when the fire broke out. If it hadn't been by the door to take to the drycleaners it would've been ruined. Vera sank down on the bed to catch her breath. Goodness, she was going a mile a minute.

There was a knock on the door.

"Come in," Vera called.

May opened the door. "Here are some towels and a nightgown and robe I thought you might need," she said, laying them on the foot of the bed.

"Thank you, May. I don't know what I'd do without you." Vera's lip quivered. It really was too much to think of the house she'd lived in with Chester, where they raised their children, almost burnt to nothing.

"Is there anything else I can get for you?" May asked.

"No. I don't think so. I went to Target and got some underclothes and a couple housedresses to tide me over until I can get up to Wilson's in Greenfield."

"Well, you get settled. I'm going to go and start supper." May started to close the door.

"Wouldn't you like some help?"

"Now, Vera, I can manage peeling a few potatoes. And pork chops practically cook themselves. You settle in and relax." The door closed.

Vera nodded and dabbed her eyes with the handkerchief she'd found in the bottom of her handbag. She inhaled the lavender aroma and felt a little better. Where in the world would she find lavender sachets? She just couldn't abide bureau drawers without lavender sachets. It was a safe bet that May's guest room bureau had no sachets and was probably unlined as well.

Poor May just wasn't a housekeeper. She was forever reading to patients at the nursing home or gardening or volunteering at the library or taking Tai Chi at the senior center. Just last winter May had taken a cooking class from an Indian woman from India and made something green and runny for Vera to try. May swore up and down that it was spinach but Vera preferred her vegetables recognizable. How May could do all that gallivanting and have dead flies on the windowsills, unlined bureau drawers and those awful wire hangers in the closet was beyond Vera.

* * *

May made a beeline for the Jim Beam she kept in the pantry. She filled an old-fashioned glass with ice, a jigger of whiskey and topped it off with some ginger ale. She felt the carbonated bubbles popping against her upper lip as she took a healthy sip. Well, it was more than a sip.

"Give me strength," May mumbled.

She spent the afternoon all discombobulated thanks to her awful conversation with Avola. That feeling hadn't faded despite Avi having eventually called her back to apologize or rather her version of an apology which felt more like an excuse. May had learned years ago that Avola was jealous. That's why she had wanted to tell her about Vera so her appearance wouldn't be so surprising when Avola came over to pick May up for their lunch date earlier today.

Lunch had been strained, May felt hurt and Avi seemed distracted. She swore up and down that it was a bothersome upholstery job but May didn't believe it. It was awful when the two of them weren't getting along. At times like this she tried to remember their train trip to Montreal about twenty years ago.

They'd gone to a lesbian bar. It was down some alley off a street May could no longer remember the name of, in the basement of a hair salon owned by the sister of the bartender.

The ceiling was low; the place was filled with cigarette and cigar smoke. They drank and danced to some foreign-sounding music that seemed as smoky and dark as the bar. May didn't speak French and though she had no idea what was going on she never felt unsettled.

Avola had looked handsome in her navy blue double-breasted suit. Her white shirt gleamed and her red silk tie had small gold hourglasses scattered across it. Avola's dark hair was slicked back, her eyes glistening with excitement and the red wine they were drinking. She'd sewn May a dark green dress with a scooped neckline cut so low May knew she should've been embarrassed but instead felt like dessert—a wicked, high-calorie concoction that you'd never make for yourself but would order at a fancy restaurant.

There were other women there dressed as they were. Some were kissing and groping each other in the booths that lined the dance floor. May was too shy to do that but it was wonderful to dance, pressing their breasts and bellies together, turning her insides to liquid. They had barely made it back to their hotel room where they spent the next two days quenching their pent-up desire. Avi still had that power over her. That's why it was almost funny for Avi to feel jealous of Vera. But May knew Avola could never tolerate her making light of it.

And if today's argument wasn't bad enough she could feel Vera's disapproval coming at her like a thunderstorm. May wasn't able to call her on it. After all, her house had just burned and couldn't be lived in. Vera had to be upset, had to be wondering what she was going to do next.

Better start the potatoes. May was partial to potatoes. Baked, boiled, fried or mashed. White or sweet, Yukon gold, russets, red or the all-purpose. Since she'd learned she had too much potassium in her blood she'd had to cut back. Now it was rice on the plate twice a week and pasta, as Earl referred to anything noodley, twice a week. Consequently, May really went to town on her potato days. Strictly speaking this was not a potato day but a whiskey and soda could only do so much. Sometimes mashed potatoes were required. No doubt Vera would benefit from some as well. Earl would too. He'd had an auction this morning which usually made him cranky as all get-out.

May had known Vera for decades but had never cooked for her besides that shrimp saagwala she'd made as an experiment. They'd always gone out for dinner and Vera always had broiled scrod with baked potato and pickled beets. Well, she'd make mashed with lots of butter and sour cream and some fresh picked chives from the garden.

Once the potatoes were on to boil, she sliced some onion and garlic and started browning it in the cast-iron fry pan that had been her grandmother's. Now, there was a woman who could cook. Her specialty was making something out of nothing. What Gramma could do with salt pork and cabbage was some kind of miracle. Good thing too. Otherwise they would have starved. The smell of frying onions filled the kitchen. May finished her whiskey and ginger.

"Hey, Ma. Whose car is parked in the driveway?" Earl slammed through the kitchen door. "Boy, something smells good."

"How was your day, Sonny?"

"Shitty. You're not going to believe it when I tell you." Earl opened the fridge and looked inside.

"Have a drink with me. I just had a highball and I'm going to have a second." May unwrapped the pork chops, rinsed and dried them and sprinkled them with salt, pepper and a bit of paprika. She pushed the onions to the side and put the chops in the fry pan.

"Two highballs? Something go wrong at bingo today?" Earl chuckled to himself.

"Don't be a wise guy, Earl. I'm in no mood."

"Sorry, Ma. I couldn't resist. I'll make the drinks."

The sounds of ice cubes cracking almost drowned out the sizzling pork fat. Earl offered his mother her drink, his eyes glowing so she knew he had big news or good gossip. They clinked glasses and said "*Nostrovia.*"

May turned the pork chops. Good, nice and brown. "Sonny, will you get me a can of cream of mushroom soup from the pantry?" She poured the soup over the chops and added a half can of skim milk, covered everything with foil and put the pan in the oven.

"So, Ma, you'll never guess who we almost sold at today's auction." Earl drained his glass and set about making another.

"Who or what?"

"Who." Earl told her about Brad Nelson.

"Oh, that poor boy." May poked a simmering potato. Done. "Sonny? Drain these for me, would you?"

"Sure, Ma. But he wasn't a boy. He was a poor middle-aged bastard who lived at the VA and drank too much."

"Earl, if some stranger was standing in this kitchen with us they'd be thinking you and I drank too much. Maybe Brad just had a bad day. Make sure you get all of the water out. I don't want soggy potatoes."

"Brad had a lot of bad days, Ma. Not that I saw that much of him. But, when I did he was usually drinking something out of a brown paper bag."

"Thanks, Sonny." May began mashing, threw in a half stick of butter, a dollop of sour cream and a drizzle of milk. Salt and pepper. She took a taste. Perfect. Put the cover back on the pot and slid it into the oven to keep warm along with the chops.

"How about peas?"

"Okay with me."

May peeked under the tin foil. The pork chops were bubbling. She took the bag of peas from the freezer and sprinkled them around the chops, gave everything a stir and put the foil back on.

"You had a bad day too?" Earl sucked on an ice cube.

"In a word, yes. My morning constitutional was disturbed when I thought I saw something I couldn't identify floating in the river."

"Yeah, the cop who came by about Brad mentioned it."

"The worst part is…" May couldn't tell him about Avola. He knew they were friends but nothing more about their relationship. May wanted to keep it that way.

"Vera Henderson will be staying in the guest room for a while. She had a fire." May took her drink to the table and sat down.

Earl made a face. It was a mystery whether it was because of the fire or because Vera would be upstairs at the other end of the hall from his room. She surmised it had to do with their houseguest and decided she didn't want to think about it just then. He would just have to get a grip and adapt. It wasn't like she was thrilled with Vera's presence either.

* * *

Earl took the trash from under the kitchen sink and scraped the pork chop bones and hard nuggets of mashed potatoes into the bag. He rinsed the plates and put them in the dishwasher along with the glasses and utensils and anything else he could cram in. Except for the cast-iron fry pan which Mother protected with her life. After filling the soap dispenser he pushed the start button and listened with satisfaction as it wheezed to life.

"Anything else to go out to the trash?" he yelled in the vicinity of the living room where Ma and Vera sat watching the local news. Next was the national news, *Wheel of Fortune* and *Jeopardy*. No answer. Sometimes he was convinced that Mother was as deaf as a stone and then she'd hear some comment he made under his breath. Her mission in life seemed to be always to keep him guessing.

Trash taking was an opportunity for smoking. Mother forbade smoking in the house and since she didn't forbid much Earl thought it respectful to honor her wishes. Thankfully she wasn't a prude about alcohol. In fact, if tonight were any indication, there'd be a lot of highball drinking going on while Vera was staying with them.

Vera was one of those old ladies Earl didn't like. Picky and opinionated but never saying anything directly, forcing a person to guess what they wanted. Since Earl worked six days a week, he wouldn't have to put up with her much. Though having her just down the hall meant he'd have to turn down his music and not walk naked from the bedroom to the bath. Mother had already lectured him on the condition of the bathroom, returning the toilet seat to the down position being the most important detail. Apparently Vera might die if she saw a dribble of urine.

Earl dropped the trash bag into one of the barrels that stood shoulder to shoulder along the side of the garage. Good thing tomorrow was trash day. After his cigarette he'd drag the barrels out to the curb and hope some dog didn't get into them overnight.

He lit his butt and wandered out behind the garage to smoke. There was that old pile of bricks he got from one of the storage units when the guy who rented it died and the family came to take the stuff out. He'd brought them home figuring to make a brick patio or walkway through one of Mother's flowerbeds. That was three years ago and he hadn't got to it yet. Oh well, it probably didn't matter in the grand scheme of things. Who knows, maybe he'd get to it now that watching a game wouldn't be as enjoyable with Vera hanging around. Especially since Mother was often gone visiting one of her old lady friends.

The sky was pretty tonight. He wondered when he'd see You-Know-Who again. There was no rhyme or reason to her appearances. He came out here every night as a signal that it was okay to approach. But her visits seemed timed to some cosmic schedule he had no knowledge of. Earl crushed his butt into the ground and dropped the filter into a coffee can he kept just for that purpose.

Guess tonight wasn't going to be the night. Better get to those trash barrels. He didn't want to get up any earlier in the morning than he had to.

CHAPTER THREE

"Have fun in Greenfield." May waved from the herb garden as Vera drove her Buick Skylark down the driveway. "Don't rush back," she muttered.

Having Vera underfoot reminded May of being married. There were mealtimes and laundry schedules to consider, sharing the newspaper and agreeing on the television volume. It had only been a few days and already May found herself looking at the house through Vera's dirt-seeking eyes. They'd be better friends once Vera moved out.

No surprise there. May had gotten along better with her husband after he'd been killed by the bus. In retrospect, their marriage had been a mistake. Mate choosing shouldn't be allowed until after age thirty at least. By then she would've figured out she was attracted to women. At seventeen she was clueless. He was nineteen, in the Air Force and stationed at Otis Air Force Base on Cape Cod. It was a cliché, but the blue in his uniform brought out the blue of his eyes. He had a good set of teeth and wavy hair he tried taming with Vitalis. A prime example that what looked good might not be good for you.

The first couple of years of their marriage were great mainly because Frank was stationed in Texas and then volunteered to go to Korea. May was working and making decisions on her own. The trouble started when he was discharged, came back to Massachusetts and expected her to be a wife. To be fair, he wasn't as bad as some. He didn't drink too much or stay out carousing until all hours. He never laid an angry hand on her or Earl. About the only time he swore was when he tried to fix something around the house and then he'd let loose with a "Jesus H. Christ on a raft" or "shit on a shingle," something along those lines. He was a good man who spent a lot of time at home. Except that for all his being home, it was like he was never really there.

Earl had a touch of that too, more than a touch. He was like the vacant tobacco shop on East Street, windows boarded up and a No Trespassing sign nailed to the door. Occasionally, Earl would show up, just like Frank had, but mostly May might as well have lived alone.

Loneliness in her marriage had driven her to take an upholstery class at the vocational high school. She'd had the idea to learn a trade so she could earn some pin money. An additional benefit was getting out of the house twice a week, meeting some new people and feeling like there was something in her life that was just for her.

Avola LeFebre, a French-Canadian married to Louie LeFebre who owned Big Boy Liquors, taught the class. Upholstery was her specialty but she also taught tailoring and fly-tying, a talent she'd picked up from her fly-fishing daddy while growing up in Quebec. *Avola LeFebre*. The name rolled along May's tongue like high butter-fat vanilla ice cream and still had power over her.

How nervous she had been that first night of class. All through school May had been a nervous student. You'd have thought having a high school diploma, a marriage license and Earl's birth certificate would instill some confidence. She'd walked into class about twenty minutes early, she was early for everything, and stood in the doorway contemplating where to sit. Wherever she chose would be where she sat for the entire semester so it was an important decision. It had been jarring to realize she hadn't decided where she would sit for almost the length of her marriage, always letting Frank choose.

"Excuse me, madam," a woman with a sandpaper voice said.

"Excuse me." May had moved aside and looked into a pair of the brownest eyes she had ever seen, so brown they may have been black.

The woman lugged a huge piece of Samsonite luggage and made her way to the front of the room and behind the desk.

"My tools," she explained to May. "Would you mind assisting me to bring in the demonstration chair?"

"Certainly." May felt irrationally glad to be asked.

Out in the parking lot, in the back of a Rambler wagon, was a horribly floral, cat-attacked wingback found at a junk shop in Greenfield or so said Avola LeFebre, pronounced A-vo-la Le-Fay, as they had introduced themselves by then. The chair was heavy and they had dropped it three times on the way to the classroom, giggling and swearing, Avola in French.

"Please come out with me for coffee and pie after class," Avola said. "I wish to thank you for your assistance."

"Thank you, I'd love to," May had said, feeling almost giddy and not understanding why.

* * *

"That's when it started," May said aloud as she struggled to stand up from the overturned pail she used as a seat while weeding her garden. Because over coffee that evening at Harold's Diner they had both reached for the sugar at the same time and a strange electrical current escaped from Avola's fingers and zinged into May's.

The sun glinting off a car turning into the driveway caught her attention. Hopefully it wasn't Vera returning after less than half an hour. As the car moved into the shade cast by the catalpa tree May was able to see it was a police cruiser. She caught her breath, hoping all her negative thoughts about Vera hadn't caused an accident with her Buick.

A policeman no older than an Eagle Scout walked toward her.

"Mrs. Hammond?"

May nodded.

"I'm Officer Deats with the Hadley police department. I wonder if I might speak with you about your son, Earl." He removed his sunglasses.

"Is he hurt? Has something happened to him?"

"No ma'am. We're curious about his schedule. His friends. What he does in his spare time. Things of that nature."

Uh-oh. What had Sonny gotten himself involved with now?

* * *

Avola was relieved to be free of Mr. Alberti's recliner. He was happy to have his favorite chair returned to him so early in the football season. He'd paid cash which always made her happy. Uncle Sam did not need to know about every bit of money that came her way. Avola loved feeling as though she were getting away with something. A slight breaking of the rules, a bending of the law was very satisfying. If the government were to come for her she would play the part of a befuddled old lady and claim ignorance or forgetfulness. The day they penalized ignorance was the day Congress would bankrupt itself.

Avola felt like celebrating. She was glad to have that job done. Plaid was a nightmare to work with. Besides being ugly, lining up the pattern made her eyes cross. Next on the docket were some cushions for a platform rocker owned by a couple girls in Northampton. They'd chosen burnt-orange velour which should be fairly easy to work with and they were not in any rush though they did say they hoped to have it by Thanksgiving. Entirely possible unless something happened. Once one reached Avola's age, seventy-nine, something could go haywire at any time.

Speaking of haywire, she had better mend the fence with May. Avola had apologized but knew it was not enough. Yes, May had accepted the apology but her voice had sounded funny all during their lunch date. Perhaps the unfortunate Vera had tired her out or perhaps May's feelings were hurt. At this point it did not matter. Amends had to be made. It was possible that Avola had gone too far. Their argument was not so bad but she had flown off the handle. Damn the short fuse she had. Since she was a child this flaw could often rule, causing her to jump to conclusions about people and situations.

Like this ninny she was driving behind at this very minute. There he was, slouched behind the wheel, baseball cap askew playing music so loud his car was vibrating and threatening to dissolve into chassis dust. He was driving ten miles below the speed limit and turning to look at everything like he had never seen cows in a pasture or fields of corn.

She wanted to yell, "Keep your eyes on the road!" But, what good would that do? He'd never hear her over the thumping and shouting that passed for music these days. Whatever happened to beautiful music, to melody and harmony, to holding that special someone in your arms and dancing until your feet threatened to swell out of your shoes?

Maybe she would invite May to go dancing. Take her out for a nice dinner courtesy of Mr. Alberti's ugly plaid recliner. Was there anywhere to dance except for the women's bar downtown? Maybe O.L.D., Older Lesbians Dance, was having a tea dance soon. Avola would call her friend, Nan, to check the schedule.

It would be wonderful to get dressed up and go out on the town. She smiled as she remembered their trip to Montreal, so many years ago now but still filling her heart with happiness. Convincing May to go out as they had that evening might be a tall order. Going to dinner or a movie didn't bother May because they looked like a couple of old ladies out together. But, she would not be easily persuaded to dance with Avola, around other women dancing. Not polkas either but waltzing. May did not want anyone to know about their relationship. Avola was unhappy with the arrangement, had wanted to live with May which May would never allow, because of Earl she had always said.

Avola had acquiesced because she couldn't imagine issuing

an ultimatum and having May call her on it. So, she had satisfied herself with long weekends away, vacations and stolen moments. As she had gotten older it made her more and more sad because life did not last forever and the denied pleasure of living with May made her chest ache. What could she do? It was impossible to force someone to do something, especially May who had a spine of steel.

If only Earl would act like the grown man he was. The time had long passed for him to strike out on his own. The autumn equinox had just gone by, change was in the air. Maybe something would change for him. And for her.

CHAPTER FOUR

Earl minimized his spider solitaire game and watched Ed Thomas and his son, Eddie Jr., drive through the security gate after Ed entered his access code, 61558, into the keypad. They'd rented a 10-by-20 in the 300 building. Their unit was crammed with what looked like junk to him, highly organized but junk all the same. The Thomas's part-time flea market business they ran on the side stored its overflow at the Keepsake.

By scrolling through the accounts program Earl could see that they were paid up to the middle of October, used a business Am Ex account and had never been late so much as one day on rent. Customers like them were great and required minimal interaction from him. Though he did usually go out and schmooze with them a bit seeing as he and Eddie had gone to school together. Well, not quite together. Eddie had been one year ahead but they'd been on the JV baseball team. Man, that guy could pitch and was a much better all-round player than Earl had ever been. A fact that he could accept now but during school it had really bugged him. Bugged him so much that he'd really practiced and worked like hell so Coach Hanks would notice and put him on the first string and not leave him sitting on the bench, only putting him in the game when the team was either so far ahead or behind that the possibility of him screwing up wouldn't change the outcome of the game.

It was the tail end of the freshman season when Ma had told him.

She'd picked him up from baseball practice and he'd been starving as usual. He'd wanted to go to McDonald's where some of the guys always went but as usual the Old Lady had forbidden it saying it was fake food and if he wanted a hamburger so bad she could make one for him when they got home and then she'd burst into tears. Even as a stupid kid he'd known something else was going on, knew it had to be bad, but he found himself afraid to ask. So, he'd slouched in the passenger seat scared to say anything. On the way home she'd stopped at The Slice, given him ten bucks and told him to get whatever he wanted. That's when he really knew something was wrong because she'd never been a big fan of pizza either. But, he was fourteen, nothing but a stomach and a dick. He ordered a large pepperoni. It wasn't until they'd got home and he'd eaten half the pizza and taken a shower that she'd told him about his father.

After that everything, even baseball, had started to seem like more trouble than it was worth. Eddie had kept with it though and gotten himself a baseball scholarship to UMASS. The summer before his freshman year Eddie cracked up his ten-speed and smashed his head all to hell. That ended baseball for Eddie and once he'd got out of the hospital he'd gone to work at his father's appliance repair business.

All this was further proof that life was the greatest crapshoot of all, a giant cluster fuck. If it wasn't for You-Know-Who it would be impossible to live life around that fact. Nothing really seemed to matter in a world where a future Red Sox pitcher turned into a walking, talking zombie and where some kid's Dad could get flattened into roadkill while he jaywalked and read the business section of the morning paper.

Earl locked the office and walked out to the 300 building. Mr. Thomas saw him coming and waved.

"Hey, Earl. How are you on this fine day?"

"Pretty good. You?"

"Magnificent. Me and Eddie here are loading up for a trip to Vermont."

Earl thought it looked more like Mr. Thomas was loading up and Eddie was sitting on the hood of the truck playing a hand-held computer game.

"Yeah? What's in Vermont?"

"My brother lives in Rutland and they're having some kind of Fall Festival or something and Eddie and I thought it might be a good place to set up."

"Rutland's nice. I used to go camping up there off Route Five somewhere." Earl pulled out cigarettes and lit up.

"Yup. We were going to wait and go up tomorrow morning but Eddie thought it'd be a good idea to go up tonight and stay at that Motel 6 he likes with the indoor swimming pool."

"Sounds great. Well, I guess I better get to work."

"Hey, before you go…what's this I hear about a dead body in a storage unit?"

"That's pretty much it. Found him a couple days ago during the last auction."

"No kidding. Boy, makes you wonder what the world's coming to. Used to be such a nice little town, now there's a dead body showing up all over the place."

"Looks like the guy got drunk and died. Nothing serious, just unfortunate."

"Terrible thing for his family. Do they know who it is?"

"Yeah, some guy from the VA. You know, we get a lot of those folks in here and some got problems."

"Yeah. Well, Earl, you take care. How's your mother doing?"

"Fine, thanks. Have a good time in Vermont, Mr. Thomas."

"Thanks. We will. Eddie likes a little road trip."

Earl unlocked the 10-by-30 in the 600 building that served as storage for Keepsake. A faint smell of gasoline drifted out. He crushed his butt into the gravel before he went in. No use having an explosion.

Sometimes he wondered how things might've been different if his old man hadn't died. Like say if Mother had died instead, not that he wanted her to die but what if the dice had rolled that way. It was hard to say. His father hadn't been one of those dads like Mr. Thomas, for example. Mr. Thomas had always gone to Eddie's games and had taken him fishing and hunting. It was like he enjoyed spending time with Eddie. Earl's old man hadn't been like that. He'd worked and when he wasn't working he was either reading or watching the tube. Sports, *Gunsmoke* or some cop show; too bad he didn't live to see cable. Between ESPN and TV Land he would've been in hog heaven.

It probably wouldn't have mattered and if it had it's not like he would ever know about it. There were basically two camps in the world. Those who thought everything mattered—Mother fell into that category—and those who thought nothing mattered. Earl belonged in the last group. He imagined there'd be people who advocated for a third camp. The people who said the truth was somewhere in the middle, that little stuff like what you ate for breakfast wasn't important and only the big stuff like bike accidents and fathers' deaths counted for anything. The middle group was a bunch of fence-riders who couldn't make a decision.

Earl climbed into the golf cart, turned the key and backed out. Time for trash detail and to make his job easier, or at least more interesting, he used a grabber he'd found in the relinquished unit belonging to an old guy who'd had a stroke and whose family didn't want his stuff. People in wheelchairs used the grabber to pick up things they couldn't reach. After weeks of practice he was able to snatch most trash bits without ever having to leave the comfort of the golf cart. Early on, during his practice sessions, he'd made a game of it by bringing out office trash and strewing it around and then backtracking with the grabber. Batteries, crushed pens and cigarette butts still gave him trouble but he was working on it.

Trash detail was a prime opportunity to look busy without really being busy. He'd smoke a bit, listen to the radio he'd rigged up to run off the battery and relax. If his Battle-Ax Boss came by to check on him she'd have no complaints. He was easy to find if one of his customers needed him because who, after all, but an employee would be tootling around in a golf cart.

* * *

May raked her herb garden too vigorously and found she had uprooted some chicks and hens that grew along the rock border. Maybe she was too upset to be gardening though she usually found it very peaceful to work in her flower beds. Of course, she never thought the day would come when she would be visited by a policeman asking after her son. Officer Deats must have a screw loose if he thought Earl had anything to do with that poor man's death. But the more she tried to tell him that the more he didn't seem to hear her. It was very difficult to dislodge an idea from a man's head.

May replanted the hens and chicks and went to sit in an Adirondack on the side porch. Her hip was aching; maybe she should call it quits and give the gardening a rest. She'd just clean off her shoes and make a cup of tea and consider Earl and his predicament.

A van tooted and pulled into the drive. Goodness, it was like Grand Central here today.

"Oh, hi Avi, I didn't recognize your van," May said.

"May, how are you today? I had it painted, looks new but no new car payment. White is better than dark maroon don't you think? Been in your garden?" Avola asked while climbing the steps to the porch and plunking herself next to May in the neighboring Adirondack.

"Yes, I'm starting to put it to bed for the winter. It's sad to think of summer coming to an end," May said.

Avola took May's hand. "What is it honey? You seem a bit down. Is Vera wearing out her welcome?"

"Yes, but that's not it. The police came by earlier."

"The police? Here? Whatever for?"

May told her about the dead body at Keepsake Self Storage. "Apparently they are investigating and came by to ask about Earl. Who his friends are, where does he spend his time and does he belong to any political organizations."

"Unbelievable." Avola wet her finger and rubbed at some dirt on May's cuticle.

"I realized I didn't know that much about Earl," May said. "The only place he hangs out is the VFW and he doesn't belong because he isn't a veteran. Years ago the men there started letting him come around because they all knew his father," May said.

"I can't imagine anyone thinking Earl capable of murder."

"I know. He asked to see Earl's computer which I didn't feel comfortable with because it's his and not mine. And his cell phone bill. I didn't even know he had a cell phone. I don't think Earl has the gumption to kill anyone let alone one of his customers at Keepsake." May shook her head.

"It is farfetched. Sometimes your son seems to barely have a pulse."

"I called him after the police left. He'd just come in from picking up trash and when I told him they were coming back with a search warrant all he said was he wouldn't be home for dinner. I asked if he was up to no-good and he said don't be silly. He was just going to play cards with the guys. I've never known him to play cards a day in his life but he could be a card shark and I'd never know."

"I'm sure they will discover Earl is as harmless as you know him to be. They probably have to search every avenue to make sure they haven't forgotten something."

"Do you think that's all it is?" May asked.

"What more could it be? May I offer a suggestion to take your mind off things?"

"There's a lot going on at the moment, and between Vera and Earl there doesn't seem to be anything I can do about any of it."

"Come to my house this evening. I will make dinner and you can put your feet up and relax. Maybe we'll have a rousing game of cribbage afterward." Avola winked and squeezed her hand.

May squeezed back. "It is tempting but shouldn't I be home in case the police come back with their warrant?"

"Life does not stop because the police have a warrant."

"You're right, Avi. Dinner with you would be wonderful. What time should I come?"

"Five o'clock?"

May scanned the street and saw no one there. She swooped in and kissed Avola's cheek. "Thank you, honey. I'll see you then."

* * *

Vera unlocked May's house and put her shopping bags on the table. She'd had such a pleasant time at Wilson's in Greenfield, wandering through the notions department, not that she needed buttons or snaps just now but she'd found it relaxing. It was painful to think of her sewing basket and button collection, so large it filled three Danish Butter Cookie tins, melted to unrecognizable lumps in the fire. She had bought a seam ripper, very handy for things including ripping seams, a few needles and spools of white, tan and black nylon thread. She remembered when thread came on wooden spools. The kids used to save those spools and cover them with glue and glitter, put them on pipe cleaners and hang them from the Christmas tree. They'd string popcorn and cranberries, make paper garlands and bake gingerbread men and put them on the tree too. Those days when the kids were small and excited about Santa coming were wonderful. His arrival was a disciplinary tool that worked from Halloween to Christmas morning.

After Wilson's she'd gone out for lunch at the Shady Glen and had really enjoyed her tuna roll and coffee. How she wished she could've returned to her house rather than May's, not that she didn't appreciate her help; it was just that it was hard to relax with things in such disarray. She noticed a note propped against the napkin holder.

> *Dear Vera,*
> *Out running errands and then to Ladies Auxiliary meeting.*
> *Won't be home for dinner. Earl out tonight.*
> *See you later, May*

It was almost three o'clock. That meant she had hours to herself. She went and got a bath towel and laid it in the bottom of the kitchen sink and filled it with hot, soapy water. Then into the dining room, which was more like May's hobby room, and opened the china cabinet. After making a little space on the table, she removed the turkey platter, the fishplates and the soup tureen and took them to the kitchen for a hot bath. Such beautiful china, creamy white with bluebells around the edges, all of it covered with dust that was so hard and crusty only hot water and soap would remove it. Imagine May letting her things corrode.

After the platter, plates and tureen were rinsed and in the drainer Vera supposed that to really do the job right she'd have to dust that top shelf. Fresh contact paper would be nice but she had to remember where she was. Honestly, it just wasn't fair. Her house, a picture of domestic perfection turned to ashes, and May's, little more than a pigsty, standing tall and true enough that the floors barely had a slant to them after 150 years.

Vera sprayed the shelf with Pledge and wiped it down paying particular attention to the corners. At home she would have used a Q-tip but there was no reason to go that far here.

The soup tureen looked brand new and gleaming after its introduction to hot water. The sight of it gave her the strength to proceed to the coffee and tea service on the second shelf. Honestly, what was May doing with china? Chinet maybe, Vera chuckled to herself. That was funny. She'd have to tell her daughter Sandy that when they talked next Sunday.

The kids, after they heard about the fire, had chipped in and gotten Vera a cell phone. Which was sweet of them and just as well because there was very little privacy in May's kitchen where her phone was located. To be fair, she'd been used to a good deal of privacy after Chester had died from emphysema. Poor man, how he'd suffered carrying oxygen around on his back like an Indian papoose. Toward the end, all he could do was lie in his recliner and reread his Zane Grey books. He was halfway through *Riders of the Purple Sage* when he died. That was the only book she'd kept when she had all of Chester's books and paraphernalia hauled away by Ernie Horschack's Junk Emporium out on route 116.

Vera was washing out the teapot when there was a knock at the front door. Who could that be? Anyone who knew May knew to come to the kitchen door.

"Yes?" Vera said, opening the door. There were three very tall men standing there, one wearing a police uniform and the other two wearing suits. They couldn't be Jehovah's Witnesses because they didn't go around with the police.

"Mrs. Hammond?" the one in the blue suit said.

"No. I'm Vera Henderson. I'm staying with May for a while."

"Mrs. Henderson, I'm Officer Marconi and this is Officer Brooks from the Massachusetts State Police Crime Unit..." They flashed their badges. "...And this is Officer Deats from Hadley police. We have a search warrant for these premises. May we come in?"

"Oh, well, I don't know. Shouldn't you wait for May to come back? I don't really feel comfortable having people in..."

"Mrs. Henderson." Officer Deats stepped forward. "The search warrant is all we need to come in. It'll be all right. I'm sure Mrs. Hammond wouldn't mind. I was here earlier this morning and told her we'd be back. She's expecting us."

"Okay. If you say so. I'm just cleaning up the dining room a bit. I hope I won't be in your way."

"No ma'am. This won't take long," Officer Marconi said as they all trooped into the foyer and dispersed like dust bunnies on a breezy day.

Goodness gracious, what was May involved in? Maybe she'd give Sandy a call right now. Some things were just too important to wait until Sunday.

CHAPTER FIVE

Avola opened a bottle of wine, a nice red she'd bought at Stop Your Whining down on Crafts Avenue. The woman behind the counter had recommended it and at twelve dollars it fit into her budget and would go well with the pot roast she was making. Poor May needed the solace of comfort food. Avola had also bought some lavender foot lotion for May's foot massage which often led to a trip into the bedroom. Avola smiled at that possibility. Sex with May was still good despite their age and the minor adjustments they'd had to make for bad knees, sore hips and reduced flexibility.

Thankfully she had had the wisdom to go to May's this morning and invite her for an apology dinner. After seeing how upset she was Avola hadn't wanted to bring up their recent argument. The important thing was to spend some time together. Avola was determined to divert May's concerns with copious amounts of charm and good humor. May was due to arrive in about thirty minutes which would give the wine time to breathe, a strange phrase as if it were alive over there on the counter by the toaster.

The pot roast had been simmering all afternoon. She'd added potatoes, carrots and onions a little while ago. A baguette warmed in the oven, the table was set with the good china she'd received as a wedding gift when she and Louie "Big Boy Liquors" LeFebre had gotten married many misguided years ago. Poor Louie, he'd married a lesbian though he didn't know it. Avola knew but had wanted to immigrate to America and marriage was the easiest way.

It was not nice what she did…in fact, it was very bad. Probably the worst thing she had ever done and it turned so ugly too. Ah well, she tried not to think about it. Thirty years ago now…one would think it would have faded into the recesses of her memory by this time. But, no, perhaps those instances of cruelty never faded especially when one was the perpetrator.

Avola was surprised he hadn't killed her. In his Big Boy Liquor Store he was jovial, always laughing or telling a joke of which he knew thousands. But, each evening he would arrive home with a few nips of Dewar's Black Label or Canadian Club or whatever some liquor salesman had given him and sit in the den watching television and drinking and brooding. It was as though he knew he'd had the wool pulled over his eyes yet he couldn't figure out who had done the pulling.

He was surprised when he found out it was Avola. Those were the days before no-fault divorce. She was happy to take the blame. Should she admit she had taken pleasure in being honest about the reason, conjugal incompatibility?

Louie laughed when she'd told him and then started throwing nip bottles at her. Avola was glad, at that point, that he never drank from fifths. She'd left that night having had the foresight to pack her things and move bit by bit over the previous days into a furnished studio apartment in a home owned by a Women's Studies professor from Smith. Avola had reupholstered her living room suite in cream and beige jacquard fabrics.

It did not end there. Louie "Big Boy Liquors" LeFebre began to drink his nips at work, quickly, while restocking the beer coolers or dusting his inventory. How did Avola know this? She could imagine. His drinking, his growing sweaty in his now unironed plaid sport shirts, and getting angry and sweatier and more angry until he could not imagine what to do next. Unchanneled anger is a terrible thing; Avola knew that, she had been known to suffer from it too.

Poor Louie. He eventually made himself crazy. He set fire to his Big Boy Liquor Store, figuring to burn himself up but even that didn't go as planned. He was rescued when a passing jogger noticed the flames and called it in. Louie spent several months in a burn ward, several years in prison for arson and was now a monk in an abbey in upstate New York where the monks supported themselves making goat cheese and wine. At that moment a bottle of the same label, Brothers of The Mountain Vineyards, was breathing on her counter. It was a very small world.

* * *

Earl was pissed to find his mother gone and that Vera had let the cops into the house and up to his bedroom. She kept saying they had a search warrant, over and over like some broken old-lady record. The cops had taken his hard drive, his survivalist manuals and his loose-leaf binders on past life regression and alien abductions. Fortunately they missed his little stash of marijuana. A good thing too. If there'd ever been a time to get stoned it was now.

"God damn it," he said aloud as he sat on his desk chair, rolling it over to the open bedroom window. He lit up a cigarette and blew the smoke outside, left the butt smoldering in the ashtray and rolled a whisper-thin joint that he lit from his cigarette. He held the smoke in, trying not to cough, until he thought his lungs would explode. Exhaled out the window, took two more hits and put the thing out. The hell with not smoking in the house. Finally something loosened in his chest and he relaxed back to finish his butt.

A rainsquall had just passed through, freshening the humid September air. A car passed in the street, tires whooshing on the wet pavement. "Mother and Child Reunion" blared from the car's radio. That song sure brought back memories.

The aliens had first visited the summer after his father died.

He and Mom had had supper and he'd taken out the garbage as usual. The air that long ago evening was warm and silky against his skin. He'd never felt it like that before or since, like something or someone was brushing against him without actually touching him. And that was before he smoked the joint he'd bought off his friend Doug.

He'd been sitting behind the garage, and had had only a couple hits because he wanted to save some for later and because he didn't want to get so fucked up his mother would wonder what was wrong with him. He'd just lit a cigarette, which Ma didn't like either but didn't bug him too much about figuring he was having a hard enough time with Pop gone.

Bats were swooping after bugs and the western horizon was getting a bruised look when there was a bright flash of light and he became aware of a humming. He didn't hear it so much as feel it as it folded around him like a blanket. A blue tube of light came out of the sky and shone on him like he was a specimen in a lab experiment. He levitated and when he was about twelve feet off the ground he got sucked up the tube into a round room about the size of the school gym, all stainless steel with a floor of white glass. He found himself standing on a black disc in the center of the room that pulsed in time with his heart, which was racing but gradually slowed to almost nothing.

A woman appeared. She was tall, maybe seven feet and very thin and had a blue tone to her skin and very black, bright eyes that blinked side to side instead of up and down.

"Welcome." Her voice sounded like a radio DJ.

"Hi." Earl was relieved to hear that his voice sounded surer of himself than he felt.

"We will not harm you," the woman said.

Earl didn't know what to say to that so he didn't say anything.

"We wish to scan your body-mind. You will experience no discomfort except for excessive thirst after the procedure is complete. You will then be returned to your planet."

"Okay," he said without knowing why.

Instantly he found himself suspended in a giant bowl of clear Jell-O-like stuff. Violet lights flashed every five seconds and he could hear what sounded a lot like the song "Mother and Child Reunion." Which should have seemed weird but didn't.

"You will never be alone," the woman said as he found himself back behind the garage, the cigarette burning down to his fingertips.

Earl knew then that he had been chosen. It hadn't been easy all these years since then to know this thing and blend in like he was just anybody else. Another car came down the street. Was it his imagination or was he hearing "Mother and Child Reunion" again? What were the chances of that? He must be hearing things. He squinted. Wait a minute. Wasn't that the same car that had just driven by? He got his binoculars from the desk drawer. Shit, it was the same car and he was hearing the same song. This was a sign. Usually when You-Know-Who wanted him to know something she came by for a visit. This time she must be hoping he'd get the symbolism and take action.

He clattered downstairs hoping to miss Vera. Not only had she let the cops in but then had lost the warrant so he couldn't see where else they had permission to search. She said she'd misplaced it while she was cleaning out the china cabinet. He'd looked all over the dining room, all through the trash, the pile of mail on the kitchen table, the recycling bin. Nothing. If only his mother would get home she might be able to find the damn thing.

On his way outside he opened the fridge for a beer, experiencing a moment of wild hope that the warrant might be in the vegetable crisper. No such luck. He settled into a lawn chair under the catalpa tree, lit a butt and tried to control his breathing. Were they going to search the Keepsake? Now that would really be a bitch because then his boss would find out and you never knew how she was going to react to anything.

* * *

A glint of sun flashed into May's eyes as she pulled into the driveway. Her heart sank as she noticed Vera's car. And there was Earl's car too. What was he doing home? He should still be at work this time of afternoon and he had said he was going out tonight play cards with some of his friends. Cigarette smoke wafted into her car from the westerly breeze clearing away the last of the showers. He must be prowling around outside somewhere. May scanned the garden and saw him lighting one cigarette from another and flicking the butt into her hydrangea hedge, something she had asked him not to do.

She supposed she'd have to speak to him when all she really wanted to do was freshen up for her dinner with Avola. She shouldn't have come home. The temptation to shift into reverse and drive over to Avi's and act like she'd never been here was almost too much to resist.

The screen door slammed. Vera bustled toward May's car waving a piece of paper. Earl charged from the other direction blowing smoke like a locomotive and striding toward her car or toward Vera. She couldn't be sure. There was sure to be a collision.

"May? May? I've got something to show you." Vera called, waving the paper like she was surrendering. May could hear it crackling.

"Is that the search warrant I was looking for?" Earl yelled.

May watched a look of alarm wash over Vera's face. Clearly Vera wanted May to have the paper and not Earl. But Earl was much closer to Vera than Vera was to May. Had May heard correctly? Did Earl say search warrant? That nice Officer Deats with the horrible chin rash had said he'd be coming back with one.

Through the windshield she watched Earl grab Vera's wrist and yank it down so he could reach the warrant. Vera, who was often tottery because she wore shoes meant for a much younger woman got thrown off balance and fell backward onto the asphalt.

"Earl! What are you thinking?" May yelled and struggled to get out of her seat belt, an invention that often felt like an octopus.

She watched as he snatched the paper out of Vera's hand, looked at it briefly and rushed to his own car. She heard the roar of his over-revved engine, the metallic grind as he forced the transmission into reverse and in his rush to get out, backed over her daylilies and into the street. The transmission ground as he jerked into drive and roared off in the direction of town.

Finally the seat belt released and she was able to get out of the car. Vera was lying on her back, waving her arms.

"Help me, May."

What was wrong with Earl? Who had he become that he would knock down an old lady and leave her like a turtle on its back? All to get a search warrant? Soap operas had less intrigue.

"Just a minute, Vera. I'm coming." May hurried toward her.

"Please, help me. I can't get up!"

"Stay right where you are. You may have hurt something." May clasped Vera's hand.

"Oh, May. I'm…I'm…" Vera erupted into tears.

"Let me call nine-one-one. I'll be right back."

"Use my cell phone. It's in my apron pocket." Vera fished around for it extracting a few wadded tissues and some Q-tips before she located the contraption.

"I've never used one. Earl…" May cringed inside at the mention of her son's name. "…wanted me to get one but I've resisted. I don't want to always be available by phone."

"It isn't always convenient I know." Vera flipped the phone, no bigger than a deck of cards, open. It chortled at her. After pressing the appropriate numbers she handed the phone to May.

"What is your emergency?" said the tinny-voiced 911 operator.

"May Hammond here!" May shouted into the phone. "My friend has fallen in the driveway and may be hurt!"

"Your address please."

"163 East Street in Hadley."

"Is she breathing?"

"Goodness, yes. We just want to be sure nothing is broken."

"Yes, ma'am. Would you like me to stay on the line until the ambulance arrives?"

"No, that isn't necessary. Thank you. Goodbye." May shouted and gave the phone back to Vera who squirreled it away in her apron.

"I'm so sorry, Vera. I don't know what Earl could have been thinking. I've never seen him act like that."

"He was very upset with me for letting the police into the house. But they had a search warrant and they said you knew about it..." Vera's voice trailed off.

"I did know about it. You didn't do anything wrong."

"I wanted you to see the search warrant because, well, it's your house after all. So, I let him think I didn't know where it was. But I did because I'd hidden it in the paper towel roll. I saw that on *Murder She Wrote*. He said I was a demented old bat."

May winced. She'd raised him to be polite to his elders. Of course, she'd also raised him to stay out of trouble and not to get mixed up with the police. Was it possible that he had gone over to the dark side when she wasn't looking?

"When I heard you drive in I rushed out to give you the warrant..."

"Now, don't upset yourself anymore by talking about it. I hear the sirens coming."

A gleaming white ambulance, lights pulsating, pulled up behind May's car. The siren stopped in mid shriek. Two young women leapt from the cab and rushed toward May and Vera. They were neatly attired in navy blue trousers and white blouses festooned with American flags and shoulder patches that proclaimed them from Emergency Response Services.

Within fifteen minutes the paramedics had loaded Vera into the ambulance and sped off to Cooley Dickinson Hospital with blue lights flashing. May had assured Vera she would meet her there as soon as possible. But first she had to call Avola and tell her she wouldn't be able to come for dinner after all.

CHAPTER SIX

May was nervous as she contemplated calling Avola. They'd just recently had that argument and she knew tonight's dinner was an apology of sorts, not that they would ever talk about it, Avi wasn't a talker so much as a doer. It was sweet of her to make May dinner and she knew the food would be delicious. Darn Earl for behaving like a heathen and darn Vera for wearing espadrilles with no arch support. She could kick herself for ever stopping home to freshen up before going to Avola's. It was all because she was hoping for a little romantic interlude and she wanted to be ready when Avola made her move.

May dialed.

"Al-lo?" Avola's voice always sounded so exotic over the phone.

"Hi honey, it's me…there has been a little problem." May said.

"Yes? Are you well?"

"Oh, yes. It's Vera. It's a long story but the short version is Earl knocked her down and I had to call the ambulance. She's been taken to the emergency room. I am so sorry but I feel like I should go and make sure she's all right." May wished she were sitting in Avola's living room having a glass of wine and smelling whatever fragrant smell permeated Avi's house.

"Perhaps you could stop by afterward? I made pot roast which I know from experience makes an excellent sandwich on rye bread with spicy mustard."

"Oh yes, I would love to. I'm sure it won't take long. I'll just make sure she is okay and I'll get a phone number for a daughter and hand Vera off to her. I shouldn't be more than an hour, two at the most." May was thrilled Avola wasn't upset. Hopefully, the evening wouldn't be a total loss.

"Excellent. I will look forward to seeing you soon."

"Me too, Avi. Bye for now," May said.

* * *

"Do not make a mountain out of a molehill," Avola announced to her kitchen appliances. It had been one of Papa's favorite sayings and had driven her mother crazy each and every time he had said it. Though he continued to say it and she continued to be driven crazy. A little drama, the same drama played out over and over again.

Avola fixed herself a plate of pot roast, poured a glass of wine and adjourned to the living room to eat with the evening news. Poor company compared to eating dinner across the table from May. Instead she looked into the beady eyes of the newscaster.

The unfortunate Vera was a molehill. Why did Avola keep seeing her as a mountain? Even though she knew this her mind fell into the well-worn groove of suspicion. Maybe the one-track mind ran in her family. Mother had certainly had one.

Avola remembered when her brother had drowned, his little body swept away by the river and never found, and poor Mother became convinced that Gasteau had not really died. At the same time she was never able to say where he was since he was not at home. Nothing anyone said or did, not even the passage of time, was able to alter Mother's viewpoint. As far as

Avola knew, Mother had died believing Gasteau would walk in at any moment.

This was a mountain that Mother had tried to turn into a molehill which did not work either.

Instead of stewing over it she decided to get started on the cushions for that nice lesbian couple. The burnt-orange fabric would be beautiful against the blond maple wood of the rocker. With any luck she would have enough fabric left for a small round pillow to support the sitter's back, a nice touch which along with word of mouth assured Avola a constant supply of customers.

She snapped off the television and returned her empty plate and glass to the kitchen sink. Dishes could wait.

* * *

Earl pressed his gate code into the numerical pad three times before he got his number right. His fingers were shaking so much it was like being jazzed on too much coffee. He watched the gate slide slowly open, screeching a bit at the midway point, and then he drove past the office to the 10-by-30 in the 600 building used for storage. The gate closed in his rearview mirror.

The warrant gave permission for the police to search his home and place of business. He knew he was taking a risk showing up at the Keepsake but he figured the cops would have to get hold of his boss to open the gate. And that could take hours because the battle-ax played in the Saturday night golf league at the Northampton Country Club and then had a three-martini dinner at the 19th hole. She never remembered her gate code when she hadn't even had three drinks. This assured him a bit of elbow room but he couldn't waste any time.

The first thing he needed was a different car. Renting one wasn't possible because that required a credit card, very traceable. The whole point of leaving was not to be followed. That's where Melvin and Serena Horowicz came in. They were in Israel for a year. Their car, a very upscale Buick, was in unit three-thirteen and he had a key because he was supposed to start it for them once a week. Perfect. He'd put his car in their unit and take their car. They weren't due back until next August. By then the cops would've found Brad's real killer and when Earl returned everyone would be glad to see him.

It took about fifteen minutes to switch cars. Now for the stuff in the 600 building. He unlocked the door and was greeted by the familiar smell of gasoline. He climbed over the golf cart and lawnmower to the back of the shed and removed the spare aluminum wall panels and brackets and piled them on the golf cart. Underneath was a tarp which covered a metal trunk he'd bought off a guy who'd rented a unit in the 500 building. He doubted the cops would ever find it but they had dogs now that could sniff out everything. In the trunk was his larger stash of marijuana which he would take with him. He didn't want the cops getting into that or his mother finding out either. Next he took his ham radio. Nothing illegal about that so far as he knew, but since 9/11 the government was interested in a lot of things it should mind its own business about. There was probably no way they could trace who he'd been talking to. Thank God it wasn't like the Internet where they could track everything you did. Next he pulled out his MREs. Civilians weren't supposed to have the meals but he'd gotten them from a buddy down at the American Legion who used them for hunting trips.

This Saturday night things sure were different from last Saturday night. Last week he'd had some beers with the guys at the Legion, not having a care in the world. This week he was about to become a fugitive from justice. Maybe he'd make *America's Most Wanted*. He picked up the few remaining bags containing antennas and receivers, some quite heavy, set them aside and reversed the process of hiding the trunk. He would make his way west and hope You-Know-Who would contact him soon and let him know what he should do next.

He'd been at the Keepsake about half an hour. Time to get moving. He drove Melvin's car to the bank and withdrew as much money as they'd let him take. He'd better go to as many ATMs as he could find in the area and empty his savings account. Then gas up the car and drive through the Doughnut Monster for an iced coffee and a cinnamon roll. He drove the back way through Hadley and South Hadley and got on 91 South by the Old Soldiers home in Holyoke. He didn't really relax until he got down around Hartford and joined the legions of cars heading west on I-84.

About eleven o'clock he got tired and decided to stop and sleep. Melvin's car was very comfortable, electronic seats that moved every which way with the touch of a button, but he didn't want to sleep in it. So he pulled in at a motel in Hazelton, Pennsylvania, paid cash and signed himself in as Greg Brady.

He got a six-pack of beer, stopped at Wendy's next door for a bacon double cheeseburger, to hell with cholesterol, and went to his room. It was nothing special but it had cable, there was a soda machine down the hall and a *Lethal Weapon* marathon on HBO. Maybe if he ate enough fast food, drank enough beer and watched enough TV he would pass out and not have to think about search warrants, pushing Vera down, running over Mother's daylily bed or the fact that he was forty-seven years old and had finally left home.

CHAPTER SEVEN

May sat with Vera in the emergency room cubicle at Cooley Dickinson Hospital. Vera was groggy from the drug they'd given her to calm her down and help with the pain in her lower back. She was stretched out on the gurney under a pile of heated blankets. May coveted one of those blankets herself, the ER was kept as cold as a meat locker.

Where was Dr. Trueblood anyway? At least May thought that was the doctor's name but did not feel wholly confident. Young people spoke so fast in this day and age that May missed about half of what anyone under age thirty said to her. Dr. Trueblood, or whoever she was, had used that hearty, strident voice people often used when speaking to the elderly. It was distracting. May always found herself wondering what the speaker's real voice sounded like when they weren't working so hard to sound cheerful. May nearly jumped out of her skin when Dr. Trueblood jerked open the curtain separating their cubicle from the rest of the emergency room.

"Mrs. Henderson?" Dr. Trueblood spoke loudly. "Mrs. Henderson?" She crossed to the gurney Vera was sleeping on.

"Has she been like this long?"

"Ever since she got back from X-ray," May said, admiring Dr. Trueblood's wavy auburn hair.

"Oh, well, perhaps you can answer a question for me. Do you know how to reach her next of kin?" Dr. Trueblood looked at May over the top of her reading glasses.

"Her kids set up her cell phone on speed dial and since she has eight children there'll be eight numbers in there. Just be careful not to dial her youngest, Heidi. Vera and Heidi don't get along since Heidi became a pagan priestess and joined a collective in Leverett."

"Oh." Dr. Trueblood looked confused. "The thing is Mrs…"

"Hammond. May Hammond."

"Mrs. Hammond, the thing is Mrs. Henderson has a fractured coccyx."

"Coccyx? That doesn't sound good," May said, also thinking it sounded rather obscene.

"Well, it's not life threatening but it is uncomfortable and unfortunately, untreatable. We'll give Mrs. Henderson something for pain and a doughnut. That should help."

"A doughnut? Doctor, Vera has borderline diabetes. I don't think sweets are a good idea though it might cheer her up."

"No, Mrs. Hammond. You misunderstand me. I meant a doughnut she should sit on."

"Like when you have hemorrhoids?"

"Exactly. The coccyx, or tailbone, is very sensitive and sitting on the doughnut will relieve some of the pressure."

"Of course." May wondered why the doctor hadn't said tailbone to begin with. She was probably just out of school and had to prove she knew something.

"I'm writing a prescription and here are some care instructions." Dr. Trueblood thrust a paper toward May.

"When can she go home?"

"When she wakes up. I'll send a nurse in to help her get dressed. Have a good evening." The doctor disappeared behind the swirling curtain.

Having a good evening seemed impossible. May was anxious to get to Avola's and feeling a bit resentful. Earl was Lord knew where. Vera had a broken tailbone because of him. Uncharitable as it might be, May knew that Vera was going to be a difficult patient and would expect May to put up with it because Earl was the reason for the problem to begin with. Hopefully, Vera's prescription was for something potent. The minute she could get on Vera's cell phone she was going to call her children, even the pagan priestess would do, and let them work out a way to take care of Vera.

"Hello?" someone said from the other side of the curtain.

"Yes?"

"Can I come in?"

"Sure."

The curtain skimmed open revealing the tall, ponytailed paramedic from earlier.

"Why, hello there," May said.

"I just wanted to stop by and see if everything was all right with your friend here."

"That was sweet of you. Vera will be fine. She has a broken tailbone but there doesn't seem to be much they can do about that."

"No ma'am, one of the vestiges from the past when we all had tails." The paramedic stepped to the side of the gurney and gently touched Vera's arm.

"Mrs. Henderson?" She shook Vera's arm.

Boy, they really must have dosed her up, May thought.

"Mrs. Henderson?" The paramedic's fingers slid to Vera's wrist.

* * *

The next thing May knew she was shuttled out of the cubicle and given a chair in the waiting area. A nice nurse, the one with red hair that didn't look entirely natural, said Vera had suffered a medical event requiring immediate attention. Medical event sounded ominous but wasn't very informative. May imagined medical people swarming around Vera like bees around a hive.

Goodness she hoped Vera wasn't dying. At that thought May felt tears prick her eyelids. She felt terrible for being so uncharitable a few moments ago.

May wasn't much for praying or church-going but she knew Vera was a devout Catholic and attended Mass weekly. It might be a good idea to say a prayer, for Vera's sake and maybe a small one for Earl, wherever he was. She adjusted herself in the molded plastic chair and tried to think of a way to start a prayer. "Dear God" was probably a good place to start though it rang false. Who really knew how dear he was and if he was a he at all. Maybe she should pray to the Virgin Mary, Catholics really liked her.

May closed her eyes and whispered, "Dear Virgin Mary please don't let Vera…"

"Excuse me, Mrs. Hammond?"

May's eyes popped open when she heard Dr. Trueblood's voice.

"Yes? How's Vera?"

Dr. Trueblood sat in the chair next to May. Uh-oh, she thought. It's never good when a doctor sits down to talk with you though to be fair she looked exhausted, her brown eyes were red rimmed behind her glasses.

"Mrs. Henderson appears to have had a stroke."

"A stroke? But, she was fine when she came in."

"Yes, well…in any case we're going to admit her to ICU, run some tests and see what's going on." Dr. Trueblood patted her knee and stood up.

"Can I see her?"

"She's unconscious. You should consider going home and getting some rest."

"Thank you, Doctor," May said, watching her disappear into the emergency department. She supposed she should have asked if Vera was going to be okay. It was probably too soon to tell.

"Mrs. Hammond?" The nice red-haired nurse hurried up with two plastic bags and Vera's purse.

"You might want to take Mrs. Henderson's things with you. She won't need any of this in ICU."

"Of course. Thank you." May stood up and gathered her purse and Vera's belongings. Too bad it wasn't like the grocery store where you could take a shopping cart out to your car with you.

"Excuse me."

May turned around to see the woman paramedic walking toward her, ponytail swinging as she hurried to catch up to May.

"Can I help you out to your car?" The paramedic smiled, blue eyes crinkling at the corners.

"Thank you. What is your name? You've been so nice throughout this whole ordeal." May relinquished Vera's bags.

"My name is Lisa Tompkins."

"Well, Lisa. It's nice to meet you. It seems Vera has had a stroke."

"I'm sorry to hear that."

"Now I've got to call one of Vera's daughters. The oldest one. I hope I can remember her name by the time I figure out how to get her on Vera's cell phone. I'm not looking forward to it at all."

"I imagine not."

"Especially since I really don't know if Vera's going to be okay. When my friend Lynette had a stroke she couldn't use her left hand. The poor thing used to make the most beautiful crocheted afghans."

"I don't know how your friend will do but at least she was here when the stroke occurred so they were able to provide treatment quickly. That is sure to improve her outcome."

Improve her outcome. May would remember that phrase. It sounded knowledgeable and comforting at the same time. The hospital doors opened exhaling them into the dark September night. May inhaled the cool air.

"Where is your car?"

"Over there near handicapped parking." May pointed to the area behind the smoker's kiosk, a good two hundred feet from the hospital. Even now, after nine o'clock at night there were people wearing brightly colored scrubs, drinking coffee and blowing great clouds of smoke.

"I'm always amazed that medical people smoke," May said. "They of all people should know better."

"Lots of stress in the medical profession," Lisa said.

That was probably true, May thought, all that living and dying and in such untidy ways too.

"I'm sure you're right. Poor Dr. Trueblood looked very tense when she told me about Vera. This is mine." May gestured to her cornflower blue Honda Civic.

"Can I put this stuff in the backseat for you?" Lisa asked as May unlocked her car.

"Yes, dear. Thank you so much." What a nice, young woman.

"I know a little something about cell phones. Would it help if I showed you how to place a call?" Lisa held out her hand for the phone.

"Yes, it surely would. I'm not used to being so helpless but Vera having a stroke has just knocked me for a loop."

"Have you known each other long?"

"Yes, all our lives. We went to school together." May felt tears fill her eyes. Poor Vera. She drove May around the bend but it was hard to imagine life without her friend.

"I'm sorry about Mrs. Henderson." Lisa patted May's shoulder.

"Thank you, dear." At that moment the name of Vera's eldest daughter flew into her head.

"Who would you like to call?" Lisa opened the phone.

"Sandra Battistoni."

* * *

Nothing like a trip to the ER to make a person grateful, May thought as she pulled into Avola's driveway and got out of the car. The light was on in Avi's workroom, her converted double-wide garage. She must be working while she waited for May to show up for the promised pot roast sandwich.

Hopefully poor Vera's stroke had nothing to do with what Earl had done. She had seemed fine one minute and not the next. Health problems could crop up anytime but they were more numerous the older you got. It was scary. It was dangerous to think about it too much because it made it just about impossible to enjoy living. However, an evening at the emergency room really brought it home to roost.

The night sky was beautiful out here, it was darker and the stars more twinkly than at the hospital. May loved spending time out here at the western edge of Northampton near Look Park where Avi's house was located. It was peaceful, surrounded as it was by trees and seeming removed from everything even though it was only five miles from town. The best part, it wasn't in Hadley where it seemed like everyone was too interested in everyone else's business. That was the nature of small towns. Out here May felt anonymous. She could keep her love of Avola tucked away in a place that belonged just to her.

May took a deep breath. What a long night and it was barely nine thirty. Thank goodness that nice paramedic Lisa had helped her use Vera's cell phone or she never would have been able to get through to Sandra who was on her way to the hospital. May was officially off duty and could relax for the rest of the evening with Avola.

"Star gazing, my dear?" Avola's voice cut through the dark.

"I guess so…it's restful after the hospital…" May felt Avi's arms go around her and a kiss on the cheek.

"You were longer than I thought you might be. Is Vera okay?"

May told her about the stroke and calling Vera's daughter.

"Such terrible news. Come inside. I will make you a sandwich and a cup of tea unless you prefer something stronger."

"Thank you, honey. That sounds wonderful."

They walked inside and Avola ushered May to a chair at the kitchen table. Avola's house was perfumed with the smell of cooking. May felt tears prick her eyelids. Goodness, she was a basketcase tonight.

"You sit down, May. What would you like to drink?"

"Is that wine I see on the counter?" May slipped off her shoes.

"Yes, a coincidence of a wine from the winery Louie 'Big Boy' Liquors ended up at. But, it is good. I will pour some for each of us."

"Thank you, sweetie. Oh, what a night. Between Vera and Earl I feel like I haven't had a moment's peace." May dabbed her eyes.

"You are sad?" Avola brought two glasses of wine to the table and sat down.

"I don't think so. I'm just all done in."

"I understand. Here, put your feet in my lap. I will rub the weariness away."

May offered her right foot and whimpered when Avola attacked her arch with her strong thumbs. The wine unknotted the tight feeling in her chest.

"Oh, Avi, that feels so good. If you keep this up I might never leave."

"Then I will never stop. I will ply you with foot rubs, wine and sandwiches until you agree to stay with me forever." Avola chuckled and kissed May's big toe. "Your left foot is next in my diabolical plan."

"I'm sure I could be persuaded to stay over tonight…" May giggled. Her left foot was ticklish.

"Wonderful. We will start there and then…who can say?"

CHAPTER EIGHT

Earl supposed there wasn't any danger in doing a little sightseeing. It really would be a shame to cross a good part of the good ole USA without seeing, for example, the house made of teacups in Waylay, Indiana.

He glanced in the rearview mirror pleased to see that his goatee was coming in nicely and the reading glasses he got at Walgreens and kept perched on the end of his nose really made him look different. Along with parting his hair on the other side he hardly recognized himself. It was exciting being someone else or at least acting like he was.

His mother would probably enjoy visiting the House of Teacups. She drank a lot of tea. Maybe they had a souvenir shop. There was a good idea, getting her a present, especially after running down her lilies and then not calling since he'd left. She was probably worried about him but he didn't know how to get in touch. If he called and the FBI was tapping her phone he'd be in deep shit. Maybe a prepaid cell phone or he could send an anonymous postcard.

Earl turned onto Teacup Lane. It wasn't much more than a dirt track through a pasture leading to a stand of trees. By the looks of the road there weren't too many tourists who came this way. He had a brief moment of wondering if this was such a good idea and then dismissed it. What could happen at a House of Teacups?

The dirt track emerged onto an overgrown lawn that surrounded a small clapboard house. Teacups dangling from their handles covered every square inch of the house from the peak of the roof to the bottom sill. Teapots sat on top of the porch railings and the fence posts of the picket fence that surrounded a small vegetable garden. He'd never seen anything like it.

Earl pulled over and killed the engine. Was anyone home? Did he really want to meet somebody who'd spent God knew how much time hanging teacups from their house? He got out of the Horowiczes' car.

"Hello? Anybody home?" All he could hear was some crows haggling in the trees. Too bad he didn't have a camera.

The front screen door screeched open and an old man, bent over like a comma, struggled through the door and stood at the top step. Two canes kept him from toppling over.

"Ayup. Y'all here to see the teacups?"

"Yes, sir. Are you open today?"

"Son, I live here so I'm always open. When I'm dead is when I'll close."

"Great." Earl walked toward the comma-man.

"The tour is two dollars."

"Okay."

"But, you don't have to pay me until after the tour. Satisfaction guaranteed don't you know."

"Sure thing," Earl said.

"Now, if it's all the same to you I always start the tour with the teapots. Strictly speaking I know it's called the House of Teacups but I took some creative license with it."

"Yes, sir."

Keepsake Self Storage 57

"Now this here teapot was my dead wife's. She was partial to anything with pink flowers on it." Comma-man gestured toward the porch railing with a cane tip.

"And that one next to it with that there Mickey and Minnie Mouse on it my dead wife's dead sister got in Disney World."

His voice droned on threatening to put Earl into a coma. Though he didn't see how he could escape without offending Comma-man. Besides he owed some penance to the elderly since he knocked that busybody Vera down and killed his mother's lilies.

"Are you listening, son? Usually I get a laugh when I tell the story about the Roy Rodgers and Dale Evans teapot."

"I'm sorry, sir. I guess my mind wandered a bit. I was thinking about my mother."

"Ayup. I understand. Memories do take the mind away that's for sure. Since I hit the century mark my mind's gone most of the time, especially when there's nothing on television."

True, Earl thought. He'd been thinking more about the past since he'd left Hadley than about his future, which lay in front of him like an empty dinner plate.

"What say we cut the tour short and wet our whistles?" Comma-man settled himself into a bentwood rocker.

"Sounds good to me."

"Open that there screen door and just inside on the floor is a jug. Bring it out if you don't mind."

Earl got a whiff of old dust when he retrieved the brown and tan earthenware jug. It was difficult not to take a moment to stare at the stuffed deer heads gazing glassily down at him from the living room walls.

"We might as well drink out of one of these here teacups. Pick whichever one you want. I'm partial to bone china myself, feels good against the lip."

Earl gave the jug to Comma-man who set it on the floor between his feet.

"I'm not sure I know what bone china is."

"You kidding, son? Must be you were brought up drinking out of mugs."

"Yes, sir."

"Well, see that yellow flowered cup with the ladybugs painted on it? Over yonder to the left of the satellite dish?"

"Yes, sir."

"Bone china. Now, see that one four rows down that says Waffle House on it? That there is mass produced ceramic."

Earl plucked the cups from their pegs.

"Son, don't you think since we're gonna drink some of this here applejack that you ought'a know who I am and I ought'a know who you are?"

* * *

Avola felt so good this morning she thought she might be able to slipcover Northampton City Hall, spires and all. Somehow she had been able to persuade May to stay the last couple of days with her. It had been lovely. They had cooked together, popped popcorn and played Scrabble and spent some time in Avola's queen-sized bed. May had decided to go home this morning after breakfast. She had said she was feeling guilty about enjoying herself when poor Vera was soon to be transferred into rehab and with Earl rambling around the countryside. Avola supposed it just spoke to her own selfishness that she didn't feel guilty at all. She just felt happy to have had May all to herself. They had plans to get together for lunch the day after tomorrow when Avola returned from a business trip to the Highlands Inn in Bethlehem, New Hampshire.

Avola was going up to get a love seat and ottoman the girls who ran the place wanted reupholstered before next spring's wedding season. Avola had invited May to come along but she had elected to assuage her guilt by going home to put the flower gardens to bed before the frost that was sure to come within the next couple of nights. May was getting some straw from a farmer friend of hers and had plans to get the plants all tucked in. Avola knew that May was also busy with her volunteer and senior center activities, though she couldn't help but feel disappointed in May's choices.

The Highlands Inn, where Avola was traveling to, was a beautiful spot with a lovely view of the mountains, especially at this time of year as she had seen when she had been there before with May. The leaves would be turning and the White Mountains offered a feast for the eyes. A perfect setting for a romantic interlude and because it was a lesbian B&B it was relaxing, especially for May who always worried about who was who and what was what.

Avola and May usually went up two or three times a year for a long weekend. When the owners got wind of Avola's profession they had begged her to take them on. With over twenty rooms there was always something to slipcover or reupholster. The owners and Avola had developed a good system. The girls bought the fabric and they bartered Avola's time with free accommodations, a very workable arrangement that had resulted in turning a professional relationship into a personal friendship. Though this was a short trip she knew they would be planning a special time, perhaps a lovely meal or a show at the local theater. That was why she was disappointed about May's decision. Spending time with a couple that got along as well as the girls from the Highlands did made Avola lonely for being there with May.

She knew she should content herself with the glow of their recent time together. Since Earl had been gone these past three weeks, May was much more willing to be at Avola's home. It seemed like they had spent more time together recently than they ever had. One would think that it would be enough but it seemed as though the opposite were true. The more time they spent together the more Avola missed her when they were apart. Perhaps it was destined that she always wanted more of May than May was willing or able to give. Avola wondered if she was one of those women who were never satisfied.

* * *

May went out the kitchen door and stood in the weakening sunlight for a moment. Someone in the neighborhood had a wood fire burning; such a nice and comforting smell. Oh, it was good to get out of the house and into the garden. Today she was planning on digging up the cannus to tuck them away in the dark, cool north corner of the basement. Their roots would never survive a New England winter.

She wondered where Earl was. Maybe he was mad at her and that was why he hadn't called. Perhaps he blamed her for the search warrant. Who could say? She worried about him. He might be a grown man but sometimes he didn't seem equipped to handle the world.

She saw a flash out of the corner of her eye. Was that an owl up in the pine tree? If only she had her binoculars. With her eyes trained on the spot in the foliage May walked closer and closer to the tree. Perhaps whatever it was would move again.

All of a sudden she was falling forward. She couldn't catch herself and fell onto her hands and knees in amongst what would have been the lily bed in the summer. Her heart was beating so hard in her chest she could hear it throbbing in her ears. Maybe this was what a heart attack felt like. She took a couple deep breaths and her galloping heart settled down. May crawled to the park bench she'd installed under the dogwood tree and hoisted herself onto it. Gosh, her ankle hurt. What had she fallen over? That damn birdbath which she temporarily relocated while she transplanted the bee balm, invasive as all get out but beautiful nonetheless. She should have been looking where she was going and not hoping to see the owl she thought was living in the pine boughs.

Would she be able to walk back to the house? She tried to stand up but that left ankle didn't seem to know what to do anymore. What she wouldn't give for one of those cell phones. This settled it. She was going to get one for the future though it wasn't going to help her out of her present predicament.

"Yoo-hoo," May called out. Maybe a neighbor was outside. Unlikely, since most of them worked during the day.

Maybe Lou-Lou hadn't delivered the mail yet and if she hadn't maybe she would look in May's direction and...who was she kidding, Lou-Lou took her job as a federal employee very seriously. Wouldn't you know Avola was out of town and not due back until the day after tomorrow.

"Is anyone there?" Exactly who was she talking to? Impossible to say but she hoped someone was listening. She couldn't imagine that the deity spent much time worrying about an old lady who had fallen in her garden.

"Hello? Hello?" What she wouldn't give for a meter reader, a delivery person or even a Jehovah's Witness though they weren't so likely in cooler weather.

Maybe there'd be a traffic jam up at the intersection just a couple houses west of hers. It happened a couple times a day. If she waved and yelled like a mad woman maybe someone would see her, unless they were listening to their radio or talking on a cell phone.

If worse came to worst she could crawl across the lawn and driveway to the kitchen door, if her knees were up to it. They'd probably give out halfway there and she'd be stuck on the ground, which had to be worse than sitting on a park bench. Unfortunately, the *Hampshire Gazette* was no longer an afternoon paper; she couldn't hope for the paperboy until six thirty tomorrow morning.

Well, this might be it. She'd always said she wouldn't mind dying in her flower garden. She should have been more specific. She should've said she wouldn't mind dying in her garden on a nice spring day when the forsythia were thick with blossoms or even a humid August evening when the only things to see were the fireflies and swooping bats.

Avola was a big believer in guardian angels, convinced that her younger brother, Gasteau, who was a boy when he'd sunk under the ice after a skating mishap never to be seen again, was looking out for Avola from somewhere above. There were endless stories illustrating Gasteau's care, everything from finding money to a winning poker hand to numerous first class airline upgrades. May didn't know if guardian angels were able to switch their allegiance in cases of emergency. Avola hadn't mentioned his intercession recently. Surely, spirits didn't stay suspended between the worlds forever. It was worth a shot.

"Gasteau? Are you there? You don't know me but I'm your sister Avola's friend May." She probably didn't need to shout.

"Anyway, I could really use some help here. I don't care who…" That probably wasn't the best thing to say or even admit. Not caring was dangerous.

"Okay, Gasteau, send me a capable rescuer." Anticipation coursed through her like drain cleaner.

Suddenly there was the sound of car horns blowing at the intersection up the street. After a few moments the traffic going by began to move slower.

"Yoo-hoo!" she yelled and waved her hands. No one stopped. This was frustrating. May was just wishing she'd thought to tuck her emery board in her pocket when a Jeep turned into her driveway. Thank Gasteau.

"Hello. Hello," May called.

A tall woman with loose brown hair got out; May couldn't place her exactly but knew she knew her. The woman waved and walked toward the garden.

"Hello." The woman waved back. "It's May isn't it? I was just wondering how your friend who had the stroke was doing." She bent to pick up May's gardening gloves.

That's who it was. The young woman who'd driven the ambulance the day Earl knocked down poor Vera and had helped May call Vera's daughter.

"It's nice to see you," May said. "I'm ashamed to say I've forgotten your name."

"Lisa."

"It's nice to see you again. Vera is going to rehab and doing pretty well except no one understands a word she says."

"That sometimes happens." Lisa sat next to May on the bench.

"I'm sure Vera is very frustrated. She loved to talk more than almost anyone I know," May said.

"Progress is slow after a stroke."

"So I've heard." May wondered how to bring up needing to be rescued. An oh-by-the-way-I-think-I-sprained-my-ankle seemed kind of abrupt.

"It's funny, I was just running some errands and saw your house and it reminded me of your friend and I saw you out here and just thought I'd stop." Lisa shook her head like she didn't really understand it herself.

"Do you believe in spirits, Lisa?"

Lisa shrugged.

"Not ghosts so much as people we know who've died and look out for us from the other side." May expected Lisa to get that glazed over look younger people sometimes get when they talk to old people.

"I'm not sure. Why?"

May told her about Avola's brother.

"Did you see Gasteau?" Lisa asked.

"No and I'm not really sure I believe in him but I was desperate so I asked for help."

"Help with what?"

"Oh, I had a little fall," May said.

"Where? Out here? Was that why your gloves were over by the birdbath?"

"That damn birdbath was the culprit. Anyway, I can't seem to stand on my foot." May was embarrassed to admit to the infirmity, it just fed into the stereotype of being old.

Lisa dropped down on her knees.

"Which ankle?"

"The left." May thought there was nothing like falling to make you feel like a complete idiot.

"Hmmm." Lisa pressed her ankle gently. It was swelling and turning the color of a Concord grape.

"I think I should take you the urgent care place on University Drive. Just to be sure it isn't broken," Lisa said.

"Oh no, dear, I couldn't ask you to do that. Besides, I'm sure it isn't necessary."

"It's really no trouble. I can't just leave you here. That wouldn't be right." Lisa rose to her feet. "They'll take a quick X-ray, just to be sure, and I'll have you back home before you know it."

May felt herself being persuaded. The ankle was starting to throb. She'd have to remember to tell Avola about Gasteau sending her a capable rescuer when she returned home from The Highlands Inn in New Hampshire. No use troubling her until then.

CHAPTER NINE

The applejack burned all the saliva out of Earl's mouth, seared his esophagus and hit his stomach like a hot rock. After about three minutes the fire radiated into his brain and made the edges of everything fuzzy. The effects of the second sip were less purely distinct but just as powerful.

"Jesus," Earl said. His voice sounded smooth as a river rock.

"I know what you mean, son. You know it's good liquor when it makes you blaspheme."

"Mind if I smoke?"

"No, you go right ahead. I'll enjoy smelling it but my smoking days are over."

Earl sat on the top step and lit up.

"So, you never did say what your name was."

"Brad Nelson." Earl wondered why he said it the minute it was out of his mouth. The name seemed to hang in the air waiting to be noticed. "What I mean is…ummm…Bradley is my first name but I never liked it so I went with Brad."

"Pleased to know you, Brad. My given name is David Hawthorn but folks around here call me Thorny."

Earl raised his eyebrows. "You don't seem thorny to me."

"Well, I used to be a mean son of a bitch. Why don't you pour us a bit more of that libation and I'll tell you what happened."

Earl poured.

"See that there barn out yonder. It don't got a teacup on it?"

Earl nodded.

"I built it myself mostly. Oh, once in a while my brother or cousin would come by and help, especially if my wife was fricasseeing chicken. Anyhow, one Sunday I was out there working on the roof. It was hotter than hell and the sweat was running in my eyes, burning and stinging something awful. Anyhow, I decided to call it quits and stepped out onto the ladder except the ladder wasn't there. I fell twenty feet onto a pile of scrap wood. Next thing I knew I woke up on the couch in the parlor and it was nearly a week later."

"Wow."

"Well, Brad, I don't mind telling you that it gave me quite a turn. First off I thought I was dead and the undertaker just hadn't put me in the box yet. But then I realized I smelled bacon and coffee. Now, I don't know if it's true, but I got an idea that when you're dead you ain't smelling bacon and coffee."

Thorny urged the applejack toward Earl with his foot, which Earl took as a sign to pour the third round.

"About that time my wife comes out of the kitchen. Now, I can't explain what happened next all I can do is tell you what happened next."

Earl wondered if aliens had visited Thorny too.

"Up till then my wife and I hadn't exactly got along. We'd had to get married and then the wife miscarried and something happened with her female parts so there never would be any young ones. A course she was heartbroken and I felt bad but I also felt taken advantage of. I was mean and surly and everyone hereabouts took to calling me Thorny like I said. But that morning when I saw my wife coming toward me, well, she was the most beautiful thing I'd ever seen. All them cantankerous feelings I'd had just went out of me. I sat up and ate three eggs, a half-pound of bacon and close to a dozen bakin' powder biscuits." Thorny drained his teacup for the third time.

"Holy smoke." Earl finished off his cupful.

"Brad, I'll have one of your smokes if you're still of a mind to share."

After the third round Earl found he needed to lie down. Thorny's porch was very comfortable and the need to sleep was becoming irresistible. Soon he'd be snoring and farting on a stranger's front porch somewhere in East Bumfuck, Indiana. A recipe for disaster when you considered he was a fugitive from justice.

Applejack was a burglar. It snuck up behind you, knocked you witless and made off with all your valuables.

"Brad, I believe I've been hit between the eyes."

"I was just thinking the same thing."

"I'll be right back." Thorny grabbed hold of the rocker's arms and hauled himself out of the chair in what looked to Earl like slow motion. How was that old man able to move? He must have the constitution of an ox. Or he was used to drinking this shit.

"You need some help?" Earl asked to be polite though he doubted he'd ever be able to move again.

"No, thank you, son. I'll make it eventually. Getting old turns everyone into a turtle." He teetered upright, grasped his canes one in each hand and made his way to the porch door and disappeared into the gloom of the house.

Earl supposed he ought to make his excuses and find his way down the road. Look for a Super 8 or Red Roof Inn and pack it in for the night. Or was it still daytime? He thought about looking at his watch but didn't think he'd be able to lift his arm.

Perhaps he'd been poisoned. Or maybe Thorny's homemade liquor had turned him into a paraplegic. Was it possible that the Teacup House was a front for a gang of psycho killers? Not that Thorny seemed like one of those but everyone said Ted Bundy was a nice enough guy to all those women until he raped and killed them.

How long had Thorny been gone? Was it his imagination or did it seem darker than it had a few minutes ago? Great, now he was going blind. That applejack was turning off all his bodily functions one by one. First it would be his eyesight. His hearing would probably be next. He'd no more had that thought than he heard a deep rumble coming from somewhere.

He heard the shuffle-shuffle-plonk-plonk of Thorny's progress through the house. The distant rumble grew closer. Didn't they say that blind people had hearing like a dog? That must be happening to him. Relief washed through him. He wasn't losing all his senses. A toilet flushed and the shuffle-shuffle-plonk-plonk signaled Thorny's return trip. The screen door screeched open.

"Might want to shut your car windows, Brad. Looks like there's a thunderstorm coming." Thorny lowered a plastic Winn-Dixie bag toward Earl's face. Uh-oh. Here it comes, he thought, closing his eyes.

"Want some peanuts?"

Earl took the bag; hugely relieved he could move his arms and that Thorny hadn't knocked him out to do a psycho-killer routine. Maybe a snack would bring him around.

* * *

May felt like a barge caught on a sandbar. She lay back in her recliner with her sprained ankle resting on a pillow, all in an effort to keep her foot higher than her heart. She chuckled to herself. Goodness, that medication they gave her for pain at the urgent care place, oxy-something or other, was a doozy. She wondered if this was how illegal drugs made people feel. If so you could hardly blame them for using. This was much different than whiskey and soda. Feeling sorry for herself was almost impossible. Too bad Avola was up in New Hampshire because when May came down from this medication and started to feel bad about being old and broken Avi would have been able to cheer her up.

"May, do you have an ice pack?" Lisa's voice carried into the living room.

"In the freezer. I use that old bag of Sweet-Life baby peas. I've had it so long it's been taped in a few places." May marveled that she could string so many words together.

"Are you hungry?"

That required some thought. Was she hungry? She must be because she hadn't had anything to eat since her three-minute egg and rye toast at breakfast.

"I guess I am, dear." May couldn't imagine getting up and making herself something to eat.

Lisa brought the bag of peas and a towel and wrapped it loosely around May's air splint.

"How's that feel?" Her blue eyes were clouded with concern.

"Fine." May thought Lisa looked much younger in her jeans and fleece pullover than she had in her uniform and entirely too serious. "I think you could cut off my leg and beat me with it and I'd hardly notice."

Lisa laughed and fiddled with the ice pack a little more.

"Thank you, dear, for everything you've done. I don't know if Gasteau, God or serendipity is responsible and I do appreciate everything you've done for me. But don't you have somewhere else to be?"

"No. Not really." Lisa got the afghan from the back of the couch and laid it over May's lap and legs.

"You don't sound too sure of that," May said.

"I'm in a period of transition at the moment." Lisa pressed her lips together.

A ping sounded from the kitchen.

"I'll be right back," Lisa said.

People didn't seem to know how to talk anymore. A period of transition was a way to say something without actually saying anything. It was possible that Lisa thought she was prying and was too polite to tell May to be quiet and mind her own business.

Lisa returned with a tray bearing two plates and two glasses. "I hope you don't mind but I made us a couple sandwiches with the leftover meatloaf you had in the fridge." Lisa passed a plate to May.

"Mind! I'm grateful. And a pickle too." May's stomach growled in anticipation.

"Good meatloaf," Lisa mumbled.

"Thank you. I got this recipe years ago off an onion soup mix box. It's Earl's favorite."

"Earl?"

"My son," May said. It took all her restraint not to add "the loser." She alternated between being sad he was gone and angry he hadn't called to tell her where he was.

"Does he live here?" Lisa asked.

"He used to. I guess you could say that he's in a period of transition too." May sipped the ice-cold cider Lisa had brought with the sandwiches, a surprisingly delicious accompaniment. Usually she drank milk with meatloaf.

"He sends a postcard every once in a while. But that's all. I swear if he doesn't call by the end of the year I'm going to clean out his room and donate everything to the Interfaith Survival Center." May was surprised at what she'd said. She'd been trying to cut Earl some slack but to hell with that, the time for slack cutting was over. Anger seemed to be winning out.

Lisa nodded. "My brother Teddy isn't the best communicator either. Maybe it's a guy thing."

"It's been my experience and I've had eighty-three years of it, men can communicate just fine when they want something. It's when they want to avoid something that they stop talking." May crunched her pickle for emphasis.

"I'll remember that," Lisa said.

"What's your period of transition all about?" May was amazed at how nosy she was being.

"It's kind of complicated."

May shrugged, her mouth full of meatloaf.

"The person I'm living with thinks they want to…" Lisa looked up at the ceiling like she expected the words she wanted to say were written there.

"…Thinks they want to…" Lisa took a big gulp of cider.

"…Change and I don't want them to change."

"Change? Everything changes. What do they want to change?" May asked.

"Do you ever watch Oprah?"

Oprah? Where did that come from? She decided to humor Lisa because whatever change was coming had brought tears to Lisa's eyes.

"Yes, dear, I love Oprah."

"A couple weeks ago she had a show on about transsexuals. Did you see it?"

"Yes, I watched it with my friend Avola. I felt bad for those people, stuck in the wrong body," May said.

Lisa nodded and blew her nose into her napkin.

May took another bite of meatloaf and waited for Lisa to say something. After a thorough chewing, half a pickle and a swallow of cider it became clear that Lisa wasn't going to say any more.

"Let me see if I've got this right. The person you live with wants to change bodies." It really was impressive that May was able to grasp what was going on through the persistent haze of medication.

"Yes, a woman to a man. But, I want her to stay a woman," Lisa said.

May considered Lisa, eyes swollen, nose red and runny and lips all puffy. She looked just like May had looked that time she and Avola had broken up over that loose-limbed woman who had taken Avola's quilting class. Sally Whitcomb. May still felt her blood boil even after sixteen years.

"Are you and this woman in the life together?" May thought she should take pain medication more often. This was the most interesting conversation she'd had in years.

"Yes, we are…were. I don't want to be with a man." Lisa rushed out of the living room.

May could hear the almost slam of the bathroom door. The poor thing.

* * *

Just buck up, Lisa thought as she hunkered on the edge of May's bathtub pressing a cold, wet washcloth against her swollen eyes. Breakups sucked. She and Joanie or Johnnie as she now wanted to be called, had spent that morning doing the final yours-mine-you-can-have-it bit over the books, the CDs and the sock drawer. It was gut-wrenching. Johnnie had begged Lisa to understand that he just couldn't live an inauthentic life. Lisa got that. But neither could she. Lisa wanted to be with women. They had arrived at an impasse where Lisa didn't even feel capable of friendship at the moment. Hopefully that would change.

Most of the furniture was Johnnie's because he had that high-powered human resource position at the Humanity Savings and Loan. EMTs didn't make a lot of money but it was work that Lisa really liked and was good at. It was hard to accept that the division of her and Johnnie's seven-year relationship could fit in the back of Lisa's Jeep.

Before Lisa had been compelled by some unknown motivation to stop by May's earlier this afternoon she'd been on her way to look at a roommate situation in Northampton. But now it was too late for that, she'd get a motel room for the night, which she really couldn't afford, and start over again in the morning.

Starting over, both literally and figuratively, was more than Lisa could bear. Just a few weeks ago she had been fantasizing about her and Joanie—Johnnie—would she ever get used to his name change, going on an Olivia cruise in the spring to some turquoise-watered paradise for their birthdays, which were only two months apart. That was until Joanie had dropped the Johnnie bomb at the costume party to benefit the homeless shelter.

"What do you mean you want to be a man?" Lisa had asked, feeling surreal in her Marge Simpson outfit.

"Not just for dress up but for real," Joanie hissed, her Homer head nearly bobbing off.

"Why can't you just be a butch dyke for Christ's sake?" Lisa had shouted and shoved a carrot from the crudités platter down Joanie's pants. "Use that. It'll save you money at the surgeons!" Lisa had stormed out of the party and gone home where she made herself sick on the bite-sized Snickers bars she'd bought for the upcoming Halloween trick-or-treaters. Joanie had never come home. Johnnie had returned home after three days.

Anger was easier to express than grief. Now all she felt was a sadness that filled up her core making breathing difficult, almost any song on the radio made her cry and eating was next to impossible, until tonight's meatloaf.

May was a welcome distraction, though Lisa was sorry the old lady had sprained her ankle. It was interesting she'd used the phrase "in the life." That was an oldie but goodie. Maybe there was something more between May and her friend Avola than friendship.

There was a tentative knock on the bathroom door.

"Are you all right, dear?"

Lisa leapt up and jerked open the door.

"May, how'd you get here by yourself?"

"When nature calls a person must do what she must. Besides which, I had a walker in the coat closet. I got it when Earl put his back out so bad a few years ago he couldn't stand up straight. I've kept it just in case. I know hopping would be better, but this eighty-three-year-old doesn't hop."

"Can I help you?" Lisa asked.

"Let's see if I can do it alone. But, maybe you could stay outside the door in case I run into difficulties."

Lisa stepped aside, allowing May to lurch past and shut the door behind her. It probably wasn't a good idea for May to be alone but there wasn't anything Lisa could do about that. Old people had as much a right to make a bad decision as anyone else. Like Johnnie, who'd kept saying all through the dissolution of their household that he was still the same person inside, it was the outside that would change. Not once you start taking testosterone, Lisa had said. Then you'll have your beautiful breasts cut off, grow facial hair because all female to male transsexuals seemed to do that and have a penis constructed out of your vagina so you won't really be the same inside or outside. How could anyone be the same after all that?

* * *

Goodness, this was harder than May had ever thought it would be as she struggled to get off the toilet and then to wash her hands and dry them. Avola would be home the day after tomorrow and would be more than eager to help May. This incident would probably reignite Avola's campaign for the two of them to live together. It was wonderful to spend time with Avi but May just didn't want to turn herself over to anyone. She liked having her own place and making her own decisions and she knew if she lived with Avola that she would disappear inside their relationship. Besides, there was Earl to think about.

Perhaps she should consider hiring someone to come in a couple hours a day to help out, and then she'd probably be all right. Maybe someone from the church or the senior center would be available. She'd make some phone calls in the morning but for now she thought she'd be okay spending the night in her recliner which was closer to the bathroom than her bedroom. This was an adventure, of sorts, a challenge. Everybody needed one of those every once in a while.

CHAPTER TEN

Vera never anticipated she'd find herself in a nursing home. She figured if she ever got wind of having to go she'd, God forgive her, kill herself. Catholics frowned on suicide but who smiled on nursing homes? Everyone assured her that her stay was temporary, that she was there for rehab only. She knew it was a slippery slope.

Her roommate was a woman named Rosario Del Mar, such a foreign sounding name, she had a very dark complexion and spoke with a funny accent so Vera knew she wasn't an American. She'd tried asking where Rosario was from and was very embarrassed when instead of "where are you from" coming out "are you going to Scarborough fair" popped out instead.

The speech pathologist assured her that, with work, her word finding would improve. Vera was dying to ask if she'd ever return to normal but had no idea how that would come out so she didn't even try. Every morning she had speech therapy. After lunch was physical therapy, occupational therapy and then something called recreation. Lunch, hah. What she wouldn't give to get in her car and drive to Friendly's for a fish-a-ma-jig. Instead she ate overcooked, mushy food, all of it the color of overwashed underwear and tasting like cheap paper plates.

She'd asked her daughter Sandy for food. Of course, Sandy didn't know what Vera meant when she said "take me out to the ball park." Sandy was a love but she wasn't a creative thinker. Now, Heidi, the daughter she had a small falling out with, would've figured it out. She could hope for Heidi to visit but it was probably going to stay a hope.

They'd had words over Heidi's becoming a pagan. Pagan, schmagan—it was just another word for Satan. The trouble started when Heidi got involved with that women's collective. Whatever that meant. Vera never could get Heidi to say what they were collecting. She'd even visited once and while there was a large barn on the property out in Leverett there didn't seem to be anything in it other than old lawn furniture and rusted farm equipment. Perhaps whatever they collected was small enough to fit into their closets. Heidi got exasperated when Vera kept asking to see the collection and said "Mother don't be so concrete."

Concrete? What did having a polite interest in her daughter's life have to do with concrete? Honestly though, for all Heidi's faults she would've known to bring Vera food. If she ever got the chance to say what she meant she'd be sure to cut Heidi some slack and tell her so.

"Let me count the ways," Vera muttered to herself as she struggled with the toothpaste tube. Her right hand still worked but her grip was off so she had a dickens of a time removing the cap. Sometimes it just didn't seem worth it, all the effort it took just to do the little things. Eating was hard, peas rolled off the fork or she misjudged, missing her mouth entirely and jabbing herself in the cheek. Luanne, her OT, said she was doing great. Vera hoped to be around when and if Luanne had a stroke just to see how she handled wearing her lunch.

Vera dropped the Colgate. "Kumbaya my Lord." Now, how was she going to retrieve it? Luanne wanted her to get one of those pinchers for picking things up but she didn't have it yet, not that Sandy wouldn't get it for her if only she could tell her what to get.

Maybe she could scooch the tube out to the hall and one of the CNAs would see and pick it up for her. Nilda was on tonight and she had more on the ball than some of the others. Vera had made good progress, having gotten out of the bathroom and was near the door when she misjudged her scooch and stepped on the toothpaste. The tube exploded, filling the air with the cloying smell of overly sweet peppermint.

"Don't sit under the apple tree." Vera wanted to cry.

"My mother made apple pie," Rosario said from her chair across the room.

"One potato, two potato." Boy, what a pair they were. She couldn't say anything she wanted to and Rosario was demented and only heard what she wanted to hear.

"Mashed potatoes please. With gravy. I love chicken gravy."

Vera sat in her chair. One of her kids would appear soon for a visit. Somebody came every day, which was wonderful. Not that they could talk but it was nice to have someone familiar around. Nursing homes filled a need but were terrible places. At least therapy kept her busy. Oh well, no use complaining. She knew it could have been a lot worse.

"Hi, Mom." Sandy breezed in with a Dunkin' Donuts bag and a tray of iced coffees.

"Good night, Irene."

"I don't want to go to bed. My favorite show comes on at eight thirty," Rosario said.

"What's this toothpaste doing on the floor?" Sandy asked, crouching to pick it up.

"Don't tell stories out of school," Vera said.

"There's no school. It's summer vacation," Rosario said.

"I thought you might like a treat, Mom. So I got you a Boston Cream doughnut and a decaf." Sandy bustled around the room, wiping the toothpaste off the floor and handing out coffee and doughnuts.

"Inky. Dinky. Parlev-vous," Vera said.

"I even got you a treat, Mrs. Del Mar," Sandy said. Vera was pleased to see Sandy's kindness but wished she'd talk softer. It was almost like she thought shouting would make a difference in what Rosario heard.

"Trick or treat! Do you like my costume? I'm a witch," Rosario said.

"Very nice, Mrs. Del Mar." Sandy sat on Vera's bed. "So, Ma, I hope you don't mind but I called Heidi. I thought she should know about your condition."

"The hills are alive with the sound of music," Vera said, taking a bite of her doughnut.

"I know you guys don't exactly get along but life's too short to argue. So, she said she'd come by tomorrow night to see you. I guess she had work tonight."

"The sun will come out tomorrow," Vera said. The doughnut was the best thing she had ever eaten. She loved iced coffee. And Heidi was going to visit. Things were starting to look up.

CHAPTER ELEVEN

Earl felt himself enveloped by the blue light. At first he thought it was the residual effects of the applejack but when the humming started and he felt himself leave the ground he knew he would soon see You-Know-Who. Next thing he knew he was in the room with the pulsating floor. In a way he always felt most alive here, in the spaceship. It seemed like each cell in his body was throbbing in time with the floor. As with all his other visits the pulsating slowed and Earl could feel his heart rate slow and his breathing deepen. God, he loved it here.

"Good evening." The tall, thin, blue woman spoke. Well, not really spoke, she never really spoke, because he couldn't hear her voice just became aware of what she was thinking.

"Good evening," Earl said. He always spoke formally around her. It was a bit like visiting his great-aunt Ina Hammond who had, before she died, a fourteen-room house in Northfield and a new Caddie every year.

"We sense you are in some trouble, Earl."

"Yes, ma'am. Things do seem to have gotten away from me." He was only slightly surprised that she knew. It was hard to be surprised in a room where the floor pulsated.

"It was a mistake to steal the Horowiczes' car."

"So, you know about that too." Earl remembered that Christmas carol about Santa knowing if you'd been bad or good so be good for goodness sake.

"There is some truth to that song, Earl. We know."

Everything? Earl wondered.

"Without a doubt."

"Frankly, ma'am, I don't really know how to get myself out of the trouble I'm in. I guess I panicked."

"An unfortunate response. Humans are prone to behaviors that do not serve them."

Only humans? Earl remembered his long dead dog, Sam, who chewed shoes like they were licorice.

"You should return to your home, Earl. Everything you seek is there."

"But what about my mission?"

"You ignore the obvious at your peril." You-Know-Who blinked three times.

Suddenly he found himself back on Thorny's porch listening to the crickets sing up a storm. He felt the boards under his fingertips and the wood pressing against his back. Earl rolled onto his side and pushed himself upright. His head whirled like a bowling ball. He could still taste the peanuts he'd eaten, in fact they seemed to be lodged in the back of his throat. What he wouldn't give for a bucket of water and a bottle of aspirin. Since he had neither he lit a cigarette.

"That you, Brad?" Thorny's voice drifted out from the darkened house.

"Yes, at least I think it is."

Thorny chuckled. "You were dead to the world. I tried to waken you so you could come in and lay on the couch but there was no way."

"Last thing I remember was the peanuts."

"Well, it's three o'clock in the morning. You been out for almost twelve hours."

Twelve hours. Earl shook his head which only made the bowling ball roll faster.

"Thorny, you think I could have a glass of water and some aspirin?"

"A course. Come on in."

Earl stood up. His body made it clear it didn't like the upright position. He lowered himself to his hands and knees and crawled across the porch. Just as he opened the screen door Thorny flicked on a light. His pupils ached as they closed against what had to be a 150-watt bulb. There was Thorny in an oversized easy chair, bolstered by pillows with his feet up on the ottoman. He wore pale blue pajamas and a hooded sweatshirt.

"Gave up sleeping in the bed when I turned ninety-eight. It was too hard getting out of it and I got worried that if a fire broke out I'd burn to death. This way I'll have a fighting chance."

Earl crawled over to the couch and used the arm to help him stand up. This time was better.

"Aspirin's on the windowsill over the kitchen sink, glasses in the cabinet on the right. The facilities are off the kitchen if you're needing them."

Earl walked on the marbles he was sure were under his feet to the kitchen where he took four aspirin, drank two glasses of water and then used the bathroom. He had never seen a toilet where the tank was suspended on the wall above your head except in movies. It was irrational but if it were his he'd always be afraid that it would come crashing down right in the middle of taking a crap. After he was finished he washed his face and hands and squirted some toothpaste on his finger and moved it around inside his mouth. It didn't quite take the moss off his tongue but at least his breath tasted better.

Now, what was it You-Know-Who had said? You should return to your home. Everything you seek is there. He didn't really want to go home. He had his mission. Maybe she didn't understand the importance of that. But Earl knew. Besides, what if the police were still looking for him? How would he ever explain everything to them? Or his mother who had to be royally pissed off by this time. Or the Horowiczes, who were hopefully still in Israel. Maybe he could keep that little tidbit under wraps.

There was something else. He liked being on his own. The mission had finally been launched. Out here he was truly himself, more so than he had ever been. Well, not quite because Thorny thought his name was Brad Nelson but that was beside the point. Out here he had no past. He wasn't the guy whose father got hit by a bus. He wasn't May's son who still lived at home with his mother. Out here he was his own man. Maybe You-Know-Who was speaking metaphorically when she'd said return to your home. What if his home wasn't Hadley, Massachusetts? What if his real home was a place he hadn't been yet? It was scary to think she didn't know what she was talking about. He would just have to live through the fear and move forward.

* * *

Lisa taped the last of Vera's boxes shut and put them in the upstairs hall. Vera's daughter was coming by to pick up her mother's stuff and take it to her place in Leverett. Apparently, Vera was going to be the newest member of the collective. Lisa couldn't imagine her own mother moving to a feminist collective but May had said that Vera seemed eager to go, singing "She'll be coming 'round the mountain when she comes." Lisa thought it probably had more to do with getting sprung from the nursing home.

Vera would certainly be having an old age she'd never expected to have. Hell, Lisa could say the same thing about herself. Not the old age part but the "never expected" part. A month ago if you'd told her she would be housemates with an eighty-three-year-old woman, she would've called you crazy. She'd got on the strange train when Johnnie became a member of the transgendered community and had never gotten off.

And what was weirder? Lisa felt grateful. She'd needed a place to stay after she'd moved out of the house she'd shared with Johnnie and May's guest room was perfect, lots of windows, a nice comfortable queen-sized bed and a big closet. She'd bought a desk in a box, which she'd put together when she next got a day off. There was a bathroom down the hall with a huge claw-foot tub and all of it was private until May's son returned. But, May didn't seem too sure about him at the moment. The best part was May said they could set up a work exchange for some of the rent. And she didn't even mind if Lisa's dog Bosco moved in.

"Yoo-hoo," May hooted up the stairs.

"Yoo-hoo," Lisa hooted back. May really was a funky old lady.

"Vera's daughter is here, at least I hope that's who's here, otherwise we're being invaded."

Lisa glanced out the window. There were women pouring out of an Econoline van like clowns pouring from a VW Bug at the circus. She'd better run downstairs and let them in.

* * *

"Damn ankle," May cursed under her breath as she clunked and clattered back to her recliner. She was going stir-crazy and it was only day five of her convalescence. Thank goodness Lisa had agreed to move in. Not that Avola was very happy about that. Especially when she'd found out Lisa was one of the sisterhood. It was just like a replay of the fight they'd had when Vera stayed with May. Why couldn't Avi trust her? It was ridiculous to think of there being anything between her and Lisa. It had been four days since she and Avola had exchanged a civilized word. May was sticking to her guns this time and would not apologize first.

But, May knew living alone when you couldn't do for yourself was dangerous. She knew it was irrational but all she could think about was dying and her body not being discovered until Earl came home and who knew when that was going to be.

Goodness, what a trial that boy was and had been. She'd always hoped he'd find someone to share his life with. It really wasn't normal to still live with your mother when you were Earl's age. Lordy, May remembered how eager she was to get out of her parent's house. He'd never been that way. It was like he was from outer space or something.

If only he would contact her beyond those damn blank postcards. He probably thought the police were still interested in the Brad Nelson case. She only wished there was a way to let him know that Brad's roommate at the VA had confessed and been booked for manslaughter. What a sad story that was. Brad and his buddy had been drinking in Brad's storage unit, got into an argument and, as so often happens when Jack Daniels is involved, things went from bad to worse. Brad got clocked in the head and his drinking buddy thought Brad was dead, panicked and shut the door down locking Brad inside. As it turned out Brad wasn't dead but bled to death shortly thereafter. And the roommate was on suicide watch at the county jail awaiting trial.

Earl's latest postcard was from Old Faithful. It looked like a beautiful spot and somewhere May had never been. Too bad she and Avola were fighting. It might be nice to take a trip together across the United States. They could have all this time to together and yet all Avi seemed to want to do with it was fight and imagine May was up to no good. Why didn't Avi understand how much May loved her? So what that they didn't live together. Love wasn't about where you lived. Was it?

CHAPTER TWELVE

May heard the phone ringing from the bottom of a well. She wasn't sure who was in the well, her or the phone. It took all of her energy to focus on the phone and swim toward it through the fog and darkness that encompassed her brain. After a moment she realized it was dark only because her eyes were closed. Once they opened she found herself in her own living room. The television was on though muted and the little lamp on the desk she left on when she went out in the evening was lit. It looked like the 11:00 p.m. newscast was on. The question was which 11:00 p.m. was it? Today's or tomorrow's? She had to stop taking that pain medication.

The phone started ringing again. Who would be calling so late? She looked at the caller ID. Avola LeFebre. Oh God. May should make a wager: was she calling to apologize or would it just be more of the same?

"Hello?" May's mouth felt as though all the saliva had been sucked out of it.

"Al-lo? May? Where have you been?" Avola's voice crackled through the cordless.

"Right here. Did you call earlier?"

"Yes. Many times and each time it rang and rang so I hung up and called back and back again. I wasn't sure I had dialed the number correctly."

"I was asleep." It would be more accurate to say unconscious. It was so like Avi to act like they hadn't argued and weren't still fighting.

"You must have exhausted yourself in the garden, yes? To sleep so soundly," Avola said.

"Not quite. My ankle is still very throbby. I had to take a pain pill."

"I was curious how you were feeling and I…hoped your ankle had improved sufficiently that I might come by to see you." Avola's voice sounded strident through the receiver.

"I don't think so, Avola. I'm too tired." May couldn't believe that the first words out of Avola's mouth weren't something about being sorry for being an idiot.

"Oh. Well, I am sorry to hear that. Perhaps another time." Avola paused. "I have also been thinking that it was wonderful this Lisa person came by when she did," Avola said.

Maybe this was the beginning of her apology. It always took Avola a while to get down to brass tacks.

"It sure was," May said. "The poor thing is in a bit of turmoil with her ex. It's wonderful having her in the upstairs guest room. With Earl gone I've really needed some help around the house. She raked some leaves for me yesterday and finished putting the garden to bed. Then she made dinner, a nice shepherd's pie." May sat back and waited for Avola's response. Pain medication made for an enjoyable detachment.

"What do you really know of this woman, May?" Avola asked, all friendliness gone. Her voice as low and rumbling as thunder.

May knew she didn't know Lisa well. But, she'd witnessed her kindness over and over again both professionally and personally. Kindness trumped everything.

"She's a sweet girl. You'd think so too if you'd ever meet her." May wondered if that would ever happen. She'd heard the danger in Avola's voice.

"Did you think of me at all before you invited this stranger to live with you? I would gladly take care of you." Avola bit off each word except stranger which she gave three syllables.

"Truthfully, I only hoped it wouldn't make you angry. But, beyond that I thought of Lisa, who I couldn't turn away, and myself. I don't need to be taken care of, I just need a little help. I don't know why you worry so. I love you. I wish that was enough." May grimaced as her ankle started throbbing in earnest. She had overworked it today walking up and down the driveway. Suddenly her patience leaked away like she was a tire driven over a nail.

"You know, Avola, it seems like we are always having this same argument. I'm tired of it. I don't know if it's because I'm old or because my ankle hurts and I don't guess it matters. Don't call again unless it's to apologize." May returned the phone to the cradle. It felt good to be the one doing the hanging up on for a change.

* * *

Earl pulled into the truck stop on Route 60 westbound just outside Hereford, New Mexico. Time to pee and walk around a little bit. It was four thirty in the afternoon. Man, he could really use a cup of coffee and a piece of pie or something. He strolled across the parking lot, which seemed at least four acres across and three-quarters full of 18-wheelers, campers, RVs and dozens of cars. He loved places like this. Since he left home it almost seemed like he was in a movie. Everyone always said a place must have good food if truckers ate there though you couldn't prove it by him. The only trucker he knew, a guy from his dart league, liked to eat cold Chef Boyardee ravioli right out of the can.

Earl took a leak and then squeezed between two guys at the counter in the restaurant. The fat guy on his left needed larger clothes and the rangy one on his right looked like an extra from *Bonanza*. A waitress dropped a vinyl menu almost as large as his road atlas in front of him. There were so many choices it seemed impossible to pick.

A young waitress with an improbable hair color stopped in front of Earl. "Coffee?"

"Yes. Thanks. Cream and sugar."

"We're out of the chicken fricassee and the meatball stroganoff." She slapped down a napkin wrapped around some utensils.

Earl nodded.

"Our breakfast special is good until six." She gestured toward a whiteboard scrawled in red ink that closely resembled her hair color: 3 egg Denver omelet, bacon or sausage, home fries, toast and coffee $3.99.

"Be right back with your coffee."

"The breakfast special is pretty good," the fat guy said nodding in Earl's direction. "Hey, honey, bring me some more coffee too." He yelled after the red-haired waitress.

"Coffee sucks though," Bonanza said.

"That's because it's strong and you don't like strong coffee," Fatty said, looking around Earl at Bonanza.

"Strong is one thing and bitter is another and this shit is bitter. You'd drink gasoline if somebody told you it was coffee, you dumb ass."

"Don't go acting like you know what the hell you're talking about. You're just showing off and talking like you ain't got nothing better to do," Fatty said.

Earl was starting to wish he'd sat at the other end of the counter next to the woman with a baby strapped into a plastic infant seat.

"That's right you dumb ass, we should be out in the rig making time but no. We have to sit here sucking down shitty coffee because you think that waitress likes you," Bonanza snorted.

"Keep your voice down," Fatty hissed.

"Like she'd ever be interested in a fat fuck like you."

"Shut up, asshole."

Earl cleared his throat. "So, you guys know each other?"

"Yeah. We're drivers for TCT," Fatty said.

"And." Bonanza stressed the and. "We should be out there driving not sitting in here trying to attract the attention of—"

"Shhh. Here she comes," Fatty whispered.

"Here's your coffee." Red slammed down a mug of coffee and a dish of creamers. "Sugar's on the counter."

"Another coffee please, miss?" Fatty said.

"In a sec. I'm brewing another pot."

"Oh shit. Now we'll never get out of here," Bonanza said.

"So, what can I get you?" Red asked Earl.

"What kind of pie do you have?"

"Apple. Blueberry. Mississippi Mud. Raisin. Banana cream. Chocolate cream. Lemon meringue."

"Lemon meringue," Earl decided.

"Jeez, that sounds good," Fatty said.

"Now don't you go getting any ideas, lame-ass. Get the coffee to go because we're out of here." Bonanza stood and threw a ten-dollar bill in the middle of a plate encrusted with egg yolk.

"Yeah, okay. Can I get a to-go cup?" Fatty yelled in Red's direction.

Thank God, Earl thought.

"Hey, you got a couple bucks I can borrow?" Fatty asked Bonanza.

"I told you man, I wasn't going to pay for any more of your food. You're a fuckin' heart attack waiting for a place to happen." Bonanza stalked out.

"Here's your pie." Red slammed the plate on the counter.

"And your coffee and check." She dropped a check in front of Fatty and picked up Bonanza's grease stained ten-dollar bill.

"Uh, my friend left with all my money." Fatty stood up and fished around in his hip pocket threatening to push his pants down around his knees. "All I got is five bucks."

Red curled her lip and raised one eyebrow, gazing at Fatty like he was dried egg yolk on a breakfast plate.

"That leaves me with a shitty tip."

"I'll take care of it," Earl said.

"Really? Hey thanks, man. I'll catch you on the way back through." Fatty pocketed the five and shuffled out.

"Not if I see you coming first," Red muttered.

Earl laughed, "You must see all kinds in this place."

"You said it and most of them are assholes."

"I meet a few in my line of work, too." Earl took a bite of pie. Not bad.

"Yeah? What do you do?"

What did he do? It probably wasn't the wisest move to tell her he managed a storage facility, or used to before he became a fugitive from justice.

"I'm a rental manager in, ah, Florida. But, I'm on vacation on my way to—"

"Let me guess. The Grand Canyon." Red smiled revealing a tongue stud.

"Yeah, that's it. The Grand Canyon."

"Lots of people coming here are on their way to the big hole. That's what I call it."

"So, are you from around here?" Earl sipped his coffee.

"No. I'm from Bradford, Pennsylvania."

"How'd you end up here if you don't mind me asking?"

"Well, it's kind of a long story." Red glanced at her watch. "I got a break in a few minutes. I'll be back in a sec." She disappeared into the kitchen.

Earl marveled at himself. Usually he had trouble talking to girls but here, wherever here was, he felt like he could talk to anyone.

Red crashed through the kitchen door holding two plates, one heaped with french fries and the other stacked with what looked like blueberry pancakes. She slammed the plates on the counter next to Earl.

"You want more coffee?" Red asked.

"Yes. Thanks."

She whirled down the aisle that ran between the counter where Earl sat and the stainless steel counter attached to the wall behind which was the kitchen; the wall between had a long rectangular window cut through it. He could see a couple of sweaty, kerchief-tied heads moving around back there. Red returned with a fresh cup of coffee and a chocolate shake and sat next to him.

"Want some fries?" Red asked, covering them with a snowdrift of salt. She dispensed a small puddle of ketchup on the edge of the plate.

"Sure. Thanks." Earl selected a fry and dabbed it into the ketchup.

"Julio makes the best fries. He changed the grease this morning." Red peeled back the layers of pancake and painted each one with butter.

A guy wearing a faded, sweat-stained Detroit Tigers T-shirt burst out of the kitchen holding a plate above his head like a waiter in a fancy restaurant.

"Here's your sausage, *chica*, extra crispy like you like it."

"Thanks, Julio. You're a peach."

"Hey, man, how're you doing?" Julio looked at Earl like he was a specimen under a microscope.

Earl suspected Julio didn't really care about Earl but liked Red and was curious who Earl was and did she know him. He kind of liked being a man of mystery. "Fine." Earl dumped two creamers into his coffee.

Julio looked him over again, turned on his heel and ducked back into the kitchen.

Red diced her sausage into bite-sized chunks and dispersed them throughout the pancake layers. The finishing touch was maple syrup drizzled over the entire mess.

"My grandma ate her pancakes like this." Red took a bite, rolling her eyes with pleasure.

"Does she live back in Pennsylvania?" Earl asked.

"She used to before she died. That's kinda why I left."

"Sorry about your grandmother."

"Thanks. But it was almost a year ago. That's when I decided to go to LA. I always wanted to be on the *Star-Makin' Machine* show."

Earl knew the show. It was on Friday nights. One of the guys in the dart league had a thing for one of the judges, a blonde with big tits who was as stupid as a pile of bricks or pretended to be.

"So, how'd you end up here?" Earl asked.

"The car died and I didn't have the money to fix it. This place was hiring so I figured what the hell." Red shrugged and ate some pancakes.

"How long you been here?"

"Almost nine months."

"Cars are a real pain in the ass." Earl thought of the Horowiczes' Buick outside sweltering in the relentless New Mexico sun.

"That's for sure. For a while I lived in it out back in the parking lot. This place has showers because it's a truck stop and all and I got a meal allowance so things could have been a lot worse that's for sure." Red dipped a french fry in the milkshake and popped it into her mouth.

Earl thought Red had a nice mouth. Her lips were full and a nice pinkish shade he'd never noticed on anyone else before.

"Then one of the other waitresses here rented me her garage when her husband ran off and she needed the extra money. It's better than the car but it's not where I want to live the rest of my life, you know?"

"I can imagine."

"I figure in another three months I'll have the money I need to head for LA."

Earl nodded and finished the pie and coffee. He supposed it was time to get moving.

"So, where in Florida do you live?" Red asked.

Florida? Oh, that's right; he said he was from Florida. That was stupid. He'd never even been there.

"Miami."

"That's so cool. Not that I've been there but it looks really nice on television."

"Yeah, it's nice but I've lived there a while. I've been thinking lately that maybe it's time for a change. It can get boring being in one place for too long." He'd never spoken truer words considering how long he'd lived in Hadley.

"That's how I felt about PA. There wasn't anything to do. It seemed like everything happened somewhere else."

"As a matter of fact I know exactly what you're saying." Earl ate another fry.

"My family came from PA and everybody I knew came from there and everybody knew everybody. My father was kind of a loser so everybody expected me to be a loser too."

"What made him a loser?"

"He owned his own garage except he wasn't very good at fixing cars. He wanted to be and he sure tried hard but none of his repairs took. So, he gave up on cars and started fixing lawnmowers. That he could handle but he didn't make a lot of money. My mother had to work which really pissed her off." Red dredged another fry in milkshake.

"What's your mom do?"

"She worked at the local turkey farm in the chopping off the head department."

"Gross."

"It is gross. That's one of the reasons I left. I figured I'd head up with grease-stained fingernails like my father or blood-spattered clothes like my mother."

Earl thought that the acorn doesn't usually fall too far from the tree. Up until finding Brad in that storage unit he'd been on a path very much like his parents.

"I hope you get out to LA like you want to." He leaned forward and pulled his wallet from his back pocket.

"And I hope you enjoy your trip to the big hole."

At that moment Julio slammed through the kitchen door.

"Hey, *chica*, boss says you can go. It's slow he says."

"Cool." Red leapt off the stool. "Hey, if you're leaving do you mind giving me a ride home?"

"You asking me?" Earl asked.

"Yeah, usually Julio brings me but he's on until seven. Right, Julio?"

"He never lets me leave early." Julio stared at Earl. "How do you know this guy isn't some ax murderer or something?"

Wow, thought Earl, did he actually look like an ax murderer? Better than looking like an insurance salesman.

"Julio, you worry too much. I'll call you from home. Besides, I can tell about people. He's harmless." Red bused her dishes into a tub under the counter.

Harmless? He was offended. Why couldn't he look a little dangerous like Julio?

"Yeah, you call me *chica* and if the number on caller ID ain't the number I'm expecting I'm gonna fuck him up."

Earl wasn't sure he even wanted to take Red home. She could be a whacko. When you thought about it what young woman got into a stranger's car after sharing a few french fries? Red must not have any sense of self-preservation. At this point he didn't really know how to get out of it without pissing everybody off and Julio didn't look like a guy you'd want to piss off.

"Let me go get my stuff." Red followed Julio back into the kitchen.

Earl put fifteen dollars next to his coffee cup to cover his and Fatty's bill and edged toward the door. He should make a run for it. It would look suspicious but what the hell it's not like he knew these people. Strolling would be better, a casual reach into his pocket for a cigarette, fumble for a light, open the door and stop and fire up the smoke then take a drag and amble across the parking lot. He wanted to turn and see if Red was behind him but he knew from the movies that was a sure way for the person looking for you to find you. Take another drag and get beyond the third row of cars and drop the cigarette, make an oh-shit and drop to one knee. From that vantage point Earl risked a look behind him.

There was Red scanning the parking lot.

Why the hell was he doing this? She was just some waitress that needed a ride home, for Christ's sake, and here he was acting like a scaredy cat.

He stood up and waved. Red waved back and headed in his direction.

"I thought you left without me."

"Now, why would I do that? Just wanted a butt and thought I'd get the AC going."

Earl unlocked the passenger door of the Horowiczes' Buick. "Wow, nice car."

"It belongs to my uncle." Earl said. "Yup, good old Uncle Morty. He's a furniture salesman in Miami. He owns Furniture World on Ocean Street." There had to be an Ocean Street in Miami since it was right on the beach.

"I'm Melissa." Red stuck out her hand.

"I'm named after my Uncle Morty Lefkowicz. Pleased to meet you." Earl shook her hand.

* * *

"*Merde.*" Avola slammed her hand against the steering wheel as she saw the constellation of brake lights flashing before her. Her foul mood would not be improved by a traffic jam. Her back was in a spasm because of that potbellied easy chair in the back of her van. She'd had that horrible argument with May. And now she was stuck in traffic on 91 South somewhere between Deerfield and Northampton.

She was trapped with no exit for miles, no idea what was causing the traffic tie-up and an urge to get home rivaling that of a migrating Canadian goose. She hated losing control, hated not being in charge and really hated having no way out. May was always telling her to calm down, urging her to join her for Tai Chi at the senior center, as though Avola wanted to spend her time with a bunch of old people gyrating in slow motion. Strictly speaking she knew she qualified as elderly but she couldn't see the point in focusing on that and being forced, through proximity, to listen to people talk about cholesterol lowering medications or replacement joints. Her needs were simple; all she wanted was her upholstery business, a few friends and May.

She never should have called May asking after her health but she just could not stop herself. That old saying about absence making the heart grow fonder never seemed to apply to May. If Avola were honest with herself and she might as well be since she was stuck in this damn traffic jam, she had called May to say more than hello, she had called to see what she was doing and if May missed her.

Avola had a fantasy, which she would never admit, that there would come a time when she asked what May was doing that she would reply missing you or waiting for you to come over. But all she ever heard was what May was actually doing. And May was always doing something.

Last night during their phone call she'd expected nothing more than a garden update or an anecdote from the senior center or something the Unfortunate Vera had said while trying to say something else. Even more than getting hung up on was the stunning revelation that May was enjoying having an absolute stranger in her home. An interloper lesbian and her dog would be living in the upstairs guest room forever it seemed, making herself indispensable in the garden and cooking May casseroles. All because May had a feeling the Interloper was a kind woman. Hah. She was probably nothing more than a gold digger and May was too gullible to know it.

Honestly, May had no instincts for self-preservation. She traipsed through life as though nothing could go wrong or if it did go wrong she would come out of it with barely a scratch. Usually Avola found that part of May's personality amusing. However, this Lisa-person could be dangerous and she was a lesbian. That fact made Avola doubly uncomfortable. It wasn't likely that anything would develop between May and Lisa but stranger things had happened. She just didn't want May hanging out with any other lesbians unless Avola was there too. It wasn't May she didn't trust, it was everybody else.

CHAPTER THIRTEEN

Earl wondered what he was waking up from. For a moment he thought he was back on Thorny's porch recovering from the applejack. His head was heavy; a throbbing tennis ball seemed to be growing over his right ear. He tried to touch it but wasn't able to move his arm though he could move his fingers. Where the hell was he? A couch? It was upholstered but it couldn't be a couch because there was a window above and behind his head and over his feet. A car! He was in the backseat of a car. Whose car?

Shit, had he been in an accident with the Horowiczes' car? He couldn't remember anything but he'd heard that sometimes happened if events were too traumatic. This was going to be very hard to explain to Melvin and Serena; they absolutely loved their car. A car Earl had wrecked somewhere in…where had he been…oh yes, New Mexico.

Jesus, you'd think if he'd been in an accident bad enough to throw him into the backseat that there'd be flashing lights and rescue personnel milling around and he'd have been taken to the hospital. Unless he was in a ravine and surrounded by coyotes that were just waiting to tear him limb from limb and feed his tender flesh to their babies. Or he'd die out here and some archaeologists would find his moldering carcass when they were out looking for Indian ruins.

Earl tried to sit up which made his head feel like a yo-yo on the end of a string. He tried again but seemed to be stuck to the upholstery. Maybe he had bled so much that it had dried and was acting like an adhesive. Could he be dead or almost dead and having an out-of-body experience? He closed his eyes and waited to be sucked into the light.

Wait a minute. Was that music? No, it was talking. Talking, coming closer.

"Julio, maybe we should take him to the hospital."

"*Chica*, listen to me. He don't need no doctor. He's just a little unconscious but he'll wake up."

That was Red or Melissa, as he now knew her and that cook from the truck stop. And then it all rushed back at him like a car without brakes. He'd been sitting in Melissa's apartment talking and smoking a joint when he'd heard the door open behind him and just as he was turning around to see who it was, whammo.

"I feel bad. He was a nice guy." Melissa's voice sounded plaintive.

Was? Why were they talking about him in the past tense? He tried to sit up again but all he did was tear his shirt a little.

"Don't try to get up, man." Julio peered at Earl through the car window.

"Okay, okay."

Melissa slapped Julio's shoulder.

"Be nice, Julio. Morty is probably just confused." Melissa reached into a small bag of potato chips and popped one into her mouth.

Earl thought that was an understatement.

"Just explain what's happening," Melissa said.

"You explain things, *chica*. I'm not so good at explaining things."

Hopefully someone would explain.

"Okay, Morty. It's kind of a long story."

"I'm all ears," Earl said.

"Do you remember being at my apartment?"

"Sort of."

"See, I told you. You shouldn't have hit him." Melissa slapped Julio's shoulder.

"I know. I know. It sort of happened by mistake."

Mistake? A mistake is when you knock over a glass of milk not when you knock someone out.

"Why?" Earl asked.

"Why what," Melissa said.

"Why knocked out?" Earl had never been as thirsty as he felt right now.

"Okay, Morty, here's the story. You came into my apartment to have a beer, though we ended up smoking a bone even though I never thought an older guy like you would smoke herb, but that's beside the point. You were just getting ready to leave for the Big Hole when Julio came in because he got off work early, which like never happens. He saw you sitting there, freaked out and hit you with the iron."

"I didn't freak out. You got to tell the whole story."

"You mean the part about the border patrol?"

"Yeah, and I didn't get off work early. I left early because I thought they were looking for Illegals, you know?" Julio said.

"I was going to tell Morty that." Melissa crunched a chip.

"Be sure to say that we need his car to go to LA to my cousin's."

"Okay. Okay."

"And how we super-glued him to the backseat."

"It was Gorilla Glue," Melissa said.

"Whatever, *chica*. And tell him when we get to LA he can have his car back and go to the Grand Canyon like he was going to. No problem. It's just a little detour."

"Where now?" Earl asked.

"You want to know where we are now?" Melissa leaned her head back and shook the chip crumbs into her open mouth.

Earl nodded which didn't feel so good with the welt on the side of his head.

"We don't exactly know, Morty. Julio wanted to keep to the back roads. We kind of need a map."

"Up. Need to get up." Earl tried to sit up and then remembered the Gorilla Glue. That stuff really was as good as advertised.

Julio held up a hunting knife for Earl to see.

"I think we'll have to cut you out of your clothes, man."

* * *

May understood the merits in the way animals dragged themselves off into the woods to die. No muss or fuss, carcass swallowed into Nature's giant gulp. Rex, the shaggy mutt who belonged to her father had done just that. At least that's what she'd been told. Maybe Dad had felt sorry for Rex in his decrepit state and had put him out of his misery. May understood that too.

Not that May wanted to die. She just wanted to feel better. Being laid up with her ankle was giving her too much time to think. Couple that with Earl having gone missing and her phone call and subsequent fight with Avola and May was feeling grim. And old. Whatever that meant. Maybe it meant having no options beyond what kind of soup to have for lunch or what to watch on TV. She would give her eye teeth just to be able to go for a walk. It wasn't in her nature to feel sorry for herself but here she was, doing just that.

It didn't help that it was winter, dark by late afternoon with the constant litany of freezing rain and nor'easters on the weather forecast. The holidays had been awful with Earl gone and Avola and her fighting. Winter had always been her least favorite season which she usually offset with activity. Besides physical therapy a couple times a week to strengthen her ankle there was precious little of that.

Too bad Vera wasn't living close by like she used to so they could have had dinner once in a while. But, she was still out at her daughter's house in Leverett. Heidi had called recently to say that Vera was doing better though still had trouble with word finding. Apparently she was fitting in, cleaning up a storm and taking care of the collective's chickens. Next time they came into town they'd drop by a dozen eggs. It seemed Vera had the magic touch where chickens were concerned and they had more eggs than they knew what to do with.

If only she'd hear from Earl. It would help just to know he was okay and not in some car wreck on some back country road without a friend in the entire world. May didn't expect him to come home, he was entitled to live his own life and if that meant wandering around the countryside that was fine with her. It was normal to want to have your own life and make whatever you could out of it. It had just taken Earl longer than most boys to do it. Maybe the business with poor, dead Brad Nelson was a blessing in disguise. If only he'd take the time to fill in one of those postcards and let her know what he was up to.

Avola was another matter. When they were first together May had been surprised by the intensity of love she felt toward Avola. Her need for Avi had caused an ache in her body that she enjoyed but it also scared her. All the feelings she'd been sure everyone else felt that were turned off inside her had suddenly erupted. Like a seed that germinates, shoots out of the ground, grows into a bush and blooms overnight. As long as they'd been together it still surprised her how stubborn Avola could be. She could always win an argument with May just by waiting her out. May had never liked the discomfort of not getting along. It made her chest hurt so she always gave in.

She remembered that time at the Girl's Club. In the flats of Holyoke, it was in the back room of a beer joint. Men went in the front door and women went through the back. It was a dump with cracked linoleum on the floor, a plywood bar with the same linoleum on the counter and bathrooms which made you wish for something as nice as what you might find in a gas station. Draft beer cost fifty cents and there were pork rinds, pickled eggs and popcorn for snacks. Blinking Christmas lights were strung along the ceiling and a DJ, a woman with forearms like spring hams, spun the tunes. She was great and was able to mix things up enough to keep the women, who ranged in age from eighteen to sixty-eight, happy. The Girl's Club was it for women's dancing. She and Avola went about once a month and May felt fairly safe she wouldn't run into anyone they knew.

She'd been up at the bar buying a round of drinks for the table. She and Avola had struck up a conversation with a couple of gym teachers from Springfield and the four of them had decided to share a table. While May was waiting for the drinks she'd got to talking with a woman sitting at the bar who looked like Cary Grant in *North by Northwest*. The woman even sounded like Cary with a smooth, amused way of talking. May had laughed, a lot. Suddenly Avola had appeared at May's side, glaring at the Cary Grant woman and saying she'd finish getting the drinks. May had merely said "What are you, jealous?"

Avola had turned on her heel and stormed out of the club. May had realized she'd spoken out of turn and took off after her trying to apologize. But it was as though Avola were deaf. They got into Avola's car and Avola turned up the radio so loud it was impossible to talk. When Avola dropped May off at home she had refused to come in even though Earl, who was still in high school, was staying over at a friend's house, and they could have had some private time together. May spent a horrible night alternating between fear and anger. Fear that she'd driven Avola away and anger because she hadn't done anything wrong. Finally at six o'clock in the morning she had driven over to Avola's house. Avola was still married to Mr. Big Boy Liquors LeFebre then. Fortunately, he was a heavy sleeper and didn't hear May drive in. But Avola had.

Avola had gotten into May's car. May had apologized. Avola had said she had a quick temper which was as close as she'd ever have gotten to saying she was sorry. Then they had started kissing and petting, only stopping because they were afraid of being caught by Louie.

Over the years things had never really changed. There was always something that would set Avola off, they would argue and be apart for a few days and then May would apologize and Avola would say nothing beyond acknowledging her quick temper, like it was normal and nothing more inconvenient than a stone in May's shoe. This time would be different. She would not be made to feel guilty for doing the charitable thing and providing a home to someone who didn't have one. If Avola would have slowed down and met Lisa she would see that there was nothing to be concerned about. May had asked some of her friends who were Pink Ladies at the hospital if they knew anyone who knew anything about Lisa. Besides Lisa being a paramedic, she volunteered for So What! I'm Not a Purebred Dog Rescue and helped to staff the First Aid tent at the Look Park Athletic Club events in Northampton. Since she'd moved in the house had livened up. Her dog Bosco was well trained and enjoyed sitting next to May's recliner watching cable, and she had repotted all of May's houseplants. Lisa was a dear girl.

Avola would have to apologize first this time. May would not give in, no matter what.

* * *

Lisa could tell when Bosco was really listening. His eyes never wavered from her face and his ears rotated in her direction. She knew that every dog owner believed their dog had special powers but Bosco really did. He seemed to know exactly when his opinion was required.

They had been out for an evening walk at the dog trail behind the old Northampton State Hospital. Lisa liked bringing him there because he could run off leash and commune with his doggie buddies. He seemed to really like a standard poodle who was owned by a cute dyke named Mo.

Mo had asked her if she wanted to go out for breakfast this coming Saturday after their morning walk. Lisa could barely believe it. Just when she had vowed to stop thinking about dating, to give herself time and stop worrying about it. It figured. That's how the universe seemed to work. The minute you stopped worrying about not having something you got it. Not that she had anything, really, just hope and a date which was more than she had this morning.

She and Bosco were on their way back to Hadley. Lisa had promised to pick up a veggie pizza at Sergio's for her and May to share for supper. May needed a pick-me-up and really liked pizza. Having an injury was difficult for people who were normally pretty active. Plus her son Earl was still gone missing and she and her girlfriend, Avola, had had some kind of phone argument. Lisa wasn't really sure what it was all about, only that they weren't getting along at the moment. Lisa certainly understood how that could make a person feel.

It was hard to imagine being with someone for decades.

"My track record isn't that good," Lisa said to Bosco who sat in the passenger seat with his head out the window. The dog needed a breeze no matter the weather. He turned to look at her as if to say, tell me something I don't know.

"You don't seem to miss Johnnie much." Lisa rubbed his ears. "That's because he is a cat person," she said, wondering how she could have missed the whole transsexual thing. True, Johnnie was really butch but that didn't mean much. There were plenty of butch dykes who didn't want to become men. Jesus, the things you could miss knowing about a person even after living together for six years.

It was time to stop perseverating about the whole Johnnie thing. She needed to reroute her brain with a new hobby or something and no matter how tempting, that hobby shouldn't be Mo, no matter how cute she was in her even cuter jeans tucked inside a pair of dark green wellies.

Lisa swerved into a parking spot right in front of Sergio's. She left Bosco to guard the idling engine and ran inside.

* * *

The ten-minute ride back to May's filled the car with the steamy aroma of hot cheese, dough and the alchemy of mushrooms, broccoli, onion and eggplant.

"My mouth is watering," Lisa said, smiling as Bosco licked his lips.

Lisa pulled in May's drive and parked next to May's car. She got the pizza and invited Bosco out of the car, hoping he could be trusted off leash the short distance to May's door. It was impossible to manage a pizza and his leash. Just as she was thinking it was too dark for the squirrels to be out, Bosco's ears perked up and he let out a woof.

"Leave it," Lisa intoned in her best alpha dog voice. She watched him hesitate, could almost see the wheels turning in his head as he sniffed, considering his next move.

May opened the door. "Come on, Bosco." She waved a cookie in the air.

"Thanks May. I guess he decided a cookie in the mouth beats a squirrel in the bush," Lisa said as she walked through the door.

"I even managed to set the table. I feel quite proud of myself," May said.

"That's great, May. I hope you haven't been overdoing it." Lisa put the pizza on the table.

"I can't wait to overdo. I'm in that recliner so much I feel like I'm growing into it. All this sitting around is really getting to me."

"I can imagine. I know I wouldn't like it much either. What can I get you to drink?" Lisa asked.

"I always think beer goes with pizza but I don't know if there's any in the fridge." May sat in her spot at the table.

"Oh, I think there's a couple in here." Lisa opened the door and squatted down for a better view. "When did you last have pain medication? I don't want to knock you for a loop."

"I've given those up. I don't want to become one of those addicts I've been watching on that intervention show. Did you ever see it?" May opened the pizza box. "One slice or two?"

"Two. I'm starving." Lisa brought two Coronas to the table. "Glass?"

"Yes, dear. Should we give Bosco a slice?" May used her egg spatula to ferry the slices to Lisa's plate and her own.

Bosco let out a yip.

"I guess that's a yes," Lisa laughed.

"Actually, I think it's because someone just drove in."

* * *

Avola stormed across May's porch and up to her kitchen door, knocked once and banged through like she was entering a barroom badly in need of a scotch. The door flung backward crashing into the wall, vibrating on its hinges and rattling the glass. A dog started barking.

"May? You home?" Avola yelled, at the same time as she saw May seated at the table and a young woman holding the collar of a dog who was growling deep in his throat.

"Ha! You must be the interloper." Avola's voice echoed off the walls.

"Avola! What are you doing?" May struggled to stand up. The young woman touched May's arm.

Avola felt anger surge through her veins when she saw the interloper touch May's skin.

"I'm Lisa. May's new housemate."

"Housemate? Looks like more than housemating going on. How cozy you both are," Avola said, her brain filled with swirling images of the Interloper and May together. A movie playing too fast inside her head.

The dog continued to bark, the hair on the back of his neck standing up.

"Let me put Bosco in the bathroom," Lisa said, straining to lead the dog away from the kitchen.

"Avi, what has gotten into you? You are acting like a lunatic and with no good reason." May shook her spatula in Avola's direction.

"Don't brandish your weapon at me. You are the lunatic, letting a complete stranger into your home. You could be murdered in your bed by this…this…gold digger!" Avola yelled, waving toward the bathroom where the woman had disappeared.

"Avi. Stop this right now. You are embarrassing me in front of Lisa," May said in a voice Avola could not remember ever hearing.

"Embarrassing you? Already you are casting me aside in your mind; I can hear it in your voice, replacing me with a younger model." Avola stood in the kitchen unsure of what to do next. This was not how she had envisioned this scene. It was supposed to go differently. May should have agreed that the interloper would vacate the premises immediately and that Avola should move in. Instead, May was siding with the girl and her dog and pushing Avola aside like a dinner plate she was done eating from.

Anger bubbled under Avola's skin like an erupting pox. She swept a place setting off the table, scattering pizza slices onto the floor. There would be no cozy dinner now. And no beer either, Avola thought as she threw the Coronas across the room where they shattered against the fridge. There would be nothing left when she was through.

"Avola LeFebre, you leave this house right now. I am sick of your jealous nonsense," May yelled.

Lisa stepped back into the room and looked at Avola. "I'll call the police unless you leave."

"Don't threaten me. I have had enough of May's nonsense too. I will not be toyed with any longer." Avola screeched, jerking open the kitchen door and kicking the storm door open. She launched herself off the porch and into her van, barely touching the ground.

From a great distance where one part of her watched the other part, Avola noticed she had left the engine running when she'd arrived, so anxious had she been to get to May. But all eagerness to see May was over now. She had to leave, to get to where she would be safe, where she could put herself back together in privacy.

In her haste to be gone, Avola put the transmission into drive rather than reverse and rammed her van into the back of May's Honda. *Mon Dieu*. This was not a good development; May would never believe this accident was accidental now that they had had this argument. She knew she should tell May what had happened but she could not. She had to go home, go home, go home. Besides, this really wasn't Avola's fault and wouldn't have happened if May had done things correctly.

"That'll teach you," Avola said as she backed out and turned her battered van in the direction of home, trailing radiator vapor like a steaming locomotive.

CHAPTER FOURTEEN

Lisa's cell phone woke her up. Damn that cheerful ringtone. She had worked the three-to-eleven shift last night and had really hoped to sleep in a bit. She glanced at the caller ID. Johnnie. What the hell did she, he, want? The landmine of the pronoun, it reminded her of when she'd first gotten involved with women and hadn't yet come out to her family. A simple conversation about going to the movies was a nightmare of remembering to convert the she to he.

The call went to voice mail. The message would determine whether or not Lisa called back. She needed time to formulate her response to the situation. Anything to avoid her own emotional meltdown. Johnnie seemed totally unaffected by emotion.

It had been almost six months since they'd broken up. Her rage had subsided into a barely perceptible glow, a well-banked fire as opposed to an acreage-consuming, uncontrolled conflagration. Now she felt sad. Not every-day-all-day sad when it was an effort to get up and eat breakfast. It felt more like a low-grade infection, nothing that kept you home from work but made staying up late nearly impossible.

She knew it was probably too soon to start thinking about dating. But, that was all she thought about. Especially since Mo had asked her out. She liked butch women and Mo was definitely butch. Not the old-fashioned version like Avola was to May but a more modern version. Was there such a thing as a new-age butch? There was someone out there for her and she just had to trust that the right one would show up at the right time. She still wasn't sure if Mo was the one but she might be. Time would tell.

Clearly, sleep was out of the question. She raised her head to look at Bosco looking back at her.

"You ready to get up?" Lisa asked. Bosco thumped his tail into the mattress in response. He could go from sleep to sixty mph in no time flat. She pulled on her sweats and bathrobe and headed downstairs with the dog leading the way.

The kitchen smelled like toast. May must have gotten up already but she wasn't anywhere to be seen.

"Just a sec, Bos. Let me start the coffee and pee and then I'll take you out."

Bosco wasn't listening. He was glued to the kitchen window overlooking May's garden. He sure liked May. During the day when Lisa was at work Bosco spent his day next to May's recliner. If Lisa was working the night shift he slept at the foot of the stairs where he could keep an eye on things.

His tail was wagging slightly, a sure sign he had a squirrel in his sights. Lisa was sure Bosco thought squirrels were put on the earth for his enjoyment, living stuffed toys he never tired of trying to catch. She didn't look out the window until he started to whine. Not the squirrel whine, a different whine. That's when she'd noticed May, white hair tucked under a Red Sox cap, sitting on the same bench Lisa had rescued her from last fall. She was wearing her walking shoes, corduroys and a red and black checked hunting jacket. May dabbed her eyes and blew her nose.

She was so out of it this morning she hadn't even realized May was outside. But he knew. How were human beings able to function in this world without a dog to let them know what was going on?

"Maybe she needs some time to herself, Bos," Lisa said. Bosco gave her that look that said he wondered how the human race ever got to be top dog.

"Okay. Okay. Let's go see if May needs something."

Bosco reached May before Lisa did. Dogs were fearless unless there was something to really worry about. A few tears didn't bother him. Sometimes she was such a chickenshit.

"Good morning, Bosco." May rubbed his ears.

"Bosco wanted to see if you were all right," Lisa said, feeling more than just a little foolish.

May smiled and reached into her jacket pocket and pulled out a dog biscuit. She held it toward Bosco who nibbled it as delicately as if it were a cucumber sandwich at high tea.

"Oh, I'm just feeling a bit puny. I thought it might help to get outside. I've never known March to be so warm," May said.

"Is there anything I can do?" Lisa asked.

"No, dear. It's nice having you here. I'm grateful every day that you moved in."

"I am too," Lisa said. And she was. May was better now. She no longer needed a walker. She sometimes used a cane outside the house but not always and was able to drive herself around. Lisa no longer needed to be here, she wanted to be.

"I guess I'm just feeling at loose ends," May said.

"Loose ends?"

"Restless, almost like I want to go somewhere. Silly, isn't it? You take yourself with you no matter where you go. So, it's not like things would change. Avola and I would still not be together. Earl would be God-knows-where. Things would be what they are."

"A lot has happened over the winter," Lisa said, thinking that it had seemed like the longest winter of her life.

"Maybe I need a project."

"Maybe. Work really saves me from too much time to think," Lisa said.

"Are you suggesting I get a job?" May winked at Lisa.

"Well, not bagging groceries at Stop & Shop." They both laughed.

Bosco suddenly sat up and looked toward the top of the white pine. His ears rotated, his nose working to identify what only he could hear. Sniff, sniff, blow, sniff, sniff, blow. May leaned over and whispered to Bosco who wagged his tail in response.

"I was telling him about the owls who nested in that tree last year. Something seems to be up there again," May said.

"I'm glad spring seems to be on its way. A little warmth and sunshine is a relief." Lisa yawned, wishing she'd been able to sleep in later.

"You're so right. I've had too much time to think and worry events in my mind. Until the garden takes up more of my time I'll have to find something to do. You look tired, dear."

"I am. It's always hard to chill out after the three-to-eleven shift. Now that spring is here people are going a little crazy so the ambulance has been busy. I don't think I finally dozed off until one o'clock. Then the phone woke me up this morning and I couldn't fall back to sleep."

"Something on your mind?" May asked.

"Johnnie called and left me a message about wanting my recipe for scalloped potatoes he wants to make for Easter. That got me remembering last Easter when I made those same scalloped potatoes for our Easter dinner. I just need to move on, let go of Johnnie and let him be Johnnie now. He's right; he needs to be true to himself. But, it still hurts to talk to him. That got me thinking about dating Mo and how hard it is to live a life that's real and honest. Not the kind of thinking that fosters sleep," Lisa said and laughed.

"Those topics have kept me awake from time to time. At my age I think dating is definitely out of the question." May scratched Bosco's ears.

"Oh, May. I hope not. Maybe someone will show up when you least expect it." Lisa squeezed May's hand.

"I don't know, dear. Why don't you go back to bed. Leave Bosco with me. If he can stand walking with a slowpoke, I'll take him for a spin around the block." May squeezed back.

May waved Lisa into the house.

"She's a real sweetheart," May said to Bosco, ruffling his ears. He was still distracted by the goings-on in the pine tree.

May fumbled in her pocket for the tiny set of binoculars Earl, or at least she assumed it had been Earl, had given her for Christmas. They were so small it seemed impossible they could magnify anything. They had arrived by mail addressed to her with no forwarding address. The postmark was smudged but she thought she could make out California. It had to be her screwball son.

Aside from the aggravating way they'd arrived, it was wonderful to have them. May figured they gave her the vision of a hawk. She trained them on the treetop hoping to see the movement that corresponded with the faint scrabbling sound she could now hear behind the traffic noise of the morning commute. Her arms gave out before she could see anything other than shaggy bark and pine needles.

"I don't see anything." May put her binoculars away and stood up. "Let's go in so I can pee and then we'll take our morning constitutional."

May took Bosco for a walk along the dike. The Connecticut River ran high with snow melt and spring rain. It reflected the blue sky and seemed placid and harmless, belying its strong current.

Bosco sniffed along, careful not to pull too hard on the flexi as if he knew she wasn't as strong as Lisa. This was a popular dog walking spot though quiet now. They were probably between the early, before-work walkers and the retired, take-my-time walkers which was fine with her. It was peaceful not to have to make pleasantries with people. She wasn't feeling all that pleasant lately.

A few years ago May had taken a yoga class at the senior center led by a woman who had seemed so calm she had wondered if the woman was taking Valium. It turned out that meditation was her drug. She had told that room full of old people to get into a comfortable position, harder and harder the older you got, and pick an object across the room and concentrate on the middle distance, the place between you and your object. Then breathe.

May felt like she was living in the middle distance. Since the horrible scene with Avola, who had vanished afterward like smoke in the wind, she had felt adrift. At first, May had been glad, convinced she never wanted to see Avola again especially when she found out that Avola had rear-ended her car. May was furious and had considered calling the police but in the end she had just called her insurance company. Now enough time had passed that May was worried. It wasn't as though she expected Avola to apologize…she wasn't sure what she expected. All she knew was she missed Avola despite what had happened.

Last night Avola had showed up in her dreams wearing her red track suit and asking if May wanted to go for a walk on the beach. Avola looked so much like herself, hair styled yet darker than it had been in recent years. Her eyes sparkled and a small grin played on her lips like she was waiting to tell May a joke.

May had said that she'd love to go for a walk but hadn't they better talk about what happened first. Avola shook her head and said, "No, toots. It wasn't really me. It was just some little girl who was mad because her brother died. Now let's get going. I don't want to miss the sunrise." And as only you can in a dream, she and Avola boinged to the beach and there was the sun just barely winking at them above the Atlantic.

It was so real. The briny smell of low tide, the seagulls squawking at each other over their sea bits breakfast, the wet and bumpy sand under their feet, smears of purple and pink clouds streaking the sky. It was beautiful, that inside-your-eyes kind of beauty that brought tears into your eyes and made you feel like everything was perfect. May was filled with the feeling that they were going to be able to stand there forever.

May guessed that dream had been a message. It was hard to imagine that people and the love they shared just stopped. But was the memory of love enough to repair the damage caused when love took a turn for the worse?

* * *

Earl pulled the Horowiczes' Buick into the Infinity Diner's parking lot. Finally the mission was nearly complete, data gathered and all of it pointed toward Roswell, New Mexico, as the location of his one, true home. You-Know-Who had been oddly quiet for months which Earl took as a sign that he was going in the right direction.

Now he was here. The alien head-shaped streetlights were humorous. The alien crossing crosswalk signs and spaceship-shaped street signs were very tongue in cheek, part, no doubt of a lucrative marketing campaign. Nearly every store sold something to do with UFOs. Even the door to the Infinity Diner was painted black and decorated with stars and planets like the Milky Way. WE ARE NOT ALONE was etched into the casement around the picture window. He felt the goose bumps pop because that's what You-Know-Who had been telling him for years. This was definitely a sign.

He pushed open the door and stood in amazement looking at the variety of miniature spaceships decorating the place. There was memorabilia from *Star Trek*, *Lost in Space*, *My Favorite Martian* and *Star Wars* glued to every available surface. The wait staff was dressed like crewmates from the Starship Enterprise.

"We're packed this morning. Sit anywhere you can find room, honey, " a very effeminate Dr. Spock said as he rushed by with two cups of coffee and a plate of something green.

Earl selected a small table in the front window where he could view either the street or the restaurant, whichever was more interesting.

"You look bewildered," Dr. Spock lisped so close to Earl's right ear he jumped.

"I am. I am. I've just never seen anything like it," Earl said.

"The food's good too. Today's breakfast special is Out of This World Waffles with Spaceship Sausage Links. Want something to drink?"

"Coffee."

Dr. Spock nodded, dropped a menu on the table and scooted off.

Earl planned on finding the tourist office after breakfast to check out what there was here to see. He didn't want to miss anything. Then he would get into the outskirts where there were less people around and set up his equipment. His information gathering had been tiring these last few months but worth it. Earl felt exhilarated and was thinking he deserved some time off, maybe some pool time at his motel, have a few beers and relax.

Dr. Spock returned with coffee. "Cream and sugar is on the table."

"Thanks." Earl looked up, startled to see a woman in flowing purple robes standing beside Spock.

"This is my friend, Sister Starlight. She wondered if you'd be open to her joining you at your table."

Earl was too stunned to do anything but nod yes.

"Thank you." Sister Starlight's voice was so soft Earl strained to hear her.

"I'll have tea," she said to Spock who hurried off to do her bidding.

Earl knew he was staring at Sister Starlight but he wasn't able to stop himself. She had a beautiful, open face and an expression like an angel in some old-fashioned Italian painting. Her hair was long and dark brown and tied back with some elaborately jeweled band. The robe was scoop necked and made of some slippery looking fabric that seemed to vibrate. From her neck hung a heavy, silver five-pointed star that dangled between her braless, Earl was pretty sure of that, breasts.

She extended her right hand. He reached out and took it, still unable to speak.

"So nice to see you again," Sister Starlight murmured.

"I…I don't think we've met before."

"Yes, we have." She chuckled. "I can't wait to tell you all about it."

* * *

A hawk experimented with the air currents high above the Cathedral of the Extraterrestrial. At least Earl thought it looked like a hawk but in this part of New Mexico it could have been anything flying overhead. The sun was hot for mid-April. Back home in Massachusetts he'd still have needed a spring jacket; here it was chilly at night but got hot during the day.

Earl leaned against the Horowiczes' car, lit a cigarette and waited for Sister Starlight to finish talking on her cell phone. He couldn't actually see a cell phone, just assumed there was because she was sitting in her car, jabbering away while waving her arms around. It was probably one of those hands-free models.

He'd never met anyone who'd started his or her own religion. According to Sister Starlight she hadn't actually started this one but was only doing what she'd been told to do by someone named Bogee, or something like that, from the Zeleron Galaxy. Three or four times a month Sister Starlight was retrieved by Bogee and taken to Zeleron where she met with the Zeleronic Council to discuss plans for the Cathedral, community outreach and congregational recruitment.

She thought Earl would make a wonderful director of marketing. That was exactly how Sister had put it, a "wonderful director of marketing." No one had ever thought he'd be wonderful at anything before.

When he'd told her about his visits with You-Know-Who aboard the alien spaceship, Sister Starlight had clutched his hand and told him in that soft, whispery voice that Bogee was tall and blue too.

She'd said that the last time she was in Zeleron she was told by the Council to expect a visitor. Someone who wouldn't look like what he was or even know what he was. Sister Starlight would have to look beyond the presentation for an aura of indecision, which would be her clue. Apparently he had that in spades. She would have to imagine the eventuality of purpose this visitor would be capable of. Earl whispered the words "eventuality of purpose" to himself because he liked the sound of it so much.

"You must forgive me, Earl, for keeping you waiting," Sister Starlight whispered in his ear.

"No problem. I've got all day," Earl said.

"Let's go inside where we can have some refreshment and more conversation." She took Earl's cigarette out of his mouth and crushed it under the heel of her open-toed sandal. That's when Earl noticed her purple toenails. She tucked her arm through his pressing her braless breast against his upper arm as they walked together across the parking lot to the back door.

The Cathedral of the Extraterrestrial looked nothing like Earl imagined a cathedral might look. No confusion here with Notre Dame or even Jimmy Swaggart's Glass Castle. In fact, it looked a lot like a converted horse barn. A detail proven to Earl when Sister Starlight unlocked the door and the faint tang of horse manure tickled his nose.

The horse stalls had been converted to office cubicles, their doors labeled with a name and designation. Samantha Preston was Community Outreach Coordinator and next door to her there was a bleached out rectangle above the Director of Marketing placard. Sister Starlight led Earl toward the front of the building to what must have once been the tack room. He noticed the title of Inter-Space Liaison over her name.

On a shelf above her desk was a stuffed ET about the size of a bear cub, arm reaching toward the ceiling fan, fingertip glowing. Just like the movie Earl thought, remembering how much he'd hated the film. He felt like it trivialized his experiences on the spacecraft. To say nothing about those darned peanut butter candies.

"Just my little joke," Sister Starlight murmured, gesturing toward ET.

Earl was relieved.

"Our gathering place is upstairs where hay was once stored. One of our congregants put in some skylights. At night it's a bit like being launched into the heavens." Sister Starlight waved toward a couch. "Please make yourself comfortable."

Earl sat on the edge of the sofa, continuing to scan the two walls of books. Some of the authors like Joseph Campbell, Carl Sagan and Stephen Hawking, he recognized but most he had never heard of. A few books were written in languages that didn't look familiar.

"Can I offer you some iced tea or lemonade?" Sister Starlight asked.

"Lemonade would be great."

"Please wait here and I'll be right back." She skimmed from the room.

Earl cast his mind back to his last visit from the alien. He had been hung over on Thorny's applejack and You-Know-Who had told him to go home, an order he had disobeyed. All his trials and tribulations, Melissa and Julio for example, were nothing more than inconveniences set in place to strengthen his resolve to complete his mission. Here with Sister Starlight he could be open about his alien abduction and not worry people would think he was a screwball. Once he got to know her better he would tell her about the mission.

Suddenly he heard a clattering on the wood floor outside Sister's office. She soon bustled in pushing a small cart loaded down with a pitcher of lemonade, several glasses, an ice bucket and a small bowl filled with sugar cubes.

"May I pour?"

Earl nodded.

After sitting on the couch next to Earl, she plucked five ice cubes out of the bucket using very ornate silver tongs and plunked the ice into a tumbler. She poured lemonade over the ice causing lots of little, crackling explosions.

"We, at the Cathedral of the Extraterrestrial, believe that this earthly reality is just an illusion. The Larger Truth is waiting to be experienced."

Earl nodded. It sounded like music to his ears.

"With proper indoctrination and procedure we can shed our earthly perceptions and experience all The Universe has to offer. You, Earl, because you have been visited by Those from The Great Beyond can, no doubt, understand this better than most. Are you ready to enter into your new life?" Sister Starlight paused as though listening to something Earl could not hear.

"Yes, I am ready," Earl whispered.

"Sugar?"

Earl nodded again, mesmerized by the ritual.

Sister Starlight took up smaller tongs, gently grasped a cube and dropped it into his glass, whirling the whole thing up with a crystal stir stick. Earl noticed each sugar cube had CET pressed across it in that fancy writing people put on wedding invitations. She made herself a glass too.

"A toast to new beginnings." Sister Starlight touched her glass to his.

"New beginnings." Earl took a long drink. It was some of the best lemonade he'd ever tasted with just the right touch of sweetness.

* * *

Earl noticed, halfway into his second glass of lemonade, the spines of the books on the shelves across from him. The "the" from *The Prophecies of Nostradamus* changed places with the "the" from *Hiking Through the Himalayas*. He blinked his eyes. It had to be fatigue. No doubt all he needed was a good night's sleep.

He realized it was more than that when all the vowels in all the titles began to pulsate in time with his heart rate, a heart rate which increased with this latest observation, along with the sweat gathering on his upper lip like the condensation on a cold glass. It would really be embarrassing if the future Director of Marketing passed out across The Inter-Space Liaison's lap.

"Excuse me, Sister. Is there a restroom I could use?" Earl watched the words float from his mouth and explode like over-stressed helium balloons.

"Of course. In the hall opposite my office." Sister Starlight's words didn't float as well as his but bounced around on the floor in the breeze from the ceiling fan.

Earl stood and kicked Sister's words out of the way; he knew it would be very impolite to step on anything she'd said, and made his way toward the bathroom.

What was happening to him? It'd been hours since breakfast at the Infinity Diner so it couldn't be the sausages and waffles. Thankfully, the bathroom was as dark as a tomb. It was comforting not to see anything because what he was seeing wasn't behaving exactly right. But, what if there was something here that he should see? Like the floor disappearing. Because that's what it felt like was happening. He couldn't feel anything under the soles of his feet. He wasn't even really sure that his feet were still attached to his ankles.

Part of him knew this line of thinking didn't make any sense. Floors didn't disappear like melting snow. Maybe if he could find the sink and follow the drainpipe to the floor he could be assured that everything was as it should be.

* * *

When Earl came to he was lying on someone's unmade bed. He was naked and covered with a chenille bedspread with ballerinas twirling across it. His clothes were draped over a chair across the room. The bed was shoved under the eaves, a slanted ceiling canted away from him. It was a cozy room with lots of light streaming through the dormer windows.

Gosh, all he'd seemed to have done on this trip was wake up from something. There was Thorny's applejack and Julio knocking him out with Melissa's steam iron and now, this. The last thing he remembered was drinking some lemonade…and then…nothing. It was a lot like high school algebra class, there was some problem he was supposed to understand but couldn't quite grasp what all those equations were supposed to mean.

He squinted at the ceiling. There were little bumps all over it. Earl looked around for his glasses and found them on the nightstand. The bumps turned into ceramic figurines in the shape of tiny spacemen. Glued to each space helmet's visor was a Polaroid of someone's face. Jesus, who were all these people?

On closer inspection none of them appeared to be famous, just ordinary people, some good-looking, some not so much. He was enjoying the astronaut gallery when he found himself looking at his own little Polaroid face. It was creepy considering he had no idea when the picture was taken. Odder still was how happy he looked apart from his dime-sized pupils.

He needed a cigarette, to take a leak and drink about a gallon of water. He wouldn't say no to something to eat either. He got out of bed and put on his clothes but when he went to open the door, the doorknob just turned around and around. It couldn't be pulled open either.

Was he locked in? What were these Cathedral of the Extraterrestrial people thinking, locking up a grown man in a bedroom with a chenille bedspread and hokey astronauts glued to the ceiling? Where was Sister Starlight? What had he gotten himself into this time?

CHAPTER FIFTEEN

Avola sat on the deck overlooking Cape Cod Bay wrapped in the extra wool blanket from the closet. It was probably senseless to bring hot coffee out to enjoy the early morning because the chilled air cooled it almost immediately. But, the sky was not to be ignored. The gray pearlescent luster reflected her mood perfectly. A whisper of pink flirted with the horizon. The sky was of two minds, as was she. Still, after spending most of the winter at her friend Margarite's place in Provincetown and gazing at the pewter sea, she was no closer to a decision but had had plenty of time for introspection.

If an emotion were capable of being someone's shadow then anger was Avola's. She had always been angry. It was so old within her that it seemed to have been seeded in when her father's sperm met her mother's egg.

Life's circumstances, she realized, had fed this proclivity. She was the middle child and had to endure her older sister, Mary Christina, lording over her and her younger brother Gasteau's charm. But he had been her playmate and she had loved him with a single-minded devotion that surprised her then and had never been replicated except by her devotion to May. He had been cute and fanciful and a boy, the baton holder for the family name Dugas.

Maman had labeled Avola's faults as impatience and restless indignation and they were often fodder for her mother's endless lectures until Gasteau's death. After which Maman barely spoke except to ask occasionally, her voice as querulous as an ancient hag, "Is your brother coming home soon?" and then subsiding into silence when confronted with a truth as relentless as the ticking of the hall clock.

Mary Christina had been useless in the family drama, promised to the Sisters of St. Joseph and given to visitations by the Holy Ghost; she played up an ethereal nature which handily excused her from household duties, a situation that further angered Avola.

Papa had had to work so his absence from home was excused. Avola knew with the certainty of sunrise that he worked much more than their financial situation required. When he was home he disappeared into his study with the dog and a bottle of brandy, falling asleep, more often than not, on his chaise lounge placed against the double windows overlooking the street. A circus parade could have passed by their house, a uniformed cavalry or Jesus Christ dragging his cross and it would have made no difference to the people behind the clapboards.

The anger, like rhizomes knotted under Avola's skin, could never be expressed. It wasn't done in her family. Happiness, before Gasteau's death, could be expressed as long as one realized that it couldn't last. Sadness was allowed, in small allotments, except for Maman who wallowed in it like their neighbor Mr. Benoit's pigs wallowed in mud. Anger was forbidden, seen as a shortcoming, a character flaw as noticeable and unattractive as a goiter or hunched back.

Even with all this historical data there was no excuse to be found for how she had treated May. Avola had begun and discarded numerous letters apologizing and asking for May's forgiveness. They all seemed inadequate and did nothing to assuage Avola's shame and guilt. She missed May and wanted her back, or failing that to at least be friends but unless she could find a way to approach May even that would never happen.

Margarite had offered a wonderful respite. She ran a guest house and Avola had earned her keep by reupholstering and slip-covering some of the guest house furniture before Margie opened for business in mid-April. Avola's mortification over her scene with May had been so acute she had closed her shop and house and like a dog with its tail between its legs had fled to safer territory.

She and Margie had been friends for over forty years, longer even than she had known May, and they had seen each other through some ugly things. Avola and Louie "Big Boy Liquors" LeFebre's divorce, Margie's many marriages and divorces and not to forget her three children, all by different husbands. They were all grown now but had had stormy childhoods and worse adolescences.

Thankfully, there was nothing she and Margie could not say to each other. Avola knew her friend would accept the evidence of Avola's bad behavior and find a way to love her anyway as she had done for Margie many times. Friendship was sometimes about bearing witness to the ugliness each of them was capable of and not forsaking the friendship because of it.

Avola heard the slider open behind her.

"I don't know how you can sit out here. I started a fire in the woodstove to take the chill off." Margarite walked to the railing and looked out, blue eyes studying the horizon.

"The view is worth the chill." Avola grimaced at the temperature of her coffee.

"It's true. Maybe." Margarite shivered, pulling her wool hat down to her eyebrows obscuring her short blond hair. "I know I never get tired of the view. Hard to believe I'll be open in a couple weeks and the hordes will descend and I'll be so busy I'll forget what this view looks like."

"I don't know how you stand it. I would be driven around the bend," Avola said, thinking her friend reminded her of a small bird rushing here and there.

"Most times I love it and when I don't I remind myself it's only five months with seven months off to recuperate."

They watched the pink smudge expand along the horizon, widen and incorporate a smear of blue. Seagulls began to take to the skies trying to ride the air currents. The sound of waves rushing the shore seemed louder; the tide was turning.

"I have to go home, I think," Avola said.

Margarite nodded.

"I will finish the cushions in the window seat of the Captains Courageous Room today or tomorrow and then be on my way."

"Are you going back to Northampton?"

Avola shrugged but she knew she would. She had already called her handywoman and asked her to get the house back up and running. She craved seeing May. She would apologize and hope it would be enough.

"You're hoping to reunite with May, aren't you?" Margarite asked.

"You are a witch and it's not the first time I say that either." Avola smiled at her friend.

"You may have burned that bridge, honey. Maybe you should aim for friendship and see if you can fly that kite," Margarite said.

Avola nodded. She loved Margie but with three divorces she wasn't sure her romance advice could be trusted.

"I will start with an apology and hope the rest will take care of itself. May has always said I could never admit when I was wrong or jealous or angry. I am hoping she will see that I am sincere." Avola watched the ocean change from pewter to slate blue. It would be a beautiful day.

"It's a wonder you've managed to keep that woman as long as you have, Avola. There isn't a woman on this earth who doesn't appreciate an apology, especially one so well deserved. You got a heart of gold don't be so afraid for it to shine. Let May see that you know what you've done and you're willing to do anything to get her back."

Avola knew Margie was right. She'd spent her whole life afraid of losing what she had and all that fear hadn't kept it from happening.

"Shall we breakfast?" Avola stood.

"Hell, yes. How about some bacon and eggs, I got some of those sweet rolls you like so much from the Portuguese bakery."

Avola smiled. Too bad Margie wasn't a lesbian. She would have made a great wife.

* * *

"Hey! Let me out of here!" Earl simultaneously yelled and pounded on the door until his palms vibrated and his voice sounded like it did after he went to that Pink Floyd concert when he was in high school. He got down on his hands and knees and listened at the crack under the door. Nothing. No sound coming from anywhere. It seemed like the bedroom he was stuck in wasn't part of a house but floated in the air like a tethered balloon.

It was time for him to take the bull by the horns, as his mother would say. Since all the windows were nailed shut and he didn't have the tools to take the door off the hinges, he was going to have to get violent. Not a bad prospect given his aggravation level. Earl scanned the bookshelf for a hefty specimen, settled on Bullfinch's *Mythology* and practiced swinging it like a batter waiting for the pitch.

The windows on the south side dropped a good two stories to hard-packed dirt. The west window overlooked a porch or something with a gently sloped roof. The better escape route was a no-brainer.

He crouched, swinging his arm back and forth to gain momentum, spun around a couple times like a discus thrower and let the Bullfinch's fly. The target cracked. The book dropped to the floor like a stone. Since he'd made headway he tried a second time. The window broke and the book ended up splayed open on the porch roof. He cleared the glass away, folded the chenille bedspread a few times and draped it over the windowsill. He hated using somebody's ballerina bedspread but didn't see any choice.

The view out the window into the gathering gloom of the advancing sunset made it plain that he was no longer at The Cathedral of the Extraterrestrial. The Horowiczes' Buick was not visible from the second-story perch. There would be no quick trip to the Motel 6 where he was hoping to regroup. It appeared he was leaning out the window of a farmhouse that wouldn't be out of place in Hadley, Massachusetts.

He climbed over the sill and crouched on the roof.

"This is where I need to take my time," Earl whispered to himself, shifting his weight off the wallet in his back pocket. Instantly he knew that barely perceptible movement of hip started a slip, which turned into a slide that Earl tried frantically to stop. He grabbed at the chenille bedspread but since it wasn't anchored to anything it did absolutely nothing to stop his descent. He rammed into the Bullfinch's with his knee, surprisingly painful, picked up speed in an odd, slow-motion kind of way, until he, the book and the bedspread were shrugged off the roof into a spiny, New Mexico shrub very like a plant porcupine.

"Holy shit!" Earl yelled and vaulted out of the bush onto whatever passed for grass in the southwest.

"Where the hell am I?" Earl asked.

"That's what everybody asks though you're the first one who has ever broken out through the window," a voice boomed from somewhere behind him.

Earl screamed, picked up the bedspread and Bullfinch's and took off across the lawn. He ducked behind a pickup truck that seemed to materialize out of nowhere.

"Who's there?" Earl called back toward the porch.

No answer. The voice had sounded a lot like You-Know-Who but louder like she was talking through a bullhorn. Could he have imagined the whole thing? After all, he was in a weakened state being tired, thirsty, mystified and needing to pee. To say nothing of what falling off a roof had done to him. Earl squinted back toward the house. No movement. But it was getting dark, the shadows were gathering and though he had no idea where he was he knew that he needed to get himself somewhere else.

First things first. He folded the bedspread and put it and Bullfinch's in the back of the truck. While he was taking a leak against the front tire he noticed the keys glinting on the dash.

Before he allowed himself to really think about what he was doing he eased open the door and jammed the keys into the ignition. The engine roared to life. He shoved the transmission into drive and took off like a checkered flag had been waved at him. A glance at the porch as he barreled by yielded no information. Creepy. He depressed the accelerator until he thought he might push it through the floor.

Just as Earl was thinking he was driving down the longest driveway on the planet his headlights reflected a sign in the distance. Relief flooded his chest. It was too far to read but it was comforting to be close enough to something that somebody thought they needed to put up a sign about it.

If he could just locate the Cathedral of the Extraterrestrial he'd retrieve the Horowiczes' Buick and get the hell out of Roswell. He'd been so sure that this was the place. Ah well, better to find out now. Maybe he should reconsider visiting Area 51 in Nevada. Roswell made too much fun of itself to be real, but Area 51 belonged to the government and goodness knows they had no sense of humor. Maybe he could get someone there to listen to him. Maybe the air force would want him to make contact with You-Know-Who. She knew a lot of stuff the military was probably dying to know like how to get from where you are to where you want to be without any effort.

Earl bumped over a cattle crossing and pulled up to a blacktopped road. The sign he'd noticed said nothing. Figured. He'd have to decide left or right.

He flipped on the radio.

"…If you're just tuning in folks, this is Clara Goodhue with Common Sense is Good Sense on KBLM radio. If you find yourself in a quandary dial 555-KBLM. When we went to commercial we were talking to Christine. Remind us of your quandary, Christine."

"My quandary is how to get myself dressed since my stroke a few months back. My left arm just dangles there."

"Which is your dominant hand, Christine?"

"My left, which makes everything doubly hard."

Hmmm, Earl thought. Maybe I should turn left.

"Are you taking physical therapy, Christine?"

"I sure am, Clara, and occupational therapy too. They have all these ideas and when I try them, well, it just seems that my left arm has a mind all its own."

Earl flicked on the left directional signal.

"That certainly is a quandary, Christine. Well, folks, anyone out there got any suggestions to remedy Christine's left-handed quandary? Call 555-WISH.

"Here's a call from Raymond. Good evening, Raymond. You're on the air."

"Good evening, Clara. Longtime listener, first-time caller."

"Welcome, Raymond. Do you have an answer for Christine's left-handed quandary?"

"I believe I do. Velcro. My business, Velcro Sensations, makes a Velcro glove, left-handed in Christine's case…"

Earl turned left.

"…Corresponding to Velcro strips on her hairbrush for example and…"

Talk radio really attracted a lot of wingnuts.

"Thank you, Raymond, for that really innovative solution. Now, let's take a call from Ann Marie. Hello Ann Marie."

"Thank you for taking my call, Clara. I don't think my suggestion will be taken seriously but I feel duty bound to make it."

"Feel free, Ann Marie. Here on Common Sense is Good Sense we recognize that one person's common sense might not be another's."

"Thank you, Clara. I believe Christine's arm has been infiltrated by a demon. She needs an exorcism. My uncle Hank had himself a stroke and it wasn't until he went to a revival at Christ in Blood Evangelical Ministries and Pastor Luke brought the Holy Spirit into his arm and healed him that he was able to go back to his taxidermist business."

Goodness, it was dark out here though there was an odd bluish glow in the distance.

"…Interesting suggestion. Well, folks, it's that time again. This is Clara Goodhue…"

Earl took a deep breath and felt himself relax despite the fact that he had no idea where he was. The blue glow was growing in intensity. Maybe there was an accident up ahead.

"…Is Good Sense. And remember if common sense were common then everybody would have some. Good night all."

Earl drove up a little hill and there in front of him, not two hundred yards away, was a hovering spacecraft, emanating a blue light. He slammed on his brakes, which proved to be the wrong choice because the truck hit a patch of sand and skidded in a slow arc until he found himself T-boned by the spacecraft.

"Holy shit!" Earl yelled, wondering how he would ever explain this to his insurance company. But then he remembered the truck was stolen, or borrowed, as he preferred to think of it, so it wouldn't be his insurance company at all. Of course, if the cops showed up he'd be in deep doo-doo.

Earl considered his options. Should he get out and knock on the spacecraft and try to make contact or sit tight and wait for them to do it? Too bad his cell phone was back in the Buick, he could call that Common Sense show he'd caught the tail end of on the radio and ask for opinions. He bet they'd never had a call like the one he'd make if he were able.

If only he could contact You-Know-Who, a word from her would come in handy right about now. But, she'd always done all the contacting which, in retrospect, seemed kind of unfair. Friendship was a two-way street. At least, he thought of her as a friend but maybe she just saw Earl as a specimen. He'd have to ask her when they next got together.

Just as Earl was thinking about opening the door a set of headlights came over the same hill he'd just driven over, slammed on its brakes and hit the same patch of sand he'd hit which set it to spinning round and round pretty much like he had. Earl braced himself for the impact by sliding out from under the steering wheel, closing his eyes and putting his head between his knees. He had no idea if this technique worked for anything beyond air travel. That's when the other vehicle slammed into the truck throwing Earl against the passenger door, which came open, dumping him onto the asphalt.

It wasn't his night. He lay in the road hoping it was all a dream induced by the drug given to him at the Cathedral of The Extraterrestrial. Any moment he'd wake up and find himself anywhere but half-in-half-out of a borrowed pickup halfway underneath an alien spaceship.

"Sir? Sir? Are you all right?" a woman called to him from the other side of the pickup.

At least, that's where he thought the voice was coming from. Perhaps the aliens were talking though he usually heard their voices in his mind.

"Sir?"

Goodness her voice sounded familiar. He turned his head toward her voice and found himself staring at the shortest woman he'd ever seen. Short like a munchkin on *The Wizard of Oz*.

"Yes. I…I'm…" Earl struggled to finish his sentence.

The woman got down on her hands and knees next to him and put her hand on his forehead.

"Should I call an ambulance?"

"No. No." Earl shook his head which didn't feel great but didn't feel as bad as when Julio knocked him out. He couldn't involve the authorities.

"I'm fine. Could you help me sit up?" Earl extended his hand.

"Of course. But, do you think that's wise? You don't want to make things worse."

Earl nodded, struck again by the familiarity of the woman's voice.

"I'm fine. Really. I wasn't even knocked out."

"Well, if you're sure," the woman said, taking his hand and gently pulling him to a sitting position.

The world tilted a bit but evened out as Earl sat there.

"Uh…have we met? I know that sounds weird but your voice seems so familiar," Earl said, looking into the woman's large gray eyes.

"I'm Clara Goodhue. Maybe you've heard me on the radio," she said. Then said making her voice sound radioey, "If common sense were common then everybody would have some."

"Yes. That's it. I heard your show tonight for the first and only time."

"Really? Well, KBLM isn't far from here. I'm on my way home from work," Clara said.

"Wow. That's unbelievable," Earl said, knowing he should let go of her hand but not really wanting to.

A long moment passed.

"Can you stand, sir?" Clara asked.

Earl shook himself like a dog.

"Call me, ah…" Gosh, what should he call himself this time? There were so many names but suddenly he couldn't seem to think of any.

"Phillip…Phil. Phil Phillips the Fourth. But Phil will do."

"Can you stand, Phil?"

"Yes, Clara. I think so." He liked saying her name.

With her help he struggled to his feet. The top of her head was level with his belly button.

"Well, I guess…" Earl struggled to think of a way to keep the conversation going.

"Yes, Phil." Clara looked up at him; her gray eyes seemed to glow.

"Do you know where we are?" Earl asked, willing to risk sounding like a complete idiot if it meant prolonging the conversation.

"Don't you?"

"Well, I have a general idea…" His voice petered out.

"What were you doing in the middle of the road, Phil? There's not much traffic out here at night, God knows, but…" Clara looked around.

Earl realized that Clara didn't see the alien spacecraft glowing and pulsating behind her, squatting in the road like a doublewide trailer.

"More like a something, I guess," Earl said, wondering how the aliens could appear to him and hide themselves from her. Probably some elaborate cloaking device. He'd have to ask the blue woman next time he saw her. It would be great if it were something he could learn to do.

"Well, Phil, we're about five miles outside of Roswell," Clara said.

Earl was relieved. If only he could get to the Horowiczes' car he'd be home free. Well, not exactly home but the Motel 6 which was close enough.

"Do you have insurance, Phil?" Clara asked.

"Ah…no. Well, now wait…" Earl reached into the glove box hoping there was an insurance card or registration or something to save him from looking like a complete and total asshole.

"I…ah…now, don't take this the wrong way but this isn't my car. I'm sort of borrowing it." Earl couldn't believe he'd just admitted to something he didn't want her to know. Honestly, sometimes he was his own worst enemy.

Clara's eyes glittered. "Uh-huh. Well, I'll just take a gander under my hood…"

Earl knew the name Phil Phillips the Fourth screamed of fabrication. He wasn't good at thinking on his feet. And now, here he was in the desert, the borrowed truck ruined and having almost ruined Clara Goodhue's car, a local celebrity for God's sake. At least, he assumed she was a celebrity. Weren't most people who had their own radio shows celebrities? The good news was Clara's car still ran and the spaceship had vanished. The aliens must not have insurance either. He was hoping she'd offer to give him a ride back to town. But, with a name like Phil Phillips the Fourth he didn't think it was likely. If only he'd chosen to be a Tom Harrison or a John Blackburn.

At least the stars were bright. As long as Clara pointed him toward Roswell and he kept his feet on the pavement, he should make it back to the Horowiczes' car by sunup. Besides, a walk would do him good. He needed to regroup.

He watched Clara Goodhue shining a flashlight at her damaged radiator which was leaking greenish fluid at a slow but steady pace. The least he could do would be offer to pay for the repair.

Clara let the hood fall shut and jumped off the front fender. "Well, Phil, I think we can make it back to Roswell. I can't tell where the leak is. But we'll take it slow and see how far we get."

"I appreciate the ride," Earl said. "You've got to let me pay for it."

"Let's see what my mechanic, Richie, says and then we'll talk." Clara got into the front seat.

Earl was curious to see how someone so short was able to drive a car. He figured it would be adapted something like Jimmy Sadowski's car. He'd broken his back snowmobiling and was paralyzed from the waist down but since his car was outfitted with hand levers he could get around just fine. Earl promised himself he wouldn't stare but he couldn't guarantee he wouldn't ask questions. Was Clara just short or was she short short like a dwarf? Were dwarfs and midgets the same thing? Was her house sized for her? What about getting luggage into an overhead compartment on an airplane? How did she use public restrooms? Weren't the toilets too tall for her?

Maybe that was too personal. He should probably be quiet, be grateful she was giving him a ride and give her a couple hundred bucks in traveler's checks and fade away like the bad dream he was to her.

"So, Phil…are you in Roswell on vacation?" Clara asked as she started the wheezing engine.

"Well, ah, yes…in a manner of speaking. My Uncle Tom Harrison needs help at his winery in ah, California, and I thought it was time to try something new. You know how sometimes you just get the itch to do something different?"

"Yes. I've moved around quite a bit myself. What's the name of your uncle's winery?"

"Ummm. Blackburn. John Blackburn Wineries. He thought it sounded sophisticated."

"Really? How interesting," Clara said.

"Yeah, and while I was driving across the country I thought I'd stop in Roswell and see what the hubbub was about. You know, the whole alien thing. I thought those programs on A&E and the Travel Channel were pretty interesting." Earl cleared his throat. "So, ah, Clara, do you happen to know where the Cathedral of the Extraterrestrial is?"

"I've heard them mentioned around town but I don't quite know where they're located. Why do you ask?"

"Oh, I left my car there earlier and I can't quite remember how we got from the Infinity Diner to the Cathedral," Earl said.

"We?"

"Sister Starlight and I. We had breakfast together and she invited me to see the cathedral. She said there were some fascinating things going on there. So, I thought what the hell. I'll be working pretty hard once I get to the winery…" Earl's voice trailed off.

"And what happened next?" Clara asked.

"Sister showed me around and said I seemed like someone with unrealized potential and I might fit right in there because I seemed open to the power of the Universe. We had some lemonade, really good lemonade, and I started feeling weird. I thought my breakfast maybe hadn't agreed with me so I went to the bathroom and…" Earl's voice faded.

"And?"

"And the next thing I knew, I woke up in a room with a chenille bedspread and Bullfinch's *Mythology* on the shelf and I…I…couldn't open the door. So, I broke out a window and fell off the porch roof into some cactus and somebody yelled at me but I couldn't see where they were so I borrowed that truck, had an accident with a spaceship you couldn't see before I had an accident with you. It's been a hell of a day." Earl took a deep ragged breath.

Clara was looking at him carefully. "I wonder, Phil, if you'd do me a favor?" she asked.

"Sure thing, Clara. You've been nothing but nice to me."

"I want us to swing by the hospital so we can get checked out. You can't be too careful after a car accident, however minor it might seem."

CHAPTER SIXTEEN

"Mr. Phillips, do you have claustrophobia?" the MRI technician asked.

Earl considered. He didn't like being confined, who did? But, he didn't think his dislike could be called a phobia.

"I don't think so."

"Could you please lie on the gurney with your head resting in the cradle?" The technician helped Earl stand up from the wheelchair the New Mexico Medical Center had insisted he ride in. Apparently, once you were admitted they never let you walk anywhere. He'd had so many tests and X-rays since Clara had brought him in that he couldn't remember the names for any of them. There must be something going on but no one would tell him anything.

Earl did as the technician directed, feeling foolish in his johnny and fuzzy socks. He wondered where his clothes were.

"Have you ever had an MRI before?"

"No, I can't say that I have."

"It's imperative that you not move your head. Keep swallowing and blinking to a minimum during the picture taking portion of the procedure…"

Great, thought Earl, confined and no blinking or swallowing…How long could something like this go on? He found himself reluctant to ask.

"…The first part will take around twenty minutes to half an hour. Then we'll pull you out, inject you with contrast and you'll go back for an additional twenty to thirty minutes. Put these earplugs in. The machine is noisy." The technician handed Earl a packet with two yellow sponge corks about the size of a single Good & Plenty candy. He was sure he'd never been given a pair of earplugs from a health professional before. His stomach filled with an acidic dread very like heartburn.

The technician assisted Earl in lying down, bolstering his knees and covering him with a blanket. "This is the panic button, Mr. Phillips…" The technician's voice rose to accommodate Earl's diminished hearing.

Earl was given a plastic knobby thing that felt too flimsy to stop panic. The heartburn began to expand and eat away at his lungs making it difficult to breathe.

"…Press it three times and we'll bring you right out. Please keep your arms folded across your chest and remember not to move your head." The technician packed the sides of Earl's head with washcloths and snapped what looked like a hockey goalie's mask over his face. The gurney rose up and backward until Earl slid inside the plastic tube. He suddenly felt very alone and not just a little bit scared. What could they think was so wrong with him that he needed to be unhatched like a chick put back in his egg?

"There'll be some noise now, Mr. Phillips." The technician's voice echoed through the tube.

Then it started, the jackhammering of concrete and Earl was the concrete. How in the hell was he going to handle five minutes of this racket let alone the forty to sixty minutes they had planned. Maybe he should have said he was claustrophobic and he could be if he really thought about it, maybe they would have offered him a sedative or something. That's what he needed, a sedative. Any way to stop thinking that if he opened his eyes he'd see that there wasn't much difference between him and one of those poor Victorian bastards who'd gotten buried alive. That's how little headroom he had.

What if the machine broke? And they couldn't get him out? What if the technician had to pee or get a snack or lost track of time? He could press the panic button until the cows came home and if there was no one to hear it what good would it do?

Earl felt his heart rate increase. Was it his imagination or were the fillings in his teeth starting to vibrate? This was a magnetic imaging machine after all, what stopped it from yanking the fillings right out of his head? He'd had some of those fillings since he was a kid and his mother had taken him to Dr. Seymour T. Greenberg, who'd had fingers like short link kielbasa.

The noise was getting louder. It sounded like Earl was in a barrel and someone was beating on it with a tire iron. That couldn't be normal. Nothing this loud and clackety could possibly be operating normally. It was just as he'd thought, the machine was broken and the technician didn't want to tell him. Probably because they had no idea how to fix it and he was just going to waste away inside this contraption being MRIed to death.

Earl took a deep breath. His heart was going to burst through his ribs. How long had it been since he'd swallowed? It seemed like hours he'd been allowing the saliva to pool in his mouth. What was he supposed to do with it? Drool? Nothing made a person want to swallow more than being told he shouldn't. And why shouldn't he if this machine was killing him. At this rate he'd drown before they found out the machine was broken.

His nose itched. And so did his right ear because that plug was in too far so it was making his head feel too full on one side and empty on the other. His fillings were getting hot and coming loose. He could feel that much with his tongue. They were definitely coming out. Would they ricochet like BBs around this tube where there was barely room for Earl and his own skin? He was going to die. Soon. In a johnny. In New Mexico. Alone. In a tube with drool pouring out of his mouth. He never should have let Clara talk him into going to the emergency room.

Earl pressed the panic button.

* * *

The MRI showed a giant, fuzzy lump growing off his brain. Just like a burl you occasionally saw growing off a tree trunk. Lou North, his buddy from the VFW, made salad bowls from tree burls and charged a couple hundred bucks for them too. Earl considered telling the neurosurgeon, Dr. Saltus, about the burls but he didn't look like the kind of guy who walked in the woods much.

Earl watched Dr. Saltus's mouth move and wondered why he couldn't understand anything being said beyond the words "emergency surgery." He'd been fine and felt great, more or less, before the MRI and now felt shaky and a little weird. Probably because now he knew he had a "brain tumor" though the surgeon called it a something "amoma." Before, he had nothing wrong except a problem locating the Horowiczes' Buick. He supposed he should be writing all this down…though he wasn't sure why except it was something his mother always did and it seemed to help her. He wished she were here now.

It was scary to hear a stranger tell you there was something growing on your brain and that they were going to shave your head, crack your skull open and go in and get it. Earl recognized the words "shunt" and "brain swelling." Dr. Saltus said Earl needed a Health Care Proxy and a Durable Power of Attorney in case "something happened." Did Dr. Saltus mean he might die? It was surprising that a doctor who had the guts to fish around in somebody's brain didn't have the guts to say "you might die." Maybe dying was the least of it. What if his brain got fucked up and he couldn't talk or walk or think anymore? Jesus, if that happened he hoped Dr. Saltus would drop his brain on the floor and walk away.

The only person he knew around here was Clara Goodhue and it wasn't like they were friends or anything. His mother was back in Massachusetts but he supposed the hospital could call her if something went wrong. He should probably phone and give her a heads-up. He'd been gone around six months and had been sending back blank postcards from everywhere he'd been. He'd figured she'd figured they were from him. His mother was no dummy.

"Do you have any questions, Mr. Phillips?" Dr. Saltus asked, finally using a few words in a row that Earl was able to understand.

"Uh…I…uh…"

"Okay. Well, a social worker will be in to help you fill out the necessary paperwork. Since this is a teaching hospital we're hoping you'll consent to allowing interns to follow you."

"Ah, I guess…"

"Wonderful. Well, get some rest and I'll see you bright and early tomorrow morning. I'll prescribe something to help you sleep tonight in case you experience some anxiety." Dr. Saltus shook Earl's hand and departed the room so quickly his shoes squeaked.

* * *

Earl thought he must have been a baby when he last felt breezes on his bald head. They'd sent in a student nurse to shave his head a couple of hours ago. Now he was sitting in the hospital courtyard feeling all shivery and goose-bumpy, waiting for his last meal before surgery.

There must be one cookbook used by hospitals across the United States. He remembered the food at the hospital near his house in Hadley tasting just as lousy as the food here in New Mexico. He'd taken one look at the Salisbury steak and gravy and knew he'd starve before he'd eat any of it. Luckily for him there was a pizza place that delivered. He and another guy, Peter, a tall skinny guy, had ordered up the carnivore's special. Peter was going to be having brain surgery too except he didn't have a tumor like Earl, he had some vascular problem and an eighty percent chance of croaking during the operation. That's why

Peter wanted lots of meat. Who could blame him for wanting to taste pepperoni one last time? Peter said he'd been one of those exercise freaks and had eaten nothing but organic veggies, whole grains and fish…now, all bets were off. Peter's only regret seemed to be that the pizza place couldn't deliver beer so he was settling for a two-liter bottle of Coke. Earl wondered if Peter was hoping the pizza would kill him.

Earl hadn't thought to ask Dr. Saltus what his chances were. He wasn't sure he wanted to know. He was glad he'd had his little cross-country trip, including all the weird shit that had happened and his mission was mostly accomplished. It was better than finding out he had a brain tumor and still being stuck at the Keepsake. At least, now, he felt like he'd lived a little bit.

"Hey, pizza's here." Peter waved from the bench nearest the parking lot.

"Great." Earl ambled over, surprised that he was feeling a little hungry.

They pooled their cash and paid the delivery guy including a big tip.

"Want to eat in my room?" Peter asked.

"Sure. Lead the way." Earl followed him, carrying the bottle of soda, into the hospital and down the hall into a room two doors away from his. They settled in, Earl in the visitor's chair and Peter in bed, eating and watching a rugby game on ESPN. Earl could barely hear the announcers over the sound of chewing and burping.

"Hey, would you mind if I used your phone?" Earl asked. He didn't have one in his room.

"Go ahead. Is it local?"

"No, I thought I should call my mother in Massachusetts. But…"

"Wait. Use my cell. What the hell…I don't want to die with minutes on my phone." Peter laughed and took another piece of pizza which was limp from the combined weight of pepperoni, hot and sweet sausage, ham and bacon.

"Thanks, man. I appreciate it," Earl said, taking the phone.

What should he say? "Hi Mom, it's me Earl. I've got a brain tumor." Jeez, any way you sliced it there was no easy way to tell her. Better not think about it too much…just dial. Earl listened to it ring.

CHAPTER SEVENTEEN

"Hey, Ma. It's me."

"Earl, honey? Is that you?" May couldn't believe it. She turned off the evening news and sat up straighter.

"Yeah. How've you been?"

May thought Earl's voice sounded different, but maybe the connection was flukey. "I'm fine, Sonny. It's awful nice to hear your voice. You doing okay?"

"Yeah…well…that's kinda why I'm calling. I…uh…they, the doctors I mean, gave me an MRI after a little fender bender I had. Just to make sure I was okay and…" Earl's voice faded away.

May's stomach tightened. "Yes? What's wrong?"

"I got a brain tumor, Ma. I have to have surgery tomorrow morning and I…I…just wanted to hear your voice and…say I love you and I'm sorry if you've been worried about me…just so you'd know…in case something happens."

A brain tumor?

"Where are you, Earl?"

"New Mexico Medical Center in Roswell."

"I'll be there just as soon as I can get there, Sonny. You hold tight. I'll see you tomorrow evening."

"That's great, Ma. I…I…I just hope I'm still here." Earl's voice sounded thick like he was trying not to cry.

May felt her eyes fill up. Her poor boy, scared and alone, it was too much to take in. "I love you, Sonny. I'm sure you'll be okay." Though May wasn't sure, brain surgery wasn't like having your appendix out.

* * *

It had turned out that Clara Goodhue's car wasn't beyond repair. Richie found her a rehabbed radiator from a junkyard and had put a rush on the repair. It wasn't like she could use his loaner, after all. So, to show her appreciation she paid the bill in cash and got him a six-pack of Guinness Stout, Richie's favorite beverage.

Now, she was back at KBLM, drinking her preshow coffee and scanning the Internet for possible subjects for discussion. She liked to be prepared just in case it was a slow night and the callers were few and far between. Thankfully, that didn't happen too often and was unlikely to happen tonight because they were a couple nights away from the full moon. It was also springtime and that inevitably brought up people's relationship concerns. Put those two things together and it could be a wild night on the radio.

"Hey, Clara. Ready for action?" Her producer, Sally, peered over the cubicle wall at her.

"Oh, yeah. Just let me print this off and I'll be right there." Clara hit the print button and heard the whir of the printer across the room.

"I don't think you'll have to worry about dead air tonight. The crazy vibe is in the air. I stopped by the Infinity Diner on my way in and it was just crawling with a tour group from somewhere, all of them dressed like ET."

"This town is just too weird sometimes. Speaking of the Infinity Diner, have you ever heard of Sister Starlight and the

Cathedral of the Extraterrestrial? I met a guy last night who asked me about it."

"Oh, a guy, huh? A weird guy or a regular guy?" Sally asked.

"A weird guy. Not dressed like ET, maybe, but strange in any case. He told me an even stranger story about meeting this Sister Starlight during breakfast and her taking him to the cathedral where it sounds like he was drugged and kidnapped. But, since he sees alien spacecraft, perhaps I should consider the source."

"Jesus, where do you find these weirdos?"

"They find me. My guess is all dwarfs have a force field that pulls them in, if I can be so bold as to borrow a descriptive metaphor from *Star Trek*."

* * *

"Good evening, folks. Clara Goodhue here with Common Sense is Good Sense. If you have a quandary you'd like some help with call 575-555-KBLM. And remember, if common sense were common then everyone would have some." Clara could see from the phone extension on the console that all three lines were lit up and ready to go. Sally screened the calls but they had agreed to have a pretty loose policy.

Line 1. Chrissy prob. w/ boyfriend, not too wacky. Sally instant messaged.

"Hello, Chrissy. What is your quandary?"

"Hello, Clara. Longtime listener, first-time caller."

"Thanks for calling, Chrissy. What can we do for you?"

"Well, it's kind of embarrassing but my boyfriend, I'll call him Jerry but that isn't his name. Chrissy isn't my real name neither but I don't want anybody to know I'm calling, if you get my drift. Anyways, last night Jerry came home from quote, unquote, working late. He smelled like perfume and had lipstick smeared on his face. He wasn't even drunk neither. He said he wasn't with nobody else but that he was at a karaoke bar with a couple guys from work, after work you know, and this drunk woman rushed him when he was singing that Rod Stewart song

'Maggie Mae.' It took two people to pull her off him. So, I'm wondering if you think he's telling the truth?"

"Thank you, Chrissy. What do you think, listeners? Do you think Jerry was mauled by a woman at a karaoke bar? Or is there some other explanation?"

Line 2. Weirdo talking about a Phil Phillips??? He sounds confused and almost hysterical.

Shit, thought Clara. She'd thought for sure they'd have committed Phil Phillips the Fourth by this time.

Line 3. Paul answering Chrissy.

"Good evening, Paul. Thank you for calling Common Sense is Good Sense. What is your advice for Chrissy?"

"Hey there, Clara. I regularly go to karaoke bars, been to 'em in practically every state in this here great country of ours and I can honestly report that I've never seen that happen. No matter how good the person is. I think something else is going on if you catch my meanin'."

"Thank you, Paul."

Line 1. Tom answering Chrissy. Weirdo line 2.

"Good evening, Tom. Thank you for calling Common Sense is Good Sense. Do you have some advice for Chrissy?"

"Hi, Clara. I love your show. I drive a truck, overnight deliveries don't you know. Your show really breaks up the monotony."

"Thanks so much, Tom. What is your advice for Chrissy?"

"Anything is possible. At least once. If he gets attacked again I'd be suspicious and throw him out on his ear."

"Thank you, Tom. Keep your eyes on the road. I heard there were some spaceships in the area last night."

"Like I said, Clara. Anything is possible."

Weirdo, line 2. Susan for Chrissy, line 3.

"Hello, Susan. Did you call to offer a woman's perspective to Chrissy's quandary?"

"You bet your cute petoot I did. This guy is leading Chrissy down the garden path. It's more likely that the woman was singing and he attacked her. Tell Chrissy to check the police reports for assaults at a karaoke bar and get herself checked for

STDs 'cuz I bet he's given her the gift that keeps on givin', if you know what I'm sayin'."

"Thank you for that insightful comment, Susan."

"You're welcome, honey. I just love your show."

PLEASE take weirdo, line 2.

"Good evening, Phil. What is your advice to Chrissy?"

"Clara? Is that you?"

"Yes, this is Clara Goodhue with Common Sense is Good Sense. Remember, Phil, if common sense were common then everyone would have some."

"You got to help me, Clara. They're saying I have a brain tumor and they want to cut my head open. I was fine yesterday until I got to that emergency room. I called my mother, she's eighty-three, just in case something happens. Do you think maybe that MRI is wrong and that big, white blob on my brain is just a glitch with the machine, which almost pulled the fillings out of my head?"

Paula for Phil, line 1. Joe for Phil, line 3. No one gives a shit about Chrissy.

"That's quite a quandary, Phil…"

"And that's another thing, Clara, my name isn't Phil Phillips the Fourth I just used that name because I didn't want the cops to find me. But, now, I want you to know that my real name is Earl. In case something happens to me in surgery, I just want you to know my real name. Earl Hammond from Hadley, Massachusetts."

Jesus, did he really use his real name and address?

"We're going to take a moment from this interesting development for a word from one of our sponsors, Richie Rochelle from Richie's Auto Rehab. He has some advice on preparing your car for the summer season."

Clara had one minute.

"Earl, we're off the air. I'm sorry to hear about your brain tumor. I can't begin to imagine what—"

"No, Clara, you can't but mostly, I just wanted to tell you my real name and tell you how sorry I am for messing up your car and everything."

"My car is fine and I'm sure you'll be fine too…"

"I hope you're right. But, if I'm not I just want you to know that it was real nice to meet you." The line disconnected.

10 seconds. Paula line 1. Joe line 3. Ricky line 2. Get busy, girl. Earl good for ratings.

* * *

May was never so happy to see a Best Western Hotel in all her life. She had already been by the hospital to see Earl but he was in the midst of a neurological evaluation and the doctors asked her to wait outside. They said he was fine and would be available for visitors in about an hour. May wasn't happy about having to wait to see her boy. She had thought about insisting but didn't want to make them angry so early in Earl's recovery. So, she'd decided to check in at the hotel, drop off her luggage and head back to the hospital.

The day had been exhausting what with worrying about Earl and all that folderol at the airport. The need for security was understandable but there had to be a way they could do it without making people feel like criminals. Removing her shoes was especially frustrating. Imagine having her eighty-three-year-old feet with their two corns, a bunion and an ingrown toenail out there for anyone to see. There was a reason the senior center offered podiatry services twice a month. Old people's feet were a mess.

Once you got your shoes off you had to go through the metal detector or X-ray machine, depending on how dangerous you looked, which she didn't, thank goodness, unlike that poor man just in front of her who'd had a colostomy bag. May supposed it must've been all his medical supplies, poor guy, as if having to do your business in a bag wasn't enough of a cross to bear. After that she had to gather her shoes, her cane which Lisa insisted she take in case her ankle got tired—it was X-rayed twice because they thought it might be hollow and filled with explosives—her purse, carry-on and sweater, and find a bench to sit on so she could put her shoes on. It was exhausting and she hadn't even seen a plane yet.

Her room had a queen-sized bed, a television so large she figured she'd be able to watch the late evening news without her glasses. There was a comfortable easy chair and ottoman which overlooked a cactus and rock garden. Thankfully the hospital was just up the block, easily within walking distance, and there was a restaurant called The Hacienda just off the lobby.

Lisa had reminded her this morning when she'd dropped her off at Bradley Airport to be sure to ice and elevate her ankle as much as possible so it wouldn't act up too much. May had a few minutes and decided to take her advice before going back to see Earl. Lord only knew when she'd get back to the room tonight. She'd also take a couple aspirin so she'd be fully fortified in case she had to do some insisting on Earl's behalf. She'd give those people their hour and then she was going to see her son come hell or high water.

Poor Earl. She'd always known she'd see him again though she certainly was surprised by these circumstances. Before this latest turn of events she'd imagined him just turning up one day. That whatever he'd been doing while he thought the police were thinking he had killed that poor Brad Nelson…well, that he'd get it out of his system, return to his senses and come home. But, here he was in the middle of the desert, in the neurological ICU in the hospital in a coma of some sort. Dr. Saltus had said over the phone that he didn't know why Earl, who he called Phil Phillips for some unknown reason, was so unresponsive. There was no medical reason which if he knew Earl like she did shouldn't come as any surprise.

* * *

Earl looked like he'd been hit by a truck. His eyes, his whole face was swollen and puffy and there were smears of dried blood around his hairline. Or where his hairline would've been if he hadn't been shaved and his head wrapped in a bandage like a giant white Q-tip. He was propped up against a few pillows and surrounded by various beeping and flashing machines that May supposed were either keeping him alive or proving he was alive.

Poor Earl looked as close to dead as she'd ever hoped not to see him.

"Hi there, Sonny." May stroked his arm and brought his hand to her lips and kissed it. He seemed very warm.

"It's Mom, all the way from Massachusetts." Nothing. No flicker on his face.

"Where have you gone, Sonny?" May asked, searching around for a chair. There was one in the corner piled with spare pillows and bedding. She took the stuff off it and dragged it over to his side and settled in.

"The flight from home was long but okay. Though the seats seem to have shrunk since the last time I was on a plane. You remember when I went to Hawaii with my friend Avola? On that trip we got food, not that it was very good but it did require utensils to eat it. Now they give you a few peanuts and some pretzels and call it a day." May wondered how long she'd be able to keep the one-sided conversation going. Suddenly she felt more tired than she had ever been.

"Oh, hello there." A middle-aged woman wearing pink scrubs hurried into the room. "I'm Tracy Reed, Mr. Phillips's nurse."

What was it with this Mr. Phillips thing? Had Earl changed his name to throw off the police?

"I'm May Hammond, Earl's mother. Why do you refer to him as Mr. Phillips?"

Nurse Reed scanned the chart. "Are you the May Hammond the patient named as his Health Care Proxy and Power of Attorney?"

"Yes. He's my son. I have his health insurance information," May said, knowing she could barter medical information for payment information. Brain surgery couldn't be cheap.

"Phil Phillips the Fourth is the name he was admitted with. Apparently Mr. Phillips, ah Hammond, was admitted after a minor traffic accident. A Ms. Goodhue brought him in. According to her he seemed confused because he'd told her he'd driven his truck into a spaceship."

"A spaceship. Oh good Lord."

"Yes. In any case during a routine medical examination a brain tumor was discovered and Dr. Saltus, the neurosurgeon, determined that a craniotomy was required. Your son has not achieved full consciousness post-surgery, much to everyone's concern." Tracy Reed RN slid a pen out of her pocket and proceeded to write on the chart.

"Is it possible to speak to Dr. Saltus?" May asked, wondering why Earl would think he'd been in a car accident with a spaceship.

"I'll make a note in the chart. As you probably know Mrs. Hammond, it's important for you to talk with your son. Perhaps hearing your voice will bring him around."

May wondered about that. Even when Earl was awake and in the kitchen with her at home he didn't often seem like he was really there.

Dr. Saltus was missing in action. Not that the secretary behind the big desk just outside Earl's room said that. She said he was "otherwise occupied." To May's way of thinking that sounded like she had no idea where he was and May probably wasn't the only one looking for him.

May decided to go down to the cafeteria for something to drink and a newspaper or magazine. She needed something to read to Earl. They always said hearing was the last to go. Not that she expected him to go…at least she hoped not. How in the world would she be able to stand losing Earl?

"Don't go there," May murmured inside the empty elevator. There was no sense worrying…well, that wasn't quite true. There was something to worry about. Sonny was in a coma but no one had said a word about him dying. The question was, would they?

* * *

"Hi Sonny," May said, arriving back in Earl's room. "I've got the paper and a copy of *People* magazine. If the news won't wake you up maybe hearing about these Housewives of Desperation will do the trick."

May settled into a recliner an orderly had moved into the room for her. She leaned back launching her feet into the air.

"This will make Lisa happy. She's always after me to elevate my ankle. You don't know her, Sonny, but she's such a nice girl. She moved into the guest room." May considered telling him more about Lisa, having no idea what Earl thought about lesbians. This might be a way to test the waters.

"She just broke up with her girlfriend or I suppose I should say boyfriend…anyway, she had no place to live and I needed some help around the house after I hurt my ankle tripping over the birdbath so it just kind of worked out." May examined Earl's face for any frowns or grimaces. Nothing.

"Earl, here's some bad news on the front page, a crew of six marines were killed in a helicopter crash at an undisclosed location in Afghanistan. For such a small country it seems to have more undisclosed locations than you could shake a stick at. Those poor boys. Here's a picture of the First Lady visiting a Head Start program in Philadelphia. She wants to encourage better school lunches. That's probably a good idea. You used to hate cafeteria food. Do you remember eating cheese sandwiches every day for lunch? It was all you ever wanted, American cheese with mustard on white bread. Anyway, the First Lady is, as usual, looking very put together. What a thankless job. I imagine there are days when she'd rather not get out of her pajamas," May sipped her tea.

"I had more than a few of those days this winter. Avola and I had a big fight when Lisa moved in. Can you imagine her thinking there was something between Lisa and I? Goodness; she's young enough to be my granddaughter. So, with that upheaval and my bad ankle, some days there just didn't seem any reason to get out of bed. If it wasn't for Lisa being around, and Bosco, that's her dog, I don't know what I would've done…"

"Excuse me?"

May looked up to see a very short woman with pretty gray eyes standing in the doorway.

"Yes. Can I help you?" May asked.

"I hope so. I'm Clara Goodhue. I brought Phil to the hospital after our little fender bender."

"Oh, yes, so I heard from the nurse. I'm May Hammond, Earl's mother…" May struggled to scoot out of the recliner but it seemed to be sucking her down.

"Don't get up, Mrs. Hammond. Ummm…you did say Earl?"

"Yes, I did." May pointed to the bruised body on the bed. "That is Earl Hammond, my son." *The idiot*, May wanted to add, but didn't. "I cannot imagine why he was calling himself Phil." May shook her head.

"Phil Phillips the Fourth, to be exact. It did sound a bit contrived, almost like he thought of it at the last minute." Clara moved further into the room.

"Yes, that's what Nurse Reed said. She also said he got into an accident with a spaceship. You weren't driving that were you?" May asked.

"Oh, God, no," Clara said, and laughed. "I know I shouldn't laugh but this whole experience has been so bizarre. I can assure you that I drive a normal car and never saw a spaceship. Though many people say they do. Especially in Roswell."

"Earl has always been fixated on aliens. He said they were responsible for building the Mayan and Egyptian pyramids." May shrugged, thinking he could've had stranger interests, though at the moment she couldn't imagine what.

* * *

Lisa felt like she was hovering somewhere between confusion and enlightenment. She really liked Mo and she sure looked great in her jeans, baggy in just the right way and tight in just the right spot. Her standard poodle Sam was very well trained. They walked their dogs often along the Mill River. Bosco and Sam weren't too territorial but they both peed a lot.

Mo wasn't weird or narcissistic. She had no strange food phobias and had once ordered bacon, real from-pig bacon which was no small thing in the lesbian community. There had been no shortage of conversational topics…movies segued into books segued into their respective jobs. She was a tax accountant for a sportswear company, which sounded mind-numbing to Lisa but she had never been a numbers girl.

They discussed their coming out. Lisa had decided years ago that she was never going to get involved with a woman who wasn't out…living in the closet was no way to live and she really felt that if everyone came out it would be safer for all. Of course, it was easy to be out in Northampton, Massachusetts where she'd lived until her breakup with Johnnie.

It must be a generational viewpoint…Take May for example. She'd been closeted her whole life, not that she seemed unhappy though she had mentioned once or twice feeling regretful. Regret really sucked. Lisa hoped May was doing okay out in New Mexico. She'd said in her last phone update that there was talk of Earl perhaps needing a second surgery, something involving a shunt.

Mo had seemed surprised that Lisa had known from such an early age that she was a lesbian. Lisa's clue had been the wicked crushes she'd had on the girls in her class, the more tomboyish the better. Witness Patty her first girlfriend. They'd both been twelve and lab partners in eighth grade earth science. Patty was gallant in her willingness to do the gross things like dissecting worms. Lisa repaid her by sharing her mother's homemade cookies. They graduated to sleeping at each other's houses where kissing and grinding their hips together had been a primary focus. It still amazed her that their respective parents had never clued in to the truth.

Mo, on the other hand, had had a brief marriage before she "woke up and smelled the patchouli" as she'd put it. That was funny, Lisa liked a woman with a sense of humor and a cute ass.

But…but what? Lisa didn't know. Hence the confusion. Where could she find the enlightenment? Did enlightenment always fall from the sky like a blazing meteor or could it creep up on you like a sudden chill? Lisa wished she knew what she expected in a woman. The basic problem was she was gun-shy. Johnnie transitioning had been hard. She had really been in love, crazy kind of love, and having all that yanked away had been heartbreaking and…and unsettling.

How could she be sure that the next woman she was involved with, whether it were Mo or not, was really a lesbian and a woman who wanted to stay a woman? Oh sure, she could ask, but when exactly should a girl drop that conversational bombshell into the mix? Lisa supposed it was only when the answer would matter. But wasn't that too late? She didn't want to start caring for someone only to find out they were thinking of swapping their vagina for a penis. Or what if they had already swapped…their penis for a vagina?

Lisa shivered at the thought. She needed to calm down. She was getting way ahead of herself. Next week she and Mo were going out to dinner. A nice, normal date. There was no need to rush, in fact it might be nice not to. She would take her time getting to know Mo and would strive not to worry about the state of anyone's genitals.

God, dating was complicated.

* * *

May followed Clara into the cafeteria. She sure was a speedy walker in spite of having short legs. May wondered what it was like living life as a short person. Probably as inconvenient as being old. In May's case, like most old people, she often felt invisible. Clara probably had the opposite experience. Living required a sense of humor.

Clara seemed like a very nice woman and had continued stopping by to see Earl every couple of days. It seemed impossible but May had already been in New Mexico for a week. Time had done that funny thing it did, the week had flown by but each day dragged into an eternity by lunch time. May was feeling very restless and had even considered taking the day off and getting into the rental car for a bit of a scenic drive. It seemed wrong somehow to come all this way to New Mexico and not see more of it than a Best Western Hotel and the New Mexico Medical Center. But she didn't want to be away from Earl for too long.

Thankfully, Clara had stopped by and asked May to have lunch. It would be nice to have someone to talk to. The one-sided talks with Earl were making her anxious. She couldn't seem to think of anything to talk about so she'd taken to reading to him. Right now they were midway through *Charlotte's Web*. She knew he was too old for it but he had loved it as a child and she thought it might comfort him wherever he was at the moment.

Cafeteria food required a sense of humor too. There was meatloaf or maybe it was Salisbury steak, whipped potatoes and something labeled gravy which resembled a flat, brown wall paint you might use in the basement. There was chicken a lá king, egg noodles and green beans swimming in a bath of steaming water flecked with globs of margarine. May hoped there was a salad bar. She wasn't really all that hungry, maybe a bowl of soup would do.

Clara leaned close and whispered, "This stuff looks like the crap they used to feed us in school."

May and Clara scuffled along the food line, neither of them taking anything.

"Mrs. Hammond, would you like to go somewhere for lunch? We could go downtown and get something decent."

"Yes, dear. That would be lovely. A change of scenery would be refreshing."

* * *

May wasn't entirely sure she'd describe the Infinity Diner as refreshing. It looked like a yard sale had exploded and stuck to the walls. It all appeared to be paraphernalia from science fiction movies of which she had never been a fan, unlike Earl who'd watched, mesmerized, all the reruns of *Star Trek* and its various generations like some people played slot machines.

She and Clara sat in a booth and someone dressed as a space alien gave them menus and took their drinks order.

"I must admit, Mrs. Hammond, to having an ulterior motive for bringing you here," Clara said, peering over the menu.

"Oh? Please call me May." May wondered what was in the Asteroid omelet.

"Earl mentioned, just before I took him to the ER, that he had eaten here and met someone called Sister Starlight.

Apparently she offered him a job, took him to the Cathedral of the Extraterrestrial and drugged him with lemonade." Clara closed her menu and set it aside. "He was escaping when he had the accident." At accident Clara made quotation marks in the air. "With the spaceship."

May didn't know what to say. Earl really must have lost his mind in those months and miles between Hadley, Massachusetts and Roswell, New Mexico.

"I guess I won't order the lemonade," May said.

"No kidding," Clara laughed. "I checked around and this Cathedral of the Extraterrestrial has tax exempt status as a religious entity though plenty of people think it's just a bunch of wackos dropping acid. Apparently, at least according to my friend Clovis who's a dispatcher for the sheriff's department, a certain Moonbeam Callahan was found wandering naked down Hopewell Street muttering about the Intergalactic Council meeting she was late for. Moonbeam was involuntarily committed while she came down from whatever it was she was on. Poor thing. Once she could think for herself again she went back home to Houston."

"And Earl was involved with these people?" May asked.

"Involved? Well, I hope not involved, just…"

"Excuse me, Earthlings. Would you like to order?" the alien asked, placing two cups of coffee on the table.

"I'll have the Apollo burger, please. Medium well," Clara said.

"Can you tell me what's in the Asteroid omelet?"

"Shitake mushrooms, roasted red peppers and Swiss cheese. It comes with our house-made Out of This World rye toast."

"I'll have that," May said, watching the alien waiter bustle toward the kitchen. She added some cream to the coffee and took a sip. May had never realized that her son was so gullible. Maybe the tumor Dr. Saltus had removed was responsible. Perhaps it had been pressing on whatever part of the brain responsible for giving you good sense.

"I was thinking about taking a drive and checking the place out," Clara said.

May wasn't so sure that was such a good idea. Who knew what those extraterrestrial types were up to? They could make minced meat out of a dwarf.

"I'd better go with you," May said.

* * *

The Cathedral of the Extraterrestrial looked like a barn you'd expect to see in New England. There was even a silo attached, though that part had no roof just a gigantic pulley arrangement suspended over where the roof should've been.

Clara pulled her car into the parking lot. "It doesn't look like much does it?"

"Well, it sure doesn't look like a cathedral." May thought a cathedral should have some stone work, a cross, and a gargoyle or two. There was nothing grand about this place.

"It doesn't look like anyone's around. The only car I see is that old Buick and from the amount of dust on it it's been here a while," Clara said.

"Aren't those Massachusetts plates on that Buick?" May squinted into the glaring sun. "I wonder if that's the car Earl's driving."

Clara inched her car closer. "Yes, you're right. Massachusetts plates."

"What happened to Earl's car?" May wondered where he had gotten it from and what he had done with his own.

"So, you're sure it isn't his?"

"I'm sure…well, not last I knew…but, I haven't seen him for six months or so."

They sat and looked at the car and at the cathedral, waiting for something to happen.

"Maybe I should take you back to the hospital, May. It doesn't seem like much is happening. Besides, you probably don't want to be away from Earl for too long." Clara turned her car around and headed back toward town.

"I should be getting back. Thank you for lunch. My Asteroid omelet was much better than anything I could've gotten in the hospital cafeteria."

How was it possible for Earl to drive up to this place—May just knew it was his car—and not wonder, not think that this was more than a little strange and know not to get involved? It had to be that brain tumor.

"When I get back to work I'll call Clovis and let her know what's going on. It's too much of a coincidence that there would be a second car from Massachusetts in the cathedral's parking lot."

"It does seem…" May searched for a word. Unbelievable came to mind but that wouldn't be right because here it was, whatever this was, happening.

"Weird?" Clara asked.

May nodded, thinking that the word would have to do. Goodness, in the space of a week she'd gone from her life in Hadley into a sort of homeless limbo, splitting her time between Earl's room at the hospital and her room at the hotel. And now there was this extraterrestrial business to deal with. She had a moment of wishing she hadn't come. A moment of wishing she could sleep in her own bed, walk through her own garden and chat a bit with Lisa over breakfast before taking Bosco for a walk. Something normal and predictable.

Maybe that's what had gotten to Earl. The predictability. She was eighty-three, after all, and predictability was okay. When she was his age she was having her wild affair with Avola and trying to keep it a secret. Everyone had secrets and maybe Earl's secret was wanting to get away and feeling he couldn't because of her. Maybe he didn't want to abandon her. That was ironic. If she'd had the guts not to keep her secret maybe he'd have had the courage not to keep his. Neither of them had had the life they'd wanted to have.

May watched the desert through the car window. Goodness, she hoped it wasn't too late. For either of them.

CHAPTER EIGHTEEN

Earl dreamed he was hanging wallpaper. He'd never hung wallpaper before and in this case he had no walls to hang it on. He had plenty of expensive wallpaper though, a kind of old-timey fleur-de-lis pattern… How did he know it was a fleur-de-lis pattern in his dreams when if he'd been awake he never would've known what to call it?

He was gluing up the wallpaper, adhering it to walls he couldn't see but somehow the paper stuck to it anyway. He seemed to be good at it. His pattern matched and the seams were straight. Best of all, he didn't need a ladder. He hovered in space, like a hummingbird at a blossom, so the job was going quickly. Not that he knew when he'd be done because he couldn't really tell how big the room was but, somehow, he had the sense that he would know when to stop. Dreams were wonderful that way, knowing you'd know something when you needed to know it. That kind of viewpoint in real life seemed almost impossible to achieve without mind-altering substances.

The dream was getting noisy. He could hear people shouting. The yelling was playing hell with his concentration.

His pattern was drifting off a bit and the seams seemed to be listing to the left, almost as though the wall, which he couldn't see, was collapsing. Slowly. So slowly that Earl blinked his eyes a few times to see if it was really happening.

Gosh, it was bright and when he blinked that voice got louder.

"Wake up."

Where was he? The room without walls but with that lovely wallpaper, gray and white, became blurry and porous and he could see through it. He was somewhere else, there was light and beeping and people pulling on him and moving his arms and wiping his face.

"Come on, Earl. Wake up."

The voice was so insistent, so loud and someone was patting his hand. Whoever this was yelling about waking up sounded an awful lot like his junior varsity high school baseball coach, Mr. Leonard Hanks, a man who could make a compliment sound like a reprimand.

Was Earl late for practice? Why was he hanging wallpaper when he should have been practicing bunting or hitting pop flies to the outfielders? Wait a minute, hadn't Mr. Leonard Hanks died a few years back? Hadn't he had a massive heart attack during the seventh inning at Fenway Park? The Red Sox won which everyone said was a fitting tribute to a man who lived and breathed baseball.

"Open your eyes."

Weren't they open? Earl felt sure they were. Wasn't he watching himself and his JV teammates running sprints between the baselines? Wasn't Mr. Hanks wearing his gray hoodie, the sleeves cut off and blowing the whistle that hung around his neck like a spouting whale? Earl could see the early spring sun slanting through the trees behind the backstop. The buds were fuzzy with their tiny, lime-green leaves emerging and the mown grass smell swirled around him. He tasted the salty tang of sweat when he licked his upper lip. He wasn't even tired as he ran back and forth listening to Mr. Hanks screaming, "Get a move on boys or I'm gonna kick your ass!" Earl knew he could run forever and maybe already had.

* * *

Avola knocked on May's kitchen door. In the past she would've just opened it and yelled yoo-hoo and May would've yoo-hooed back. No yoo-hooing now. Not after what Avola had done. She was determined to be polite and proper and demonstrate her worthiness to May.

A window opened on the second floor and a head popped out. Avola recognized the head as belonging to May's housemate though she couldn't remember her name.

"Hi. Can I help you?" the housemate asked.

Avola heard a dog bark. "Yes. I was wondering if May were home?"

"Just a moment. I'll be right down." Her head vacated the window and was immediately replaced with a dog Avola recognized as belonging to the housemate. In one of those memory quirks that drove Avola crazy she remembered his name was Bosco.

The kitchen door opened. The housemate stood there dressed in a bathrobe despite it being one o'clock in the afternoon.

"It's Avola isn't it?"

Avola took a deep breath to quell her nerves. "Yes, and I must apologize for not remembering your name, probably because my brain was filled with idiocy on our first meeting. Please forgive my bad behavior." Avola extended her hand.

"Lisa. I accept your apology." She shook Avola's hand. "And I am afraid May is away."

Avola felt the hope that had been growing inside her stop being a green and pulsating thing.

"Away?"

"Yes. The thing is…gosh, I don't know how much I should tell you…"

"Is May all right?"

"Yes. She's fine. Come inside. I'll give her a call. Just a moment." Lisa plucked her phone out of her pocket and walked away.

This was mysterious. Avola felt as though she'd been dropped into a theater showing a foreign movie without subtitles. She couldn't help but remember a time not so long ago that May would've told Avola what was going on before she went away. Not for the first time Avola wished that night when she had acted like an ass had never happened. It had been stupid and too costly. At their ages, she and May had no time to waste.

Lisa came back into the kitchen extending the phone. "She wants to speak to you."

"Al-lo? May?"

"Avi? Is that you?" May's voice rushed into Avola's ear and ricocheted around inside her head.

"Yes, May. I want to apologize…"

May cut her off. "Not now, Avi. I can't talk long. Earl's in surgery. Lisa will explain. But I just wanted to say that I've missed you and we'll talk when I get back."

"But, May, I…"

"I'll call you, Avi. Just sit tight." The call ended with a beep.

Avola gave the phone back to Lisa. "What is going on? She said you would explain."

"Please. Sit down while I tell you what I know, though I have no doubt it isn't all that May knows." Lisa gestured toward the kitchen chair. "I'm going to make some coffee. I'm working the three-to-eleven shift today and I need to regain consciousness. Would you like some?"

"That would be nice. I, too, feel a bit unconscious." Avola thought Lisa had a sweet smile and seemed like a nice young woman. Thinking badly of her had been yet another error on Avola's part.

Lisa launched into a story that seemed to Avola had been lifted from a movie. It seemed unbelievable that Earl had a brain tumor though it could, perhaps, explain some of his strange ideas. He had always been an odd man but to think he thought he had been in a car accident with a spaceship was lunacy. Poor May. To go through this with her son and be all alone while doing it made Avola's heart hurt.

"How horrible for May and Earl, too, of course." Avola sipped the coffee Lisa had given her. Nice and strong.

Lisa nodded. "He's been in a coma since his surgery which has baffled everyone. I guess they are hoping clearing out the shunt will bring him around."

"Where is he?" Avola asked.

"New Mexico Medical Center. May is staying at a Best Western near there. I'll write all the information down for you."

"Thank you, Lisa. And again I am sorry for my behavior. Every time I think of that evening I am filled with shame."

Lisa looked up from her writing. "I really do forgive you. I understand how desperation can impact behavior and usually not for the good. At least it never has in my case." She smiled and slid the paper across the table toward Avola.

"I appreciate your help and thank you for the coffee." Avola rose, eager to be on her way. Sitting around and waiting was not her style. Avola would go to May.

* * *

Lisa chuckled to herself as she climbed the stairs to let Bosco out of lockup. She really did understand desperation. It was just last night or rather this morning at three thirty when she had been in its grip. Thank God her only witness had been her dog and he'd take it to his grave.

Lisa remembered feeling more than a little ashamed to find herself at Burger Bliss's drive-through. Bosco was riding shotgun and hoping for his own cheeseburger. The sky was beginning to shift from black to dark gray on what promised to be a clear spring morning. She was in the market for a fish sandwich, maybe a crate of french fries and some sense.

Wednesday had come and gone without any communication from Mo. Thursday she had worked a double shift to try and keep her mind off not hearing from Mo. Friday she had cleaned May's house, mowed her lawn and taken Bosco for a long romp at the state hospital, thinking exhaustion might clear Mo from her mind. And, no, they hadn't run into each other at the dog park as hard as she had tried.

At two fifteen this morning she had awakened when she'd heard shrieking outside, something succumbing to nature's food chain. She hadn't been able to fall back to sleep, a dangerous situation that led to thinking, stewing and perseveration. Finally she had gotten up hoping chamomile tea might help and it was sometime while she was filling the kettle that she thought a drive by Mo's house was a good idea. Lisa had been able to resist the temptation up until that point. She would have been lying to herself if she acted like she'd just thought of it in those wee, dark hours that prompt sane people to behave like complete wackos. Bosco liked getting into the car no matter the hour.

As she had been driving through the nearly deserted streets of Northampton on her way to Mo's condo on Crescent Street she began to have second thoughts and third and fourth, imagining herself descending the slope into stalker territory. Hence the detour to Burger Bliss, hoping some fat, cholesterol and salt would pull her back from the abyss of bad behavior.

She had inhaled the aroma of hot grease emanating from the bag a cheerless individual working the window had given her. It smelled like the best thing in the world but made her feel, suddenly, as lonely as if she were the sole survivor of a shipwreck. She had pulled over to eat in the parking lot and burst into tears. How pathetic could one woman be? What was wrong with her?

She barely knew Mo. They'd had a few dates and dog walks and while it seemed like they'd connected, who really knew. Mo didn't owe her anything. Lisa blew her nose into a grease-stained napkin. Maybe it was too soon to date—that was clear by how much she was overreacting—even though it had been months. She must be still getting over Johnnie and not hearing from Mo had pushed all those buttons.

The one button in particular—the something's up but I don't know what—button. Lisa had remembered feeling something was up with Johnnie. At first she'd wondered if it was an affair or maybe an illness or emotional problem. Repeated questions got the same, "No, everything is fine" response which was so obviously a lie that Lisa stopped asking. Then the fateful Halloween party blow up. When Johnnie came home and she was finally able to stop crying long enough to have a conversation with him he had told her he wasn't so much a butch lesbian as a man trapped in a woman's body.

Lisa had been stunned to hear that he had been in therapy for over a year and would soon begin hormone treatments. It felt like she was just getting off the starting line in a marathon Johnnie had been running for months. They'd gone into couples counseling but Lisa had to admit that she was attracted to women and didn't want to be with a man, even one who had once been Joanie.

Bosco had whined, ever present in his cheeseburger world. Lisa unwrapped his snack and fed him pieces. He was a dainty eater, gently taking each morsel from her hand when he probably wanted to snarf the whole thing in one bite.

"What do you think, Bos? Should we do a drive-by or go home?"

He had whined. Was that a yes or a no or I want a french fry?

Bosco had more self-control than she did. If she could find a way to live her life as simply as he lived his she'd be doing pretty well. That seemed like a tall order especially at four o'clock in the morning, or whatever time it was, when you found yourself crying in a fast-food restaurant parking lot and shoving greasy french fries into your mouth so fast you could barely swallow.

Lisa had thought then that she should find a therapist. She'd decided to ask her co-worker, Mike, if he could recommend someone. She needed help to get a grip. It was important to be ready when the right woman came along.

* * *

Later that afternoon on the job, Lisa and Mike were riding along Main Street in Northampton, Mike scanning between the ambulance's windshield and the side mirrors.

"Sweetie, you girls commit too soon," Mike said, slowing at the crosswalk near Thornes Marketplace.

"As I recall, Mike, you committed to Rich pretty quickly." Downtown was mobbed with half-dressed people enjoying the late sunny afternoon. You never knew when a pedestrian would pop out of nowhere.

"You forget, I knew Rich for years. We both sang in the Gay Men's Chorus. When his douche bag boyfriend left him for that bodybuilder I knew I had to snap him up."

"I know. He is a sweetie," Lisa said.

"Yes. He. Is." Mike pulled onto Masonic Street.

"So is Mo. You know when you meet someone and it just feels like you've always known them? It felt like that." Lisa took her eyes off the street to scan her phone for incoming messages. No luck.

"I'm glad but maybe you wanted it to be something it wasn't meant to be. It hasn't been that long since you got your heart broken, sweetie. Give it time. Who knows, maybe you'll meet Ms. Right when we work the first-aid tent at the Queer Home Show in a couple weeks. A cute damsel in distress." Mike pulled into a fifteen-minute spot in front of the Assam Tea House.

Lisa laughed. "That's what I need. A butch damsel."

"Don't knock it, girlfriend. I'm dying for an iced chai. Do you want anything?"

"Yeah, thanks. Iced coffee. Cream. No sugar."

"Ummm, Lisa, this is a teahouse. Tea."

"Oh, right. Make it an iced black. Nothing fancy or fruity." She held her cell phone out the window hoping the open air would attract the little smiley face which meant text message.

"You're no fun," Mike lisped and waved a limp-wristed hand at her as he got out of the driver's seat.

Lisa laughed watching him dodge traffic as he crossed the street. He was a great guy. And a great work partner. They always had fun together no matter how difficult their shift might be. Sometimes it was low stress, less serious calls and other times it was heart attacks, car wrecks and strokes. Honestly, if her work weren't enough of an object lesson to stop obsessing about Mo then Earl's brain tumor should be.

What Lisa hadn't wanted to admit, felt desolate about acknowledging, was that she had probably bombed out on their last date. They had gone to the Smith College Museum of Art. Mo had wanted to see an exhibit titled "Women's Impressionists Then and Now." Lisa didn't know much about art and felt very much out of her element. She had no clue how to look at art let alone talk about it beyond saying whether or not she liked something. More than once she caught herself thinking the canvasses looked like fuzzy, out-of-focus smears of paint but she knew enough to keep that viewpoint to herself. Mo had gone on and on about perspective and focal points and the diminishing something-or-other and Lisa felt like she was in an advanced college course.

After that they'd walked into town to The French Pig for dinner where Lisa had never been. The menu was in French which may have been Greek for all the French she could remember despite what seemed like decades of it during high school. Since she recalled the words for potato and chicken she ordered the chicken casserole feeling that would be safe and, no doubt, very boring.

It was impossible to relax that entire evening. Lisa felt sure she would faux pas all over herself at any moment and that Mo would run screaming from the restaurant in horror. Of course that didn't happen. She was probably overreacting but it hadn't felt like the two of them were in the same groove as it seemed on their earlier dates. Their goodbye kiss had been lackluster and made Lisa's stomach clench.

"Hey, sweetie, here's your boring, black iced with lemon. Sorry I couldn't resist a wee bit of citrus."

"Thanks."

"Jesus, you look positively morose. Tell me what's going on."

Lisa told him about the date from purgatory.

"Maybe I scared her off. She's only texted me once since then saying she had to, unexpectedly," Lisa made quote marks in the air at the word unexpectedly, "go out of town on business and she'd call when she got back to town Wednesday. By my calculations Wednesday meant last Wednesday."

"Ooooohhhhh…" Mike looked at her over the top of his sunglasses.

"Yeah. Ooooohhhhh."

"Well, sweetie, maybe she was delayed." Mike pulled into traffic.

Lisa looked at him. "Mike, honey, a delay would still have warranted some communication. I think it's a kiss-off and based on our last kiss, it probably should be. Maybe she doesn't like confrontation." Lisa shrugged.

"I still say it's too soon to expect the worst. What can it hurt to give her the benefit of the doubt and assume she's telling the truth until you know differently?"

"I guess…" Lisa wanted to be convinced. It was a new perspective for her to consider. Why worry until you had to? She had been raised in a family where worrying was a skill passed through the generations.

Ambulance Number Two. Car accident corner of King and Damon.

Lisa picked up the handset. "On our way. ETA three minutes."

Mike flipped on the lights and siren.

CHAPTER NINETEEN

Earl threw himself down on the grass in the infield. Coach Hanks had said they could take five before bunting practice. Jesus, today's practice seemed to be going on forever. Not that he minded, he loved baseball and listened to as many Red Sox games as he could on his transistor radio. Practice usually went by in a snap, even when he had to fill in as catcher while Ernie Hardy had his ups. But today it seemed like time was standing still, just like in algebra class.

His ears were playing tricks on him. He could hear someone talking. Maybe someone in one of the houses near the ball field had a radio on and it was echoing funny, though it seemed like the voice was inside his own head…

"…Cathedral looked like a horse barn…poor Sonny…what were you thinking…"

Boy, he sure wished whoever it was would change the channel to some music, something with a beat to give him some energy. Not that Coach Hanks would stand for that, he hated music except for Hank Williams and Merle Haggard. Earl couldn't stand that twangy stuff.

"…Car from Massachusetts of all things…makes no sense… nice Clara Goodhue…"

The grass smelled green. Could you smell color? No, that was silly…he was just smelling the grass and it was green… greener than he had ever seen it. It was easy to be confused. Today's practice had been going on forever and that radio was blabbing on and on but none of the other guys seemed to hear it.

He was sitting next to Ernie, Tom Houghton and Neil and Jimmy and they were laughing and chatting about…what? Why couldn't he hear them when they were lying on the grass not two feet away? But he could hear that damn radio just fine. Coach Hanks would never stand for the distraction. Whoever owned that radio was going to get a ration of shit when Coach started bunting practice.

"…Finally spoke to her…Avola for years and it almost broke my heart…"

Was that the first evening star gleaming and winking at him from high above the backstop? Or maybe it was a planet. Hadn't Mr. Krol discussed that in science this morning? Mr. Krol was usually as dry as dust but he had been interesting today. Earl had always been fascinated by the night sky. He knew there was something out there beyond the infinite darkness and pin pricks of sparkling light. He longed to look behind the dark curtain. There wouldn't be anything as hokey as that little man masquerading as the Wizard of Oz but some vast intelligence that wanted to speak to him. Earl knew he would be the one who would find a way to listen.

"…I wish I had told you but was too afraid…"

He must be hearing the radio call-in talk show his mother sometimes listened to while she ironed his father's dress shirts and his school shirts. It was just a bunch of women calling in and sharing their recipes for angel food cake and strategies for getting grass stains out of baseball uniforms. In fact, it sounded a lot like his mother's voice. Maybe she was sharing her recipe for oven baked chicken.

Earl loved it, crispy on the outside and tender on the inside. She always served it with baked potatoes. Beautiful russets with fluffy white flesh and butter, lots of golden butter and sometimes sour cream and chives snipped from her garden…the cool tang of the sour cream and salty sweetness of the butter melting into the earthiness of the potato might be the most perfect thing in the world. Better even than corn on the cob or his favorite lemon meringue pie.

"…going to move you to another room…not sleeping so well…"

Earl felt tired. Maybe he'd put his head down on his mitt and take a snooze. Coach Hanks didn't seem to be in any hurry to get back to practice. That was okay by him. He stunk at bunting anyway, either hitting it too hard and getting thrown out at first base or smashing his thumb into the pitched ball.

Yes, he'd close his eyes. The night star or planet that Mr. Krol was talking about this morning was getting larger. Brighter. It was dazzling and Earl wondered if he should look right at it. Wouldn't it hurt his eyes? Or was that an eclipse? Somehow he knew it didn't really matter. His eyes wouldn't be damaged. He could see each particle of light as it came toward him. It was like driving into a snowstorm. Each tiny piece of light was bright and as they got closer the edges became indistinct as though it were going to swallow him up.

* * *

May followed Earl's bed as it was wheeled out of the Neuro-ICU toward the bank of elevators. They were going down one floor to the Telemetry Unit. The doctors were of the opinion that while Earl was in a coma he was not in any danger as he was breathing on his own, had a strong heartbeat and normal blood pressure. His condition didn't warrant intensive care—or so said the here-one-minute-gone-the-next Dr. Saltus—though he wasn't quite ready for a regular room.

May was worried that Earl embarrassed the medical profession. They hadn't a clue why he wouldn't wake up so they were going to stash him in a back room where they wouldn't have to look at him too often. At least it was a private room with a nice view of the parking lot and the distant mountains behind it. She'd been in Roswell two weeks and while it seemed like a nice little town, she missed Hadley. At home, spring would be in full swing, green and showy. What she wouldn't give to see an apple tree in full bloom, smell the teeth-aching sweetness of the blossoms and listen to the monotone hum of the honeybee.

She settled into the chair next to Earl's bed and took his hand. She looked at his face and couldn't decide if he looked peaceful or absent. This is when faith would be handy to have but all she had was tired. She remembered last November when she had asked Gasteau to intercede on her behalf and Lisa had materialized. May bowed her head hoping some words of wisdom would pop into her head.

If only it were possible to wheel him out of here, lay him in the backseat of her rental car, throw a blanket over him and drive like the dickens toward home. How long would it take to drive back east? Probably a week at the most. But, how could she keep him fed and watered let alone comfortable in the backseat of a Ford Focus?

Maybe it was possible to rent an ambulance or a plane. There had to be some way to get her son across the country. She'd ask Lisa next time they chatted on the phone. Lisa usually called every day or two to check in. Such a nice girl, though she seemed to be having some dating trouble at the moment. Not that Lisa had wanted to talk about it. She'd said May had enough to worry about without thinking about her. May had told her it was nice to think of something else, something happy, for a change. Though dating didn't seem to make Lisa happy.

"If we were to leave, Earl, what would we do about your car?" May surprised herself by speaking out loud.

That was the strangest thing. Clara's friend at the sheriff's department had run the plates on the car she and Clara had seen at that strange cathedral. It turned out that it belonged to someone named Horowicz out of Amherst, Massachusetts, the town next to Hadley. After a little more checking it was determined that the Horowiczes were somewhere in Israel where they had been for most of the last year. How was it that their car ended up in Roswell, New Mexico?

Earl was the common denominator in that equation. Maybe that was the reason he was in a coma. Somehow he knew the shit had hit the fan and he didn't want to deal with it. It reminded her of when he was a kid and he'd keep piles of dirty dishes under his bed. He'd act like they weren't growing mold and attracting ants and mice. He'd always been someone who could look right at something and deny he'd seen it. Yet he had no trouble seeing things no one else saw like that spaceship.

Clara said it looked like the Horowiczes' backseat had been vandalized, almost as though someone's clothes had been glued to the seat and then ripped off. There was some luggage in the trunk containing clothes and antennas, a few books and a lovely bone china tea set. That surprised May. What was Earl doing with a tea set? When Clara described it to her it sounded like the one May's grandmother used to have.

Grandma had used it on special occasions though what those occasions were May wasn't always able to predict. Christmas or Easter never qualified. The tea set would appear on the spring and autumn equinox or when the first tomato was harvested from the garden. May understood, without ever being told, that tea on those afternoons was a holy occasion and to take care because the delicate china cups were so thin a cross word could crack them. What she wouldn't give for tea and cookies with Grandma about now.

"Excuse me?"

May looked at Earl hoping he had spoken. No such luck.

"Yes?" May asked the young, sweet-faced Latino man in scrubs standing in the doorway.

"I am Alberto Nunez, the RN on duty this evening. We would like to do an assessment and make your son comfortable for the night." He gestured toward an orderly standing behind him.

"Of course, I was just…" Wishing things were different, May thought but didn't say. "I'll say good night then. You have my number in case you need to reach me?"

"Oh, yes, Mrs. Hammond. Should there be a reason to call I will do so immediately." He smiled. "Try not to worry. We will take good care of him."

May suspected Alberto said that to every nervous family member but there was something about the kindness in his eyes that made her decide he really meant it.

"Thank you. I'll see you in the morning, Sonny." She kissed Earl's hand.

* * *

May made it as far as the bench outside the main entrance before she lost the ability to make forward progress. Something inside her gave way and she had to sit down. It felt like she was disappearing, that a strong wind would scatter the pieces of her that hadn't quite come apart yet. She was sure that she must look like any other old lady with her purse and tote bag on the bench beside her, wearing wrinkled pants and shirt from sitting too long at Earl's bedside.

Appearances deceived. She had entered that place people go when the unexpected has happened, a new world that makes the old world nonexistent and leads into a parallel universe of the brokenhearted and grief-stricken. May fumbled in her bag for a tissue and blew her nose, dabbed at her eyes and cleaned her glasses. All her wherewithal had vanished.

* * *

Avola got out of the van and stretched. She looked at herself in the driver's side mirror and decided she looked like hell. Her hair stuck off her head in wind-blown clumps. To say nothing of the bags under her eyes, like small purple suitcases. What could one expect after driving almost around the clock for the past three days? She probably should've flown but she didn't think of that until Indiana when she realized just how far New Mexico was. It was too late by that time so she persevered. If adrenaline was a catalyst for strength then hope was the catalyst for endurance. Fatigue was making her foolish at this point, expecting she would be able to find May at a hospital as large as this but, somehow, it felt as though May were waiting for her.

The sky was orange as the sun settled below the horizon. The sunsets were gorgeous in this part of the world but it was hard to get used to the absence of green. Nothing was as verdant as a New England spring. Avola supposed the people who lived here were used to the understated beauty of the landscape except for the edges of the day, nothing subtle about the horizon then, looking as though it were painted with the guts of a blood orange.

Avola made her way toward the main entrance which was busy with people coming and going, the place looking something like a giant anthill teaming with the medically garbed and those not. She was no fan of hospitals. Who was? They could be lonely places despite all the people. Her chest tightened thinking of May in there dealing with Earl and so far away from home.

"Avi? Is that you?" an older woman said from the bench near the door.

If Avola had been carrying something she would've dropped it. May looked haggard; the twinkle had vanished from her eyes.

"May? Oh, May…" Avola rushed toward her.

They embraced. Avola inhaled May's smell, less distinct now as it was overlaid with something medicinal, but still May. Tears flooded Avola's eyes.

"Avi. Avi. Avi," May said. "I can't believe you're here. I…" Sobs overtook May's speech, muffled against Avola's neck.

"There, there." Avola held May against her until she could feel the crying subside.

"Avi, I have never been so glad to see you in all my life." May clutched Avola's hand and pulled her down to sit next to her on the bench.

Avola's heart swelled and just like that Christmas Grinch, she thought her ribs would break open from gratitude.

"May, I know this isn't the time or place and before you tell me about Earl I have to say how sorry I am about behaving so badly in your home. There is no excuse for yelling at you and being violent…I…am ashamed and hope you will forgive me."

"Avi, it—"

"Please, May, allow me to finish. Your generous nature and kindness toward others is a delightful quality and I was wrong to think there was anything more to Lisa's moving in than that. I have apologized to her. You were right; she does seem like a very nice, young woman." Avola kissed May's palm.

"I've never heard you apologize before, Avi." Amazement had filled May's face and voice.

"Yes, I know. I thought of it as a sign of weakness to admit to being wrong." She shook her head in disbelief. "I spent the winter at my friend Margie's house in P-town. You remember her, yes?"

May nodded, her eyes wide.

"She listened to my side of things or, more accurately, what was my side of things at the time. Margie is fearless and told me that I had my head up my ass, her words not mine, though they are correct." Avola took a deep breath feeling as though her lungs were expanding for the first time in months.

"Margie said I was afraid of losing you and fear was making it actually happen. That I shouldn't be afraid to show you my heart. I think I have been protecting myself since Gasteau died and it is plain to me now that one cannot fully live if always guarding against being hurt. You are the most important person in the world to me and to know that I have treated you so shabbily, well, my heart is broken with it." Avola clamped her lips together determined not to cry. "I love you, May. I hope that I haven't irreparably harmed our relationship."

"Oh, Avi. It is so wonderful to hear you say these things. Of course, I accept your apology and am so grateful to have you here with me, especially now with Earl the way he is." May squeezed Avola's hand. "As you might imagine, Avi, I've been thinking about Earl a lot these past couple of weeks. I remember him as a baby. He looked like an old man when he was born. An old man worried about not having enough money for retirement. I had no idea how to be a mother. People said I would get the hang of it but it never felt natural to me. Earl suffered for that, I think. I yelled when I shouldn't have and I am quite sure I didn't show him enough affection. Then his father died." May dabbed her eyes.

"Oh, honey, it is not as though you engineered that," Avola said, unsure of the direction of their conversation.

"No, but I was not as kind as I could've been afterward. Earl loved his father and I didn't. I did not know what love was until I met you, Avi. I was so smitten with you that I was distracted and unavailable for him. He must've felt alone. It breaks my heart to think of that."

Avola put her arm around May. She didn't know what to say to comfort May. Regret was a terrible thing.

"As I said, there is not a lot to do in the hospital except think. It occurred to me that Earl might not have made his own life because he was worried about me. He was reluctant to leave me on my own, his poor widowed mother. If I had had the courage to tell him about us maybe it would've freed him to do what he wanted. I did everyone a disservice by not being honest about our relationship, Avi."

It was Avola's turn to be astonished. "It would have been a big risk to tell him. Who knows how he would have reacted. You could have lost him," Avola offered.

"But I should have taken the risk. Love is all about risk. I was a coward, Avi, a coward. Now it might be too late. Sonny is up there or at least his body is. Who knows where his mind has gone."

"It seems we were both, in our own way, cowards," Avola said.

May smiled and touched Avola's cheek.

"Let's go to the Best Western."

CHAPTER TWENTY

May listened to Avola singing in the shower, smiling at the off-key operatic aria. Imagine Avi driving for three long days just to see her. It made her smile even though there was so much not to smile about. It was odd to feel happy and sad at the same time. But at least she didn't feel numb anymore or like she was coming apart.

There was a knock on the door. "Room service."

May looked through the peephole to see a young woman with a food trolley.

She had ordered two club sandwiches for a late supper, a pot of tea for herself and decaf coffee for Avola. May tipped her and wheeled the food toward the table in front of the windows overlooking the cactus garden. The saguaros were strung with white Christmas lights.

Avola emerged from the bathroom in her ratty flannel robe; billowing steam followed her into the room.

"I do not think a shower has ever felt so good. I must have smelled like a goat," Avola said.

"A she goat, not a billy." May smiled and set the table.

"Thank you, May. This looks delightful." Avola sat down.

"I ordered a turkey and a roast beef club because I didn't know which one you'd like."

"Let us share halves. Then we don't have to decide." Avola picked up the teapot. "May I pour for you?"

"Let it steep a little longer. You go ahead and start eating. I'm going to get into my nightgown. This bra is about to push me over the edge." May realized she felt shy about changing in front of Avola though she had done it dozens of time before. How strange. They had been apart for quite a few months, maybe that was it.

"I will wait for you, May, though a cup of coffee will hit the spot."

"It's decaf so don't worry," May called from the bathroom. She had decided to take a shower. Maybe some of her anxiety about Earl and shyness around Avola would wash down the drain.

Twenty minutes later May felt rejuvenated from the shower and from seeing Avola with her feet up, reading the paper and sipping her coffee. Avi's apology had been a remarkable thing. She had certainly seemed sincere but May supposed time would tell. Time would tell about her own vow to live more honestly and not hide her relationship with Avola.

"There you are," Avola said. "I took the teabags out so it would not become bitter. May I pour?"

"Yes, dear. Anything in the paper I should know?"

May settled in her chair and took a bite of the turkey club. She realized she hadn't eaten anything since breakfast.

"Nothing. Reading the paper from another town always seems rather strange to me."

"I'm almost ashamed to admit this but I've gotten quite addicted to reading the obituaries in the *Roswell Tribune*. It's not as though I know anyone here except Earl and Clara Goodhue. She's the woman who had the fender bender with Earl and brought him to the hospital." May sipped her tea.

"Oh, yes? She may have saved his life. I cannot imagine he was not feeling the effects of the brain tumor even if he was unaware of them," Avola said.

"That's true, Avi. She is a real spitfire." May examined Avola's face for the tell-tale squinting of the eyes and tightening of the lips that had always been the harbinger of a jealous fit. But, Avi just looked tired and interested in what May was saying.

May felt the part of her she was holding back relax and she told her about Clara's radio show and the Cathedral of the Extraterrestrial.

"That is all very odd. Not the radio show but that strange church." Avola had put down her sandwich. "It sounds like they took advantage of Earl's fascination with alien spaceships."

"I thought the same thing. Sonny has always been…" May searched for a word that wasn't too mean. "Well, you know how he's always been. Clara and I went out there, you know. It didn't look like much."

Avola's lips narrowed. Uh-oh, May thought, here it comes.

"Nighttime is when they would be most active, don't you think?" Avola asked, taking another bite of her sandwich.

* * *

Clara squatted behind some scrub peering at her quarry. The Cathedral of the Extraterrestrial glittered like gaudy cubic zirconia. She was dressed head to toe in black including one of the K-Blam baseball caps from the radio station. She'd taken the night off, her producer was playing some of Common Sense is Good Sense greatest hits, and she hoped all this skulking around would yield a good result. She had waited until nine o'clock to drive out here and had even gone so far as to park down the street and walk back.

She'd thought about asking May to come with her but had second thoughts when she'd seen how tired May seemed when she'd stopped by the hospital earlier. Earl was lying there dead to the world, his mouth open and his hands wrapped around a couple washcloths. May was reading to him from Agatha

Christie's *A Pocketful of Rye*. The whole situation sucked the big one. The least Clara could do was figure out what these wingnuts at the cathedral were up to.

She wasn't sure why she cared so much. She'd known Earl for all of a couple hours before she'd handed him off to the ER department at the hospital. There was something oddly endearing about him, especially once she realized he really was as clueless as he seemed. Genuine cluelessness was rare. Often people pretended to be clueless to get something from someone else. Talk radio had taught her that. The faux clueless were constantly calling in with some quandary which said more about their duplicity than anything else. It was nothing to her, it wasn't her real life after all and it was great for ratings.

Clara still smiled when she thought about Earl telling her about his fender bender with the spaceship, showing her the dented fender as though that clatter trap pickup didn't already have half a million dents and dings pocking its body. Earl was so earnest, it had made her feel bad that she couldn't find a way to believe him.

A metallic whirring sound cut through the night. It seemed as though the pole or pulley that was sticking out the top of the grain silo was moving. Up and down, faster and faster. Clara started to feel the ground under her ass vibrate. The top of the pole opened, like an umbrella with its stays only, and began to whirl around like a high speed pinwheel. All of a sudden a bluish white light shot out of the tip of the pole and began to pulsate.

It took a moment for her to realize it was Morse code. Thank goodness for her dorky older brother, the perfect son and Eagle Scout or she never would have caught on. WE ARE HERE. WE ARE HERE flashed into the black, starlit sky. An odd music began to alternate with the pulsing light, filling the air with a mournful wailing that made Clara want to howl like a dog.

These people must have one hell of a utility bill.

A set of headlights flashed across the parking lot. Clara ducked. Hopefully she hadn't been seen. A van backed into a spot very close to the bush concealing Clara, turning off its engine and extinguishing the lights. Nobody got out. Whoever was inside sat there staring at the cathedral's display.

Suddenly the door opened and May and another woman got out.

Oh shit, Clara thought.

* * *

May was grateful for her cane and Avola. The ground was uneven and the flashing light made it difficult to see. Dark one minute, light the next. Her pupils had no idea what was going on. The last thing she needed to do was fall and reinjure her ankle.

"Avi, slow down. I can't see worth a darn."

"Okay. I am anxious to get behind something. We are sticking out like a sore thumb."

"You're right. Head over there to those bushes."

"Sssssshhh, May," Avola hissed. "I don't want them to hear us."

"How can they hear us with all that noise?"

Avola nodded and towed May toward the bushes.

She wasn't exactly sure what she was doing here. Clara had started her thinking a few days ago when they'd come out here after lunch. Talking with Avola had really clarified things. She'd been so caught up in feeling sad and worrying that Earl might die that she hadn't left time or space for any anger which these cathedral people richly deserved. They had taken advantage of Earl. Drugging him was uncalled for. Now, it was true that Earl smoked pot when he lived at home. Oh, he didn't think she knew but she did. After all it had a very distinctive odor. He thought he was sneaky, only smoking it when he took out the trash or up in his room at night, sitting in the dark and blowing the smoke out the window.

But, putting drugs in lemonade without someone's knowledge was underhanded and wrong. It couldn't have helped Earl's poor brain and now he was in a coma…could it be more than coincidence? There was no way to know. What she did know was she wanted to yell at somebody and these strange people with this strange cathedral, flashing lights and caterwauling into outer space seemed like good candidates.

"Pssssst."

Avola stopped.

"Was that you, May?"

"No, I thought it was you." Was there someone else out here? Goodness, she hoped there was no wild creature near here, hungry and waiting to eat some old ladies. The pulsing light stopped but not the music.

"Pssst. May."

May?

"Who's there?" May whispered.

"It's me. Clara. Over here in the bushes."

Avola led May in the direction of the voice. Once they were close enough Clara stood up.

"Clara, this is my friend Avola. Avola this is Clara," May whispered.

"Nice to meet you," Clara and Avola said in unison.

"Can you both get down? We don't want to be seen," Clara said.

"Well, ladies, I'd say it's a little late for that." A man's voice cut through the air.

"Shit. Who's that?" Clara said.

"He's over there, I think." Avola gestured toward the stand of bushes north of them.

They listened to footsteps trying not to be heard walking toward them.

"I should have brought my Phillips-head screwdriver from my car," Clara whispered.

"I keep a hammer in my van for much the same purpose," Avola said.

May wished she had more than a cane to work with. When she thought the man was close enough she bumped Clara out of the way with her hip, pushed Avola aside and swung the cane just like Babe Ruth at the space where she hoped he might be. There was a satisfying thud, an umph and the sound of someone falling to the ground.

"Ooohh, nice swing, May," Avola said.

"Jesus, May. What did you do?" Clara whispered.

"I don't know. But I had to do something. Maybe we should get out of here."

"I'm with you," Clara said. "Let's head toward your van."

"I'm feeling a little bit shaky." May hoped she hadn't killed whoever it was. But, he should have known better than to sneak up on people in the dark.

Avola started to chuckle. "You continue to surprise me, May. Even after all these years."

"I surprised myself."

"Let's get going. The station isn't far. We'll go there and call the sheriff," Clara said.

* * *

"Batter up," You-Know-Who yelled across the baseball diamond. She was dressed as a major league umpire complete with chest protector and facemask.

Earl was perplexed. Last thing he knew he was having some weird dream about driving through a snowstorm and the next thing he knew Coach Hanks was yelling, "Get your asses off the grass. Let's play ball."

Earl was batting first. He rotated his shoulders as he walked toward home plate. You-Know-Who bent over and whisk-broomed off the plate until it was clean of infield dirt. The bleachers were full of people, including his mother. She was sitting between a woman he'd seen her with before and his father. Earl hadn't seen Pop in ages but he looked the same, maybe a little sleepy, like he'd just woken up.

Earl took a couple practice swings, stepped up to the plate and considered the pitcher who considered his catcher. The pitcher shook his head no twice and then nodded once. He spat on the ground, reared back and fired a fastball straight at the plate.

Earl swung and missed.

"Stee-rike one," You-Know-Who intoned in a funny, echoey voice that reverberated across the field.

Earl stepped out of the batter's box and swung at nothing a couple times. He had to loosen up. Keep his eye on the ball. Become the bat.

The pitcher and catcher reached an agreement right away. He wound up and threw. Earl swung and connected.

"Foul. Stee-rike two."

Shoot, thought Earl. Settle down. Just look at the ball and swing when it gets to you. Don't rush it. He could hear a chorus of his teammates yelling, "You can do it. You can do it." But, could he? Get on base? A single was all he needed. A grounder that bounced funny so the shortstop couldn't field it.

Another pitch.

"Ball one."

Whew. Finally a break. Maybe that would make the pitcher nervous. He seemed too sure of himself.

Another throw.

"Ball two."

The pitcher made a motion to the umpire. You-Know-Who nodded and held her arms wide signifying a time out. The pitcher and catcher met halfway to the mound and began a heated discussion. Earl took a moment to retie his shoes and sneak a look at You-Know-Who. He wondered why she hadn't spoken to him; surely she had to know who he was even though he was his fourteen-year-old self at the moment.

"Of course I know who you are, Earl," she said, filling his brain with her words.

"I didn't know you were an umpire," Earl said, thinking of the many things he didn't know about her. Was she married? Did she have kids? What planet did she come from? Where did she park the spaceship when she wasn't using it?

"I came here because this is where you are."

"Where is that, exactly? This has been the strangest practice. It seems like it's gone on for days. Do I have home field advantage?" Earl asked.

"Not yet. But you soon will."

Earl felt the same ambivalence about that as he had when she had told him to go home while he was at the Teacup House.

"It's a shame you didn't take my advice." You-Know-Who adjusted her facemask. It wasn't made for someone with a head shaped like hers.

"Yeah. Maybe I should've but…" Earl's thoughts kind of trailed off.

The pitcher and catcher finished their conversation and returned to their places.

"Batter up."

Earl stepped into the batter's box. The pitcher wound up and threw. The ball left the pitcher's hand at a pretty good clip but seemed to slow down about halfway to Earl. He watched the stitching revolve as it turned and turned on its way to him. He swung.

CRACK.

The vibration of the bat connecting to the ball echoed through Earl's palms, up his arms and into his brain. A collective "Ooooohhhh" sounded from the bleachers. The ball flew across the infield, over the center fielder's head and just kept going. Earl struggled to keep it in his sights but it disappeared from view.

"Run, you dumbass!" Coach Hanks yelled.

Earl took off running toward first, to second, around third and made for home as if he could be thrown out though he knew he couldn't. The ball was long gone. He slid across home plate just because he wanted to. The crowd started cheering.

"Saaaa-fe. The batter is safe at home." You-Know-Who's voice rang out above the crowd's.

CHAPTER TWENTY-ONE

The chocolate chip cookies were still warm from the oven. The chocolate plentiful and gooey as it coated May's lips like lipstick. Gramma was the best baker and had made cookies and gotten down her special china tea set from the cabinet and washed it in warm soapy water in the big, white porcelain sink attached to one wall in her kitchen.

It was the summer solstice, the longest day of the year and Gramma believed it should be filled with pleasure from dawn to dark. For breakfast they'd sat outside on the stone wall overlooking the east pasture and watched the sun rise and begin the task of warming the earth. They'd had strawberries and sweet, milky coffee from a thermos that had once belonged to Grandpa, a man who only existed for May in a faded, beige photograph on top of the Victrola. He'd been dead longer than he'd been alive.

After breakfast they'd worked in the garden planting a third crop of green beans and thinning the carrots. There were always weeds to pull and the tomato plants needed to be staked. Then they'd gone down to the brook and washed the dirt off their feet. Gramma encouraged bare feet in the garden. They'd had egg salad sandwiches, crunchy with spring onion, for lunch.

Gramma made rhubarb sauce after lunch while May gathered twigs and wood from here and there to start the bonfire Gramma always made on the solstice, each of them, the one in June and the one in December. It was funny how the solstice worked. On the longest day you welcomed the coming darkness and on the shortest day you welcomed the light. Gramma always said, "In the midst of darkness is the light and in the midst of the light is the dark," as she lit the bonfire. It was like going to church but better because you didn't have to get dressed up and listen to things that made no sense.

May didn't know of anyone else who even seemed to know what the solstice was. She'd learned a long time ago not to talk about it, especially at school, where very little of interest ever happened. After the fire they'd have tea and cookies to be "mindful of the sweetness of life." Even though May always knew what would happen on summer solstice she still looked forward to it, from year to year, as though it were happening for the first time.

This year she'd been old enough to chop the walnuts for the cookies. She watched her hands, hands that looked too old to be her hands, wield the knife. Her hands looked like her grandmother's hands and moved with the surety and cadence of an experienced baker. The light in the kitchen was bright but fuzzy as it can be on a humid, summer afternoon in August, the dog days of summer, but it wasn't August. It was June. Maybe it was the way the sun angled through the window that made everything indistinct and almost like it wasn't happening. But it was. May could see her hand moving, could hear the snicking of the knife on the cutting board and smell the bitter tang of the walnuts.

Where was Gramma? Somewhere nearby, May could hear her humming Christmas carols, Gramma sang them all year round, "Oh, Come all ye Faithful, joyful and triumphant…"

May was nervous. It felt like the earth had tilted on its axis, its orbit around the earth slowed and almost stopped. Though the bird, a red-winged blackbird continued to sing…a song that was the harbinger of spring sung on this first day of summer… and then she felt movement behind her and there was Earl. Still wearing his johnny and those fuzzy socks with nonskid soles they made you wear in the hospital.

"Hi, Sonny. Did you come for Great-Gramma's bonfire?" May asked, smiling at her son as he smiled his lazy, lopsided smile back at her. The same smile he'd had since he was a baby.

"You bet. I wouldn't miss it for all the world," Earl said as he crunched a walnut in his strong, white teeth.

"I'm glad you're feeling better, Sonny. I was worried about you."

"Oh, Ma, you should know there's never any real reason to worry. Everything happens as it should." Earl reached for another walnut.

May felt her eyes fill with tears.

"I thought you were going to die, Earl."

"There isn't much difference between the living and the dead. That spark that lights our eyes when we are alive continues to live on no matter what. It has been nice to finally meet Great-Gramma."

"That's right. She had passed over by the time you were born." May measured the chocolate chips.

"I'm looking forward to the bonfire." Earl snagged another walnut. "She reminds me a lot of you. I've enjoyed being your son, Ma. I know you've been concerned you weren't a good mother. But you were. I always knew you loved me."

May looked at Earl. He seemed different. Happy and…wise.

"I'm glad, Sonny." She took a deep breath. "I did, I do, love you. But I wasn't honest with you about my life."

"I wasn't always honest with you either. That's the nature of living in the physical body. After we're born, after enough time passes, most of us lose touch with the infinite wisdom we come from. When we die we merge back into it. So, don't be sad. Don't question our relationship. And be happy with Avola." He smiled and took her hands.

"You know about us?"

"Be happy, Ma. It doesn't have to be difficult."

"What doesn't?"

"Any of it."

* * *

May jerked awake, such a strange dream, so real and so unreal at the same time. She hadn't been thinking about Gramma all that many days ago and here she shows up, bright and smiling like she had been in real life.

And Earl, it was nice to see Earl even if only in her dreams. He had been so awake and vibrant, so different than he had been when he was alive… When he was alive? Why did she think that? Oh no, not…her Sonny…her boy…dead. She felt an ache in the center of her chest blossom until she wondered if she was having a heart attack. She struggled to sit up. It hurt to breathe, almost like she couldn't get enough air. The darkness in the room began to gather into itself until she could feel it around her, pressing against her, compressing her skin. She was being crushed. How could this be true and not kill her?

Just breathe she told herself, just breathe. Tears flooded her eyes and ran down her face. She pulled the blanket up to her face, trying to muffle her crying. Oh Earl. Her boy. It was too much to take in. Too much to feel. She should have died instead of him. She was eighty-three and would've been willing to sacrifice her life for his, would've run into traffic to save him, offer her still beating heart for his still one. There was so much he hadn't done and now he never would. May pressed the blanket against her eyes. Grief washed over her like a tsunami.

"May? Honey? What is it?" Avola sat up and pulled May against her.

Could she be mistaken and he wasn't dead? Maybe it was her fear of it happening coming out in her dreams. But, even as she thought that she knew it wasn't true. Somewhere deep inside she felt he was gone. She knew there was no reason to rush over to the hospital, he wasn't there anymore. She just had to wait for the hospital to realize it.

"May? Tell me what is going on?"

"Earl…passed…away." May sobbed into Avola's neck. "I…"

"Oh, May…"

It was too much…this feeling of sadness was overwhelming and there was no escaping its long grasp. It was endless, this ocean of grief… She was getting further and further from shore. There was Avi in the distance, waving and beckoning to her, waving her into shore from the deep water. The water wouldn't let go. The riptide was tearing her apart and soon she would disappear inside of it. She would be gone. Maybe she would join Gramma and Earl for the summer solstice…and Gramma would say that thing she always said about the sweetness of life and May would remind her that life was not always sweet. Sometimes things happened that were insurmountable. But, Gramma had known that and said it anyway.

"Here, honey, let me get you some tissues…I'll be right back." Avola got out of bed.

May listened to Avola cross the room toward the desk and heard the tiny click when she turned on the small lamp there. The darkness pushed against the light. Which would win? Darkness seemed more powerful, more dangerous, more enveloping. It would certainly drag her down. Poor Earl. Was he in the darkness too? All alone, cold and bereft?

"Here, May, some tissues and a glass of water." Avola sat on May's bedside.

May blew her nose. Avola extended the glass and helped May hold it as she took a sip.

"Thank you, Avi."

"Can you tell me what happened?"

"I had a dream. Earl was with my grandmother. It was the summer solstice and we were making chocolate chip cookies and all of a sudden he was there. You know how dreams are. He looked so…alive. He's never looked that…that…I don't know if I can describe it. He just seemed so *there*." May wiped her nose.

It was wonderful that he would appear in a dream with Gramma, Gramma who had passed away so, so long ago. And what had he said, it was nice to meet her. May felt comforted to think of them together. Gramma had been so much fun and had a carefree spirit. Poor Earl could use some of that. He had always seemed so distracted and worried about something.

"Maybe you should telephone the hospital, yes?"

"They'll be calling very soon, I'm sure. I just want to remember everything he said…something about us being happy." May wiped her eyes, she could feel how swollen they were.

"You and I?" Avola asked.

"That's what he said."

"I didn't know he knew about our relationship." Avola smiled.

"Me either. He also said it doesn't have to be difficult." May took another sip of water.

"What doesn't?"

"That's what I asked him and he said none of it. None of it has to be difficult."

Avola nodded.

"It made so much sense in my dream. I understood it…now I don't understand anything…I…"

The phone rang.

CHAPTER TWENTY-TWO

Avola put her and May's suitcases into the back of the van. They were heading back to Massachusetts, back to their normal lives. It remained to be seen if there was such a thing as normal anymore. Poor May. Avola wished she knew what to do for her. But sometimes, perhaps, there was nothing to do, nothing to say that didn't seem trite or ineffectual. Sometimes all one could do was bear witness and remain until witnessing was no longer required.

May had been in a daze since it had happened. Avola was glad she had obeyed her inner voice and driven to be here, otherwise May might still be sitting in that chair by the cactus garden staring at those twisted, spiny creatures as if the answers to the why of it could be read in their thorns. While they were at the hospital and afterward while making arrangements, Avola had never heard May ask why, she didn't rant and rave at God or swear vengeance on the medical community. She had just thanked everyone who had taken care of Earl and asked Avola to take her back to their room where she had subsided into the chair and into herself like a dormant volcano. Except May wasn't a volcano, there was no volatility, though Avola had the sense that there was something simmering beneath the surface. She would wait it out. Whatever May was would be fine with her.

Avola went back to their room to find May putting money into the envelope for the housekeepers. In the weeks May had been here she'd made friends with the women who cleaned the room, learning about their children and husbands. It was remarkable how May was able to turn acquaintances into friends wherever she went.

"May, are you ready to leave?" Avola asked from the doorway.

"Oh yes, I think so. Though I…I feel like I am forgetting something…" May's voice trailed off.

"Yes? Well, I will check again but I feel certain we have everything."

"I'm sure you're right. Okay. Let's go." May hooked her cane over her arm, picked up her purse, and Earl.

"Can you carry him?" May extended the urn. "I'm feeling a bit shaky. I don't want to drop him in the parking lot." May's smile didn't reach her eyes.

"Yes, of course." Avola took him in one arm and May's other arm. They made their way from the hotel and then across the parking lot toward Avola's vehicle.

"Is there anywhere you would like to stop as we make our way back home?"

"I can't think of anywhere. How long do you think it will take us to get there?" May asked.

"Maybe four or five days. I do not think I can drive the long days I drove on my way out here."

"It doesn't matter to me, Avi. I feel like I'm in that in-between place again, not quite here and not quite there."

"This is a place you have been before?"

"I felt a little like this when you and I were not getting along this past winter. With Earl gone…this feels more pronounced," May said.

"I know a bit about what you are saying, from this winter's estrangement and when Gasteau died. But," she said softly, "I also know a brother lost is not the same as losing a son."

"It'll be strange to be home without him. Oh, I know he hasn't been home in months. But then there was the possibility of his coming home…Now…" May sighed as though the effort of speech were beyond her.

Avola finished May's thought. "Now the possibility is gone."

That was what death was—the possibility snatcher. Avola thought back to Gasteau's death; of course she had been a girl, perhaps too young to understand how hope also drowned when he did, especially for her parents. Maman and Papa disappeared inside themselves, turtles in the shell of grief. She lost her family and had even lost herself, those tender loving parts crushed by the weight of hopelessness. For her, anger was all that was left, empowering and safer then grief. She wished she hadn't taken so long to let go of it.

It was interesting that May didn't seem angry. At least not yet. Sad, yes. Bewildered, yes. But not angry. Once again Avola vowed to wait and see.

Avola opened the passenger door and held it for May while she climbed in.

"Where shall I put him?"

"I'll hold him on my lap. At least for a little while," May said.

* * *

All Lisa could smell was pot as she looked down at the guy crumpled on the sidewalk like a discarded cigarette pack.

"I think I could get a contact high from him." She squatted next to him and felt for a pulse, nodding at Mike when she felt it.

"I'll get the backboard," Mike said, turning back toward the idling ambulance.

"It looks like somebody beat the shit out of him." The woman who had been across the street in a food truck came toward them. "I called it in when I got here. At first I thought it was a pile of clothes but when I got closer I could see differently."

Lisa nodded at her. The woman was wearing a white chef's apron and had beautiful hazel eyes.

"I don't remember seeing you around before. I'm Lisa and he's Mike."

"Sarah Sterling. I moved here a couple months ago but just got my truck running last week. You guys had breakfast? I make a mean breakfast burrito. Salsa's fresh."

It was tempting. Lisa had only had a banana for breakfast. Damn, there was just no time. Lisa shook her head as Mike returned and they went to work stabilizing the pot smoker for the ride to the hospital.

"No thanks, Sarah. We got to get shaking but..." Mike said.

"But, we'll be back." Lisa finished his sentence.

"We will? Oh, yeah, we will." Mike nodded so fast it looked like his head would come off.

"Great! I'll be here through lunch. Carnitas is my lunch special today." Sarah smiled and winked at Lisa.

Or at least Lisa thought she winked at her. Lisa hoped she winked at her. A butch who could cook might be the perfect combo.

The bright interior lights inside the ambulance highlighted the bruises and cuts on the guy's face. Mike worked on getting a blood pressure reading. "Looks like he gave as good as he got. His knuckles are raw and swollen."

"Maybe he hit his head on the sidewalk," Lisa said. "We'll get him up to Cooley Dickinson." She shut the door and hopped behind the wheel, waving at Sarah as she did. Sarah waved back as she cranked open the awning over her serving window. What a cutie.

Lisa flipped on the lights and siren. The patient was breathing and seemed stable enough but you never knew when that was going to change. Better to get him to the hospital quick and let them figure it out.

It was a buzz to drive the ambulance. It had a huge engine and could haul ass when it had to. The lights and siren really moved people out of the way, which was pretty cool too. Though sometimes drivers acted like they didn't hear or see anything, and that's when she drove up behind them and goosed the siren which let out a wail that made its normal screeching sound like birds singing. It was petty and very juvenile to admit how much she enjoyed that.

What a busy morning. The day had the Friday night vibe even though it was only eight a.m. Northampton was gearing up for the weekend. Lisa was out at three and had Saturday and Sunday off, a rare occurrence. May had called two days ago to tell her Earl had died. It had broken Lisa's heart to hear the sadness in her voice. She and Avola were going to be leaving for the drive back east as soon as Earl had been autopsied and cremated.

Lisa listened to Mike call in the vitals as she navigated the corner from Pleasant onto Main. The Jamaican guy who played the steel drums was already set up in front of the bagel place, serenading the passersby with "Somewhere Over the Rainbow." There was a woman dressed up like the Statue of Liberty and standing on a milk crate collecting money for something. Lisa was too far away to read her sign. Spring fever was an epidemic and the good people of Northampton didn't seem to mind.

"He doing okay?" Lisa asked.

"Yup. He's stable but it smells like he smoked an ounce of weed. He is out of it so there has to be some other substance percolating around in there."

"Hey, ummm, do you mind going back to Sarah's for a burrito after we drop him off? I didn't have breakfast." Lisa slowed in the intersection of State, Main and South giving people a chance to get out of the way.

"Haven't had breakfast, huh? If his name was Larry I bet you wouldn't be so focused on his burrito," Mike said.

Lisa could hear the smile in his voice. "Why, Mike, I don't know what you are talking about."

"In other words, girlfriend, I saw her burritos. If I was into girl burritos and that's a big if, I'd be into those. And like she said, the salsa is fresh." Mike laughed.

"The question is, Mike…are they lesbian burritos?"

"Guess you'll have to unwrap them to find out."

* * *

Lisa was in the back of the ambulance taking a supply inventory and waiting for Mike who was still inside the ER finishing paperwork when she heard a knock near the open back door.

"Hey there."

Lisa turned around to find herself looking into Sarah's smiling face.

"Hi. What are you doing so far away from your burritos?" Lisa asked, smiling more than she probably needed to because of her and Mike's conversation.

"I'm not." Sarah held up two foil-wrapped burritos. "My assistant came in and I thought you guys might be hungry. So I borrowed her car and delivered."

"Gosh, Sarah, that's sweet of you." Lisa got out of the ambulance and sat on the back bumper.

"I hope you like them."

"I'm sure I'll like them. Sarah, what do I owe you?"

"We can settle up later. I…ummm…actually was wondering if you might want to go out sometime. I apologize if you're not a—"

"Oh, I am a—" Lisa interrupted.

"Great. Me too…"A look of mortification crossed Sarah's face. "Uh duh, right?"

Lisa laughed. "When would you like to go out?" Lisa asked.

"Tonight? Tomorrow?"

Sarah had a space between her front teeth. Lisa loved that. "How about tonight? You want to meet downtown somewhere?" Lisa felt irrationally excited. Her heart was hammering in her chest like she had just drunk espresso.

"Let's meet under the awning at Thornes. We can decide where to go from there. Will six o'clock work?" Sarah asked.

"See you then," Lisa said. "Oh, and thanks for breakfast."

"You're welcome. See you tonight." Sarah waved and ran across the parking lot toward a VW Bug with its flashers flashing.

Lisa peeled foil from the burrito and took a big bite. Scrambled eggs, with bacon, home fries, cheese, salsa and guacamole.

"What you got there?" Mike had emerged from the ER toting their backboard.

"Burrito. Mine's a lesbian burrito to be exact. It's yummy." Lisa laughed and held one out to him. "I don't know what yours is."

CHAPTER TWENTY-THREE

Holly leaves prickled Lisa's face as she unloaded the bush from the back of her Jeep. She had been looking for something to get May as a sympathy gift for Earl and had been stymied until she thought to go to Sappho's Greenhouse. After Lisa had told the cute dyke in overalls about May's loss and her beautiful gardens, the woman recommended a holly bush. Apparently it symbolized everlasting life, remained green year round and had tiny blossoms in the spring and red berries in the fall. Lisa would string it with small white lights and leave it for May to decide where to plant. The woman at the greenhouse had said it should survive a day or two until May returned. It seemed like the perfect choice.

May was due home later today or tomorrow. Avola had said she wasn't sure when she'd called to keep Lisa posted on their arrival. Avola had said they were both tired and she just wasn't able to drive like the demon she had been when she drove west. Despite their first meeting, inauspicious to say the least, Lisa had grown to like her. And Avola certainly loved May, that was clear. Apparently they had mended things between them which had gladdened Lisa's heart and filled her with hope, probably irrational hope but hope all the same.

* * *

Lisa's cell rang. She looked at the screen. Why would Johnnie be calling? Usually she let it go to voice mail but, well, why not answer it?

"Hi, Johnnie. How are you doing?" Lisa asked.

"Pretty good. You?" Johnnie's voice sounded surprised as it crackled in her ear.

"Fine. What can I do for you?"

"Well, I'm…ah…kind of surprised you answered. I thought I'd be leaving a message…"

"Yeah. Well…I…"

"No worries, Lisa. I just wanted to say…ummm…I met somebody…" Lisa wasn't surprised he had. She examined herself for a flare-up of sadness or anger.

"…and Northampton's a small town in a lot of ways and I just didn't want you to hear about it from somebody else."

"I appreciate that, Johnnie. It's nice of you to let me know."

"Are you dating?" His voice sounded hopeful.

Lisa wasn't sure she wanted to tell him about her love life just yet. But, she could honestly say she was happy for him. That surprised her. It seemed like she would never get to this point and then, suddenly, here she was. It remained to be seen how much of this peace of mind had to do with Sarah.

"A bit. Well, I've got to go. Thanks for calling, Johnnie. Talk to you later."

"Okay. Take care. Bye." Johnnie clicked off.

Sarah Sterling. Much of her hope roosted with her, or maybe with them. Their date the other night had been fun. They'd met at Thornes and Sarah had said she was interested in sampling some sweets from Honey's Sugar-Free Emporium on Center Street and was Lisa game for dessert first. Her stomach had bottomed out with that question. They had strolled through downtown as Sarah chatted about Honey's mission to make desserts using only natural sweeteners like honey and maple syrup. She was interested in carrying Honey's muffins and cookies on her meal truck.

It had been wonderful. Sarah had chosen some treats and coffee to go and they had strolled to the courthouse lawn, sat on the grass near the fountain, eating, talking and people watching. There was a guy playing an accordion on the steps and the year-round Christmas lights in the trees outside the Hotel Northampton next door had transformed the evening into a fantasy first date a girl in a book or movie might dream of having. It didn't hurt that it was oddly warm for April, the sky streaked lavender in the sunset and the black flies weren't swarming. Lisa couldn't even remember what they had talked about but there wasn't any shortage of topics.

Lisa found herself obsessing about the possibility of a first kiss as they walked back toward the awning at Thornes. Would there be a kiss and if there was would it be a good kiss? That first kiss was telling. First, did she have a pretty mouth? In Sarah's case, yes. Second, could she use that mouth as a force for good? That remained to be seen, though Sarah was a good conversationalist. Third, did the kiss have that spark, that promise of more and make Lisa's insides turn to lava? Please, let it be so.

They had arrived under the awning. Sarah had taken Lisa's hands in hers and asked if she were free Sunday afternoon for brunch. Those hazel eyes were so kind and melty-looking that all Lisa could do was nod. Could I pick you up at noon, Sarah had asked. Lisa had smiled and nodded and told her the address. Sarah had then turned Lisa's hands over and kissed each palm. Lisa's insides turned to lava. She was a little afraid, in a good way, of what might happen when they actually did, finally, kiss.

* * *

May was hollowed out. The drive east seemed endless though she was grateful for Avi who seemed very tuned into

May's mood and talked when May wanted to and kept quiet when May didn't. At another time she might have enjoyed the trip but all it did was reinforce her feeling of being an anchorless boat, adrift on a ribbon of asphalt. Hopefully, she would feel better when she arrived home. Her gardens would be blooming, the birds would be nesting and she would be able to sleep in her own bed. Though to be honest she hadn't been sleeping very well. It wasn't that she wasn't tired, exhausted wouldn't be far from the truth, but whenever she closed her eyes a movie started in her mind and made it impossible to doze off.

There was Earl learning to ride a two-wheeler. In his Cub Scout uniform. As a pirate for trick-or-treat. Holding a baseball trophy. Eating birthday cake. At his father's funeral. Wearing a suit and standing next to the girl he went to the prom with. In his graduation cap and gown. His bruises from brain surgery. His dead face. Over and over, around and around until she would give up and turn on the bedside lamp and read. If you could call staring at words on the page reading. Thankfully, it hadn't kept Avola awake.

May looked forward to the day when the ache of missing Earl would lessen. She hoped those days existed but there was a large part of her wondering. She supposed they must. Other people lost children and managed to find a way to get through it. Her friends Evelyn and Gil had found a way. They even seemed to have fun, gadding about town and traveling with the Senior Spirit Chorus. Of course they were many years on the other side of it and who could say what they thought in their private moments.

"How do you think people stand it, Avi?" May asked, glancing at Avola who was concentrating on passing a motor home as big as a three-bedroom ranch. It was just getting dark. It was probably three or four hours to Hadley. May hoped Avola felt like driving the rest of the way tonight.

"Which it are you speaking of?"

"A child passing away."

"I do not know. My parents, as I have told you, did not handle it very well at all. Not having children myself I can only imagine that it must feel unfair…parents expect to outlive their children…but, I can speak of losing Gasteau. My grief for him has never left me. It is like an ember now and not the fire it once was. I hope, my dear, that it will become that way for you." Avola shrugged as if to say though it might be possible it was impossible to say when.

May hoped so too.

* * *

"Good evening, folks. Clara Goodhue here with Common Sense is Good Sense. And remember if common sense were common then everyone would have some. I want to take a moment and thank all you listeners for tuning in to the show and calling in. KBLM has added an extra phone line to help handle the volume of calls. And we have a new toll free number 1-800-555-WISH."

Line 1 Alberto. Asking what gives people the strength to go on! Too heavy for 1ˢᵗ call. Alison line 2. Girlfriend problems, lesbians good for ratings.

"Good evening, Alison. What is your quandary this evening?" Clara found herself wishing she had taken Alberto's call instead. She had been out of sorts these past few days, ever since May called with the sad news. It would be great to find out how people found the strength to go on. She'd been wondering that herself.

"Hi Clara. Longtime listener first-time caller."

"Thank you, Alison. What can we help you with this evening?"

"My girlfriend wants to have an open relationship. I am just not into that but I love her and don't want to lose her." Alison burst into tears.

Wayne line 3 advice for Alison. Bob line 4 religious wacko. Alberto holding line 1.

"That is a true quandary, Alison. Take a moment to gather yourself and let's see what the good folks out there in radio land have to say. Good evening, Wayne, what is your advice on the matter?"

"Love your show, Clara."

"Thank you."

"In regard to Alison there. My ex-wife wanted an open relationship and at first I thought hey, good deal. I mean what guy doesn't want to fu…I mean screw any woman who'll have him, know what I'm saying? But then as it went along I realized she was screwing anybody and everybody too. Made me crazy jealous and I got addicted to Oxycontin. So, in a word, don't do it, Alison. It's a slippery slope."

"Thank you, Wayne. Bob, what do you have to say on the matter?"

Alberto holding line 1 Hazel line 3.

"That woman is a handmaiden of Satan and her girlfriend is a harlot. There can be no happiness when people live such a godless and immoral life. I say walk away from each other and find peace in our Lord Jesus. He'll point you in the direction of a good man who will help you find the path of righteousness and the blessings of a marriage sanctified by God. My church, The Rugged Cross of Cal—"

"Thank you, Bob. I think we know where you're going with this. Thanks for calling." Clara hung up on him. What was wrong with her? Last week she would've let him go on and on. It would've revved up the listeners and she would have had a radio brawl. Terrific for ratings. She just didn't have it in her this week.

"Hazel? Are you calling to offer us the woman's perspective on this issue?"

"Hi, Clara. If Alison's girlfriend wants an open relationship there is nothing she can do to change the girlfriend's mind. It may just mean that they aren't supposed to be together, they want different things from life and that leaves you at square one. No matter if you're gay or straight, love can be a heartache. Just hang in there Alison honey, it'll get better."

"Thank you, Hazel, spoken like a true humanitarian. Good luck to you, Alison. A wee bit of advice from me…My mother always said if you don't respect yourself then nobody else will respect you. Take from that what you will. Good night now."

What are you doing? People on line…

"Good evening, Alberto. Sorry to keep you waiting. What is your quandary?"

"Hello Clara, I listen to your show almost every night on my drive home after my shift. I'm a nurse and ah…well, this is going to sound weird but…what do you think makes people survive? The hard stuff like death, like grief. Know what I mean?"

"Why don't you explain a wee bit more, Alberto. We don't want any confusion out there in radio land."

"We had a patient, he died and I'm used to that you know. I'm a nurse like I said…but this was unusual. He had a brain tumor and was in a coma. Nobody knew why. And then he died which surprised the hell, excuse me, heck out of everyone. Anyway, his mother was there. A nice lady, older, like maybe eighties or something. Not that that matters. Anyway, I guess it got me thinking about how people go on when something awful like losing your kid happens."

Hope you know what you're doing! Other callers hung up. Told you too heavy. Lesbians get people riled up. Good for ratings.

Clara was stunned. Alberto had to be talking about Earl and May. How many other guys with brain tumors, in an unexplained coma and dying, could there be? How many of them had eighty-something-year-old mothers in attendance?

"You heard it, callers. Anyone out there care to offer their viewpoint on Alberto's existential quandary?"

Fat chance. Depressing topic. Get Alberto talking about his sex life. That will help.

"I guess maybe we'll never know, Clara. I was just feeling… well, kind of sad about it and I didn't even know him."

"I can only imagine, Alberto. This is an unusual quandary folks, I know. Not our usual sort of topic at all but I know the listeners of Common Sense is Good Sense is up to the challenge."

Finally. Line 2 Jessica for Alberto. Line 3 Marvin for Alberto.

"Good evening, Jessica. Thank you for calling Common Sense is Good Sense. What do you have to say about Alberto's quandary?"

"Hi Clara, I love your show. Hi, Alberto. I don't know if I have any advice. I just think sometimes we just can't understand what's going on behind the scenes."

Behind the scenes! Wacko #2 of the show! Line 3 Marvin. Line 4 Theresa.

"What do you mean, behind the scenes?"

"Okay, this is going to sound weird, Clara. I'll admit it. But, I've had this feeling ever since I was a kid that this life we're living isn't our real life. That this is sort of a dream. Our real lives happen after we've died, that this is just a sort of game we're playing."

Jesus! Where do these people come from??? Milk it for all its worth.

"That's an interesting viewpoint, Jessica. But, sometimes like in Alberto's case of a child dying, that just seems like more than a game," Clara said.

"You misunderstand me. I never meant to say that it's all fun and games…but that what happens to us here isn't as real, no matter how it feels, as where we come from. Like before we're born. You know, the other world. I'm not explaining it very well."

"I appreciate the call, Jessica. Bye now."

Line 3 Marvin. Line 4 Theresa. Good going girl.

"Hello, Marvin. What is your opinion on Alberto's quandary?"

"Hi, Clara. I'm in the funeral business so I generally see people at the worst of times. It's been my experience, and I been in it for more than forty years so I've had a lot of it, that whether a person is religious or not, it doesn't matter, losing a child really rocks their world. It's like the worst thing on the planet."

"I think we all realize that, Marvin. Can you address Alberto's concern? What helps people go on in the face of the worst things that happen to us?" Clara asked.

"I guess time. The passing of time. And maybe bourbon."

"Thank you Marvin for your professional viewpoint. Theresa? Thank you for calling Common Sense is Good Sense. What perspective can you offer the listeners?"

"Hi there, Clara. I'm just passing through the area on my way to LA hauling frozen pig parts but I had to pull over and call in."

"Thank you, Theresa. We're always glad to hear from long-haul truckers."

"Well, I just want to say that I lost my little girl a few years ago. Seven years, four months, two weeks and three days ago to be exact. As you can tell, it's not something you ever forget. After she passed I felt like all the light had been sucked out of the world.

"But, one day I realized that life for her had been one joy after another. She was a happy child and just loved hummingbirds. She'd wait in our flower gardens, more patient than you'd ever think a child could be, for them to come drink from the blossoms. When she first got sick and couldn't go out, I put up a couple hummingbird feeders outside her bedroom window and moved her bed right up against that window so she could see them. They came in droves. Neighbors started calling ours the hummingbird house."

Clara was mesmerized. She knew she should say something but she couldn't think of anything as interesting as what she was listening to.

"Anyway. One day I was sitting in the garden, staring off into space when I heard this buzzing in my ear. I thought it was a bee. But, when I turned to look I saw it was a hummingbird, a beautiful shiny green one and I just knew it was my little girl coming to say hello. It was strange but that creature hung around the garden all day."

"What a beautiful story, Theresa." Clara felt like she was going to cry. For the first time in days she felt a little bit of hope that May would be okay and that wherever Earl was, he wasn't unhappy.

"That's when I remembered her joyfulness in life and I knew I was doing her and our life together a disservice by not finding joy in life too. Slowly but surely, things got better after that. I got my CDL which I had always wanted to do. I believe our dead don't want us to die with them; they want us to live as fully as we can so when we see them in the next world our lives won't have been a waste."

And she's a truck driver? Shoot, she should be on Oprah!

* * *

Yolk oozed from the pierced, poached egg.

"Yum. This egg is perfect." Lisa smiled across the table at Sarah.

"I'm glad. I'm trying to impress you." Sarah smiled and raised her glass in a toast. "To perfectly poached eggs."

"To perfectly poached eggs." Lisa clinked her glass against Sarah's.

Lisa had never had a Bellini before this morning. Peaches were her favorite fruit; she waited each year for those few precious weeks when they were available from local orchards. A piece of peach pie could make her swoon and it was tantalizing to think there was a drink made from peach juice.

"Thanks for coming over here this morning. I had wanted to take you out but you know how car trouble can be," Sarah said.

"I'm happy to be here." Lisa felt like she was in high school and dating for the first time. Sarah made her nervous and excited. Some form of electricity was zinging back and forth between them; electrocution by Sarah might be a very delicious thing.

Sarah sat back, pushing her plate away. "My mother taught me to cook eggs. She said any man would be happy with a woman who could cook eggs. So, she taught me to fry, scramble, soft and hard boil, poach and make an omelet."

Sarah's hazel eyes softened and her left eyebrow rose when she said omelet. Lisa felt her chest tighten and her pussy tingle.

"How thorough of her. Did she teach you any other useful household tasks?" Lisa asked, sipping her drink.

Sarah smiled. "Yes, I can iron."

"That's useful. You never know when a wrinkle will come your way." Lisa pushed her plate away. The food was fabulous but she didn't think she could eat another bite.

"How about you?" Sarah stood up and took their plates toward the counter.

Lisa followed her and stood right behind Sarah at the sink. Not touching but almost.

"Laundry. There is no stain in this world that I can't get out." Lisa ran her finger along Sarah's spine, smiling as she stood up straighter. "I can also dust. I'm especially good at getting into corners and hard to reach places."

Sarah cleared her throat. "That's…useful…too."

Lisa moved away to the safety of the slider overlooking a small deck. She'd been wrong before about the electricity, it was a force field pulling her in. She really liked Sarah and didn't want to screw, whatever this was, up.

"I know how to defrost a fridge though with frost free… well, I'm not called upon to do it much anymore." Lisa felt heat gathering on her skin.

"Still…it's a talent." Sarah crossed the room to stand next to Lisa.

She wanted to kiss Sarah so much it was a physical ache, a whole body craving, the Johnnie glacier inside her thawing.

"Yes, it is." Lisa imagined kissing Sarah's neck, rubbing her face against her skin, pressing her lips along Sarah's jaw, down her throat toward the collar of her shirt…

"Umm…I made a fruit tart for dessert…" Sarah reached out to brush Lisa's hair back. "Would you like some?"

"Desperately." Lisa smiled. Yet Sarah made no attempt to move away.

"Sarah, I…know we barely know each other…" Maybe she should just shut up. Talking so often ruined things, either saying things you didn't mean or saying too much and leaving yourself exposed. Yet, she wanted to be exposed to Sarah, wanted to let the hurt slide away and be new with her.

Sarah turned toward Lisa, compelling her to turn and look into those creamy, hazel eyes.

"I feel it, too," Sarah whispered.

"You do?"

Sarah nodded.

"Oh good…" Lisa sighed with relief. "I don't think I could've survived if you didn't…" She rested her head against Sarah's shoulder for a moment, and pulled back.

"I haven't been able to stop thinking about you since I first saw you last week. I couldn't wait for this brunch…Then when my car went screwy I was so disappointed…but then you agreed to come here and…well, I wanted to show what I felt in the food…" Sarah stopped talking and smiled.

"I haven't stopped thinking about you either…" Lisa moved closer to Sarah until they were standing belly to belly, breast to breast.

"The food was delicious…" Lisa could smell peaches on Sarah's breath. All the oxygen left the room, the clock stopped, the spider plant hanging over the kitchen sink ceased making chlorophyll. There was only Sarah's mouth, only her mouth so close to her own as she hovered there, a hummingbird suspended in the here and now.

Their kiss exploded. Lisa's hot skin dissolved as the heat in her stomach spread to her clit. Sarah's hands slid down to cup Lisa's ass, pulling them closer. Lisa couldn't get enough of Sarah's mouth, that pretty mouth, so much a force for good that she could barely stand up any longer.

Lisa fumbled with Sarah's pants, groaning as she felt Sarah's hands slide from her ass, along her body and under her shirt, squeezing her breasts and then skimming down until Lisa could feel that devil hand slip under the waistband of her jeans. Sarah was wearing button-fly Levi's which made her smile against Sarah's mouth.

"Ooohhh, challenging…" Lisa murmured.

"Not…really." Sarah growled. "Jesus…let's go to bed."

Lisa pulled her down onto the floor where they melted together like hot wax without a bowl.

CHAPTER TWENTY-FOUR

Whew, it was hot. May never remembered her namesake month being so warm. If this kept up the black-eyed Susans would be blooming right alongside the forsythia. She stood up from weeding and stretched her back, remembering how much she used to enjoy gardening. Since Earl died it just felt like a chore. So what if the weeds took over and claimed everything, weeds had as much of a right to existence as anything else. Did it really matter in the grand scheme of things? The month since Earl's passing had crawled by, such a contrast with how her days had always been, busy and filled with the things she enjoyed.

May thought she'd stop for the day. The hammock swayed in the breeze beckoning her to lie down in the shade. Sleeping had been impossible of late; she always woke up at three o'clock in the morning. At first she'd struggled to go back to sleep but now she just got up, made tea and worked jigsaw puzzles until it was light enough to go for her morning walk. Some mornings it seemed like she could walk to the Canadian border and not even notice. It even happened when she stayed over at Avola's and Avi had been thoughtful enough to get some puzzles from the library.

The hammock welcomed May into its embrace. She kicked off her shoes and lay back gazing into the branches of the maple that had been growing on the property since before she'd bought the house. The green leaves undulated in the breeze and seemed to whisper to her. What could this old tree have to say to her, what could anyone have to say that would take this ache out of her heart? People tried, saying that Earl was in a better place or some version of that, comments that caused the tips of May's fingers to tingle with the itch to choke them. Really, the only appropriate comment was I'm sorry but people seemed to want to say something else they thought would be helpful. Sometimes there was nothing helpful. It was nice to know people were sorry; Earl had been well-liked around town, but it wasn't enough. Nothing was enough. Either she felt too much and couldn't stop crying or she felt numb like she had been submerged in ice water.

Avi had been wonderful, attentive but not overbearing. She and Lisa had planted Earl's holly bush and run an extension cord so May could light the lights Lisa had strung in it. What a thoughtful girl. May felt cared for and loved but it didn't seem enough to counteract the misery.

A catbird May couldn't see started to sing its complicated mating song. Such an unassuming creature but what a melodious tune, a nearby veery wasn't to be outdone, its song sounded like notes echoing down a drain pipe. Nature was comforting but that comfort had to be tempered with the knowledge that hurricanes and tornados blew through and laid waste to everything in their path. An idiot could see the lesson in that.

Nature was gentle this morning offering sympathy and inviting May to close her eyes. Just for a minute, then she'd go inside and force herself to eat some lunch.

* * *

The bonfire licked at the night, playfully chasing it away. The tug of war between darkness and light was endless, ageless, neither had the upper hand for long, round and round, first one leading the dance then the other. December was clear and cold on solstice, the stars displaying their winter constellations.

Earl stood there wearing a fedora and an overcoat that had belonged to his father and made him look serious and grown up. He was sipping hot chocolate and smoking a cigarette. The flames danced in his eyes.

"Hey, Ma." A smile cracked his face open, his teeth shimmered in the firelight.

"Earl. I never expected to see you here." May's chest expanded with disbelief.

"I know you didn't. But, I missed you and wanted to stop by and let you know I was doing okay." A second cup of hot chocolate appeared in his hand. "Have some. It's delicious."

"Thank you." It was delicious, sweet and warm in her mouth.

"Earl, honey, I…I thought you were dead."

"What makes you think that?"

"I saw you. You were dead in that hospital bed. Dead. Then you were cremated and I brought you home in an urn." May didn't want to be right, had never hoped to be wrong more at any time in her life. And maybe she was because here he was. Here. He. Was. She didn't know what to think.

"Do I look dead?"

"No, not really." This didn't make any sense.

"Oh, and I wanted to tell you how much I like the holly bush. It looks great with the lights in it. Will you light them every night? I'd enjoy that." He sipped from his cup.

"Of course, Sonny. You can see them?"

"I sure can and they are beautiful. Everything is beautiful. I love it here."

"Where is here, Sonny?"

"The place we go. It doesn't seem to have a name. But, I'm new here so maybe I haven't learned it yet." He tossed his cigarette into the fire.

"Did you see Pop?" May was almost afraid to ask.

"Yes. He's fine. He loaned me his coat so I could meet you here in winter." Earl laughed. "It was great to see him."

"I don't know what to say. This all seems so very strange." May held onto her mug like it could save her from disappearing.

"It is strange and must seem especially strange to you. I really just wanted you to know that I'm happy here. The hardest part is seeing you suffer."

"It's been terrible losing you, Earl. Something has been ripped out of me…"

"But, you haven't lost me, Ma. I'm right here. Anytime you think of me I will be standing next to you. I promise." He smiled and took her empty mug away.

"Really? It's that simple?" May asked.

"Everything is simple. It all comes down to loving each other."

"Love?"

"Love. It's the most important thing. I'll see you around, Ma. Oh and congratulations." Earl hugged her against his chest. She could feel the scratch of the wool against her cheek.

"Congratulations? I don't understand…"

"You will, Ma. You will. See you later."

May watched him leave the firelight. A shadow of him crossed the lawn and street and disappeared into the woods.

* * *

The hammock jostled as someone lay down next to her. She felt a kiss on her forehead.

"'Allo, my dear," Avola whispered in her ear.

"Avi. I must have dozed off."

"That's good. I know sleeping for you has been difficult." Avola kissed May's cheek. "I brought you something I thought you might find enjoyable on this hot day."

"It is hot. That's why I decided to take a break. What did you bring?"

"Milkshakes. One for you and one for me. I put them in your fridge. I was running errands and had a craving for a sweet. I thought you might enjoy one too." Avola smiled and shrugged.

"You're so thoughtful, Avi. I was dreaming about Earl." May scootched up in the hammock and slid over making room for Avola.

"Yes? How is he?" Avola put her arm around her.

"It's funny you should ask because he told me he came by so I would know he was all right."

"That was kind of him."

"Avi, are you humoring me?" May wondered if she needed humoring. Things were feeling a little odd at the moment.

"No. Gasteau visited me a lot. Especially at first. I think he knew I missed him."

"Did you ever tell anyone about it?" May asked.

"I was a child. My parents would have thought I was making it up, I think. I liked that his visits were just my own."

May nodded. "It was good to see him. He said he likes the holly bush, especially the lights." May was relieved that Avola didn't seem to think she had gone completely around the bend.

"I am not surprised. It is lovely."

May nodded and snuggled against Avola.

"May? I noticed something while I was out," Avola said.

"What?" May's voice was muffled in Avola's shirt.

"I drove through Northampton and there was a line of gays and lesbians at city hall getting marriage licenses. It was so beautiful to see," Avola said.

"That's wonderful. I had forgotten that same-sex marriage was allowed as of today."

"People were laughing and dancing, there was a band playing…I never thought I would live long enough for this to happen. After the decision last November I suspected the conservatives would do something to stop it." Her eyes were as wide as a kid who sees a new bike under the tree Christmas morning.

May remembered last November: Earl was alive and on his road trip. Lisa had moved in and she and Avi weren't exactly getting along.

"I never thought this day would come either. Times sure have changed," May said.

"Truer words have never been spoken. Of course the federal government is lagging behind but I am choosing to see this day as a start. That's why I got the milkshakes, I wanted to celebrate."

May smiled and kissed Avola.

"May, I…I know this is not really the right time to ask. You are sad, perhaps too sad to consider this but…"

May put her fingers against Avola's lips. "You want to get married," May said.

Avola raised her eyebrows and nodded.

"I would love to marry you. But not until the fall…I…"

Avola burst into tears.

"Avi, what's wrong? I…"

"These are tears of joy, May. I understand you want to wait and I understand why." Avola wiped her eyes using the bottom of her T-shirt.

May thought back to her dream. *Is this what Earl was congratulating me for?*

CHAPTER TWENTY-FIVE

September eighteenth gleamed under the sun. Reds, yellows and oranges were starting to overtake the green in the foliage, beginning the yearly good-natured battle. There was a cool breath in the air, a promise of winter still months away. A blue dome of sky arched over May's backyard. The sun would set in an hour but was low enough in the sky to fill the yard with shadows. The white lights in the holly bush shone. Japanese lanterns had been strung through the low branches of the trees, softly glowing pink. A podium was set up near the holly bush, surrounded by folding chairs, the circle bisected by two aisles. Gentle classical music seemed to emanate from the very air itself. Sarah's meal truck was parked in the driveway, her assistant grilling skewers of marinated chicken, shrimp and vegetables for the after-ceremony festivities.

Avola, dapper in navy blue trousers and tunic, paced the driveway and yard. She was giddy with thanksgiving, a giddiness unable to be contained no matter how hard she tried. So, rather than drive Lisa and Sarah crazy in the kitchen or bother May

while she was dressing, Avola came outside to walk. Happiness this acute was…words fell short though Avola was sure she was grinning like an idiot, an idiot for love.

May had asked Lisa to help her zip her pale blue dress and adjust the lace shawl draped over her shoulders. It would mean so much if Earl could be here, though in an odd way it almost seemed like he was. Once or twice earlier this afternoon she smelled cigarette smoke but there was never anyone there.

Sarah finished putting the last of the champagne bottles on ice in the bathtub. People started arriving, greeting Avola in the driveway with hugs, kisses and handshakes; proceeding to the backyard to ooh and ahh and finally to settle down in the seat of their choice.

Nervous excitement crackled in the air.

The justice of the peace arrived, a tall, gay man Lisa's friend Mike knew from the Gay Men's Chorus. His tie was pink, goodwill radiated from him like sunbeams. This was the day Avola had never thought would arrive. But it had arrived. May was grateful her grief had subsided enough for her to feel joy in marrying. She did feel joy. Lisa was in love with Sarah. Sarah was in love with Lisa. It was a day love ruled. The birds watching from their branches could hear it singing. The yellow jackets flew in drunken circles under its sweet influence. A rabbit who lived in the hedgerow emerged to sniff, little nose twitching at the succulent aroma.

Earl watched it all from a distance, close enough to see but not be seen. He was the slight breeze through his mother's hair, the gleam of light reflected off the sundial, the steady cadence of the cricket call, and the deep shadow in the wood. The lights in the holly bush flickered and glowed brighter which more than one wedding guest noticed but didn't comment upon because just then the first strains of "The Wedding March" could be heard.

Bella Books, Inc.

Women. Books. Even Better Together.

P.O. Box 10543
Tallahassee, FL 32302

Phone: 800-729-4992
www.bellabooks.com